# I Am Jack

# I Am Jack

## CONFESSIONS OF THE WHITECHAPEL RIPPER

By

## SHIRLEY GOULDEN

~~~~~~~~~~~~~~~~~~~~~~~~~~~~~~~~~

As for myself, I walk abroad o'nights
And kill sick people groaning under walls.
Sometimes I go about and poison wells.

CHRISTOPHER MARLOWE: "The Jew of Malta"

~~~~~~~~~~~~~~~~~~~~~~~~~~~~~~~~~

Order this book online at www.trafford.com
or email orders@trafford.com

Most Trafford titles are also available at major online book retailers.

For the Blood Drop-'WarApple' at devaintart.com
http://warapple.deviantart.com/art/Blood-drop-WP-perspective-81545961?q=gallIf

Printed in the United States of America.

ISBN: 978-1-4269-6856-3 (sc)
ISBN: 978-1-4269-6858-7 (hc)
ISBN: 978-1-4269-6857-0 (e)

Library of Congress Control Number: 2011907871

Trafford rev. 05/31/2011

 www.trafford.com

North America & international
toll-free: 1 888 232 4444 (USA & Canada)
phone: 250 383 6864 ♦ fax: 812 355 4082

Dedication

This Book is dedicated to my best Friend Shirley Van Eyssen (nee Goulden) who has been an inspiration in my life since the day I met her.

~~~~~~~~~~~~~~~~~~~~~~~~~~~~~~~~~~~~

Shirley died on the 21st July 2010 after a long period of illness. It was her dying wish that this book should be published for everyone to read and draw their own conclusions after reading it.

Caroline Bunting – April 2011

# AUTHOR'S PREFACE

In the last decade of the nineteenth century Doctor Thomas Neill Cream was hanged at Newgate for poisoning prostitutes. More recently a letter appeared in the press written by a W. Jack Heaney of Lincolnshire, stating that his grandfather had a friend, the hangman Billington, who insisted that Cream had gasped with his last breath: "I am Jack ---" before being despatched abruptly below. That Billington was apparently the only one to hear the confession in no way detracts from the veracity of his claim, since he was obviously positioned closest to the hooded and therefore slightly muffled wretch.

Intrigued and, like the Victorian police, having not a clue as to the identity of "Jack the Ripper", I decided to inquire into the history of the sinister Doctor Cream - finding that he had during the Whitechapel atrocities in 1888, to all intents, been confined in an American prison for the crime of murder by means of strychnine poisoning.

Yet an odd contradiction in Cream's character caught my attention. Raised from early childhood in Canada, he was already displaying criminal tendencies as a high-flying medical student at McGill University while also indulging in frequent bouts of religious fervour, often preaching piously at Sunday school. I felt it questionable whether such a man, doubtless convinced in that awful moment of reckoning that Divine Judgment was at hand, would with his last breath utter a false confession. Unless of course he was not merely depraved but insane - a plea which was found totally unacceptable at his final trial in 1892.

The venue of Cream's first conviction having been Chicago of the eighteen eighties, which, as a result of widespread corruption was soon to become a gangland citadel for the likes of Al Capone, I began seriously to consider whether, after all, the good doctor might not have managed to bribe his way out of jail earlier than was recorded. Particularly since one year previous to the Ripper crimes he had come into what was for those days a sizeable inheritance.

Given that under such circumstances he had been able to buy his freedom and escape to England some time before 1888, and that he certainly specialised in the sadistic murder of prostitutes, Thomas Neill Cream would undoubtedly, have been a prime Ripper suspect; but it is generally assumed that his term of imprisonment in America constituted a perfect alibi. A hardened cynic however might be disposed to question. such an assumption, readily accepting that large sums of available cash could (and can) open any doors ---even the barred variety.

Mr. A.C. Trude, a prominent American attorney who had defended Cream in the notorious Chicago murder trial went on record as suggesting that the subsequent shortening of Cream's life sentence, ostensibly to ten years, "was effected by political influence obtained by a free use of money"; and furthermore that on commencement of his sentence in 1881 the prisoner's father had furnished a well known politician with the sum of five thousand dollars, to procure, so it was implied, his unconditional release.

From which the inference may be drawn that there is nothing new in political sleaze, except perhaps the term.

Turning up Donald Bell's inspirational article published in `The Criminologist' (Volume 9, No. 33, 1974) entitled `Jack the Ripper - the Final Solution', I was encouraged to find his hypothesis outlining Cream as the Whitechapel slayer agreed in almost all essentials, with my own, particularly on the pivotal issue of Cream having been bought out or escaped from jail before 1888. Far from being an impossibility, as Bell revealed, between 1924 and 1936 when prison security was far tighter than it had been back in the eighteen eighties, it was recorded that as many as 204 convicts escaped from Illinois jails. But had Cream done so? Donald Rumbelow, in his excellent book `The Complete Jack the Ripper' M. H. Allen, London 1987) thought not, by reason of three affidavits, none of which, however, in my opinion, establishes entirely beyond doubt that Cream was still in prison until 1891. The substance of these is as follows:

1)　　　On the death of Cream's father in 1887 an executor to his Will, Thomas Davidson, applied for evidence as to Cream's guilt in respect of the murder for which he was serving a life sentence in Illinois. Davidson claimed he received "such documentary evidence as convinced me of his innocence." One wonders by what evidence he was so convinced, for during an interview with the `Chicago Tribune' of 28th October 1881, Senator Fuller expressed no such conviction: "he … believes there is as little error in the record of this case as in any criminal case he was ever connected with, and he does not believe it possible for the Supreme Court to find anything than can reverse the case. It is a case, he says, where there can be no possible doubt of the guilt of the defendant, and the crime is one that stands almost without a parallel in the annals of crime."

Davidson nevertheless pursued his efforts to secure Cream's pardon up until the summer of 1891. "...he came to me immediately in Quebec on being liberated …" While Mr. Davidson, in swearing that Cream came to him "immediately", was probably doing so in good faith, he had absolutely no way of being certain that this was so. If the prisoner had been secretly freed by the authorities in 1887, only appearing in Quebec four years later, when the pre-arranged "official" date of his release, July 31st, 1891, was announced (in low key) Mr. Davidson might have been deceived into an incorrect assumption as to exactly when Cream left jail.

2)      An affidavit from Cream's sister-in-law Jessie swore that Cream (to the best of her knowledge) had been released from prison "on or about 29 July 1891," and stayed with her family in Quebec until he had sailed for England in October 1891. This statement did not tally with one made by her husband Daniel to Inspector Frederick Jarvis, reporting from Montreal on July 4th 1892 that Daniel Cream had told him: "..the prisoner arrived at his (Daniel's) house in Quebec on the morning of 20th January last but his wife objected to his staying there as she did not like his manner ... In consequence he went to Blanchard's Hotel." Ruling out Cream's arrival and whereabouts in Quebec, it is reasonable to suppose that Jessie Cream had simply been duped by the same means as W. Davidson into believing he had recently been set free.

3)      Pinkerton's National Detective Agency said that Cream had written to them from prison in December of 1890, requesting an interview. Assuming again that there had been collusion between Cream and the authorities, letters could conceivably have been penned elsewhere by Cream from the prison... There is no evidence as to whether such an interview actually took place, but if so the Pinkerton agent, who had probably never met Cream, would be unaware that he was confronting the look-alike, paid, arguably, to serve the remainder of Cream's sentence. Had it dawned on the authorities, two years after the Ripper crimes, that they may inadvertently have loosed on the world a serial killer, some such deception would have been essential for their own protection, as well as Cream's, with the object of establishing that he was still in jail until 1891 - a cover up of cover ups, as it were. Based on the premise that there was such collusion between Cream and the authorities on the matter of his earlier release, the three affidavits have little validity.

If it appears distinctly improbable that Cream had an accomplice serving out his sentence at Joliet, I would cite an account made by the celebrated advocate, Sir Edward Marshall Hall in his biography by Edward Marjoribanks "The Life of Sir Edward Marshall Hall". At Cream's second murder trial in 1892, Hall recognised the prisoner in the dock as a former client whom he had once defended at the Old Bailey on a charge of bigamy.

Cream, confronted by a number of women all insisting it was he who had "married" each and every one of them, was advised by Hall to plead guilty. Cream eschewed his advice, insisting he was serving a sentence in an Australian prison when the offences were said to have taken place. Hall sent a cable to the Sydney authorities, and was astounded to have Cream's story verified, inasmuch as a man of his description had in fact been detained by them at the time in question. The case was accordingly dismissed, leaving a baffled Hall to conclude that Cream must have a double in the underworld willing for some reason to provide him with an alibi - a not unprecedented situation at a time when, without even an established fingerprinting system, much less more recent innovations such as DNA and blood typing, there were few reliable means of identification.

If Marshall Hall was right in suspecting that his client had a confederate to supply him with an alibi, it is highly probable that Cream would in the future, if and when necessary, make further use of such an arrangement; and he may well have done so, as soon as the opportunity arose, in order to abscond from Joliet.

As against Bell's thesis (and my own) it has been observed that Cream's established modus operandi (poisoning of prostitutes) differed from that of the Ripper. However, the ever increasing incidence of unsolved crimes does suggest that implicit reliance on modus operandi is now archaic; and should perhaps be replaced by modern methods of psychological profiling, together with assessments of the criminal's genetic makeup.

The modus operandi of both Peter Kurten, the Dusseldorf Ripper and Peter Sutcliffe, the Yorkshire Ripper, varied as follows:

Peter Kurten, murder by means of drowning, strangling, axe attacks, battering, stabbing, and in his own admission, poisoning. A criminal of Cream's (and indeed the Ripper's) devious mentality was more than capable of changing his modus operandi deliberately to confuse the police as, wholly consciously, did Kurten. Rumbelow in `The Complete Jack the Ripper' observes of Kurten: "More importantly, he thought that these variations would give him still greater sexual satisfaction." And in the same book, regarding the Yorkshire Ripper. "Sutcliffe's last six victims have a special significance. None of them were prostitutes. All of them were respectable women. This made a change in the modus operandi employed."

Cream conversely specialized in murdering prostitutes, (or probably any woman whom he might class as "low"), but not necessarily in the method of killing them. Most certainly he was strongly motivated by a compulsive sadistic urge, i.e. an intense desire to inflict suffering - his methods ranging from blackmail, and the writing of scurrilous post-cards (inflicting acute mental suffering) to poisoning by strychnine (inflicting acute physical suffering). The mere awareness of his victim's pain was sufficient to afford him intense gratification - he did not require necessarily to witness the events.

Presuming that Cream had been the Ripper, and found himself on at least one occasion uncomfortably close to capture, it would have been typical of him some four years later, confirmed sadist that he was, to resort again to strychnine as an equally if not more agonizing method than the knife - and without the attendant risks of being present at the kill.

Bell must certainly be credited with producing some remarkable material to support his case, particularly the photograph showing Cream wearing a horseshoe pin, precisely as described by George Hutchinson, considered by the police a reliable eye-witness to the suspected murderer of Mary Jane Kelly in Miller's Court. That Cream possessed and continually displayed such a pin does not of course in itself prove that he was the same man spotted by Hutchinson - the "lucky" horseshoe was doubtless a popular form of adornment at the time. However there were surely not many men established as sadists, prostitute killers, qualified surgeons, users of American terminology, (& etc) - all characterized by the Ripper - who also wore horseshoe pins!

More recently, on November 21st, 2006, in a televised episode of Channel Five's "Revealed," Laura Richards, Behaviour Psychologist attached to New Scotland Yard's Violent Crime Directorate, revealed that as a result of compiling all available witness statements made to the police at the time, she had come up with an E-Fit photograph which, when superimposed on the above mentioned photograph of Cream, matched with astonishing accuracy his jaw structure, nose and prognathous chin.

In `The Crimes Detection and Death of Jack the Ripper' (George Weidenfeld & Nicholson, 1987) while in no way intending to discredit Martin Fido's splendid book, he does seem unintentionally to underline the likelihood that Cream was the Ripper. Regarding the Ripper letters:

"The reoccurring Americanism `Boss' does not point to the murderer's nationality. Their sadistic humour does not necessarily reflect his temperament. The similarity of some letters to the handwriting of the poisoner Neill Cream does not mean that he wrote them."

Taken individually - agreed - but there again, taken collectively: Cream's background was American, he was arrested for writing sadistic postcards and - what one would assume to be a confirmation of Cream's guilt rather than a denial - a handwriting expert positively identified his writing with that of the Ripper.

It seems extraordinary that Donald Bell, who in my view put forward the most plausible theory of all, backed on solid research and sound common sense, was generally dismissed for suggesting, on grounds too numerous to be entirely coincidental, that Cream was the Ripper. Yet at least one film company produced a star-studded extravaganza based on the extremely unlikely supposition that Queen Victoria's personal physician, Sir William Gull (ailing and in his seventies) abetted by several prominent members of the British government, including the Prime Minister, had committed the ripping in an attempt to shield the monarchy from scandal. If so, with what dreaded apprehension must the poor dear Queen, presumably also in on the plot, have anticipated the visits of her Physician Extraordinary!

Again the elaborate theory, reintroduced with due solemnity by Brian Worth, O.B.E. on an I.T.V. Crime Monthly Special that the Ripper was actually an East End Jewish immigrant called Aaron Kosminski seemed to be based on the flimsiest of evidence. Though that unfortunate person, thrown in Coney Hatch Asylum for what is to be hoped were valid reasons, could read and write, he was almost certainly not wholly at ease in the language of his adopted country. How then to account for the famous letter, graphically inscribed in red ink and expressed in fluent English (or is it American?) -- a relic which, despite conflicting beliefs as to its authenticity, has been observed by this author reverently exhibited on the wall of the Black Museum at New Scotland Yard, and therefore presumably regarded by the police as genuinely from Jack the Ripper. And Mr. Worth formerly assistant head of the C.I.D.!

Worth's Victorian predecessor was Sir Robert Anderson who claimed rather feebly in his memoirs 'The Lighter Side of Life' that he was "almost tempted to disclose the identity of the murderer, but no public benefit would result from such a course and the traditions of my own department would suffer." The fact that his department had failed abysmally to apprehend the Ripper, thereby exposing the police force to stringent criticism, was undoubtedly far more damaging than any revelation he might, possibly, have been in a position to make as to the identity of the killer. Indeed, were Anderson able to name the Ripper, it would surely have been his clear duty, in the interests both of his department and public security, to have done so.

Anderson, as it emerged, merely shared a commonly held suspicion ( did not, after all, Whitechapel abound with their sort?) that the Ripper was a Polish Jew, suggesting that it was "a remarkable fact that "people of that class in the East End will not give up one of their number to Gentile Justice" - an accusation against the integrity of the Jewish community which was not backed by a vestige of real evidence and which would no doubt today be considered a clear breach of race relations.. One might be forgiven for speculating that if the Ripper ever had been brought to book it would have been by error rather than trial!

Nor were Sir Melville Macnaghten's notes, written some years after the events, any the more reassuring, since he seemed to be under the misguided impression that his main suspect, the aforementioned Kosminski, had developed homicidal tendencies as a result of indulgence, so it was claimed, in "solitary vices"; and was therefore a perfect candidate for the role of Ripper. It would seem the police were so desperate to find a scapegoat for the crimes that practically anyone who could be established as rather eccentric, foreign, weak in the head, of a poetic temperament or downright insane was in danger of becoming a suspect.

Into this category I would place among many others, the likes of Druitt the Cricketer (the rumour of his guilt only surfacing way after 1888, and then via NcNaghten and his unfounded suspicions); Pedachenko the Assassin (whose motivation for the rippings, so we are asked to swallow, was a purported plot by the Russians to discredit the British police); and Eddy the Royal (who happened inconveniently to be out of town on the night of at least one ripping).

It is surely a good deal more credible that a cunning and moneyed criminal with all the hallmarks of a psychotic killer, bribed his way out of an Illinois jail earlier than the authorities dared admit, absconded to England where he committed the Ripper atrocities, and returned to America to hide out until his supposed release in 1891. Of established sociopaths, George Chapman was in the right place at the right time and possessed rudimentary medical know-how, but no particular predilection for murdering prostitutes; the same applying to Frederic Bailey Deeming who specialised rather in despatching wives than whores. That Deeming had claimed to be the Ripper was never substantiated, and besides he did not have the professional expertise demonstrated by the Ripper -- any more than did the other butchers, bakers and candlestick makers who used knives to perform their work. Despite a certain amount of contradictory medical opinion, the majority of doctors who had examined the victims were convinced that the Ripper possessed considerable surgical skill. At the inquest on Annie Chapman, Dr. George Bagster Phillips, who was a Division Police Surgeon with twenty years of practical experience said: "Obviously the work was that of an expert - or one, at least, who had such knowledge of anatomical or pathological examinations as to be enabled to secure the pelvic organs with one sweep of the knife." Cream was a practised and qualified surgeon who had trained both in Montreal and St.Thomas's Hospital, London.

The super hyped "The Diary of Jack the Ripper" by Shirley Harrison and Michael Barrett which surfaced dramatically in 1993, purporting to be the long-lost genuine confession of Liverpool cotton-broker James Maybrick (himself allegedly murdered by his wife Florence) was exposed as a fraud by a national newspaper.

In the scholarly "Jack the Ripper. Summing up and Verdict" by Colin Wilson and Robin Odell (Bantam Press, 1987) it is observed that there is no hard evidence Cream was the Ripper. Quite so, but with the greatest respect to Messrs.Wilson and Odell, neither is there, in my submission, an iota of evidence that would stand up in a Court of Law behind any theory hitherto propounded as to the identity of the Whitechapel killer. Nor after more than a century, with the exception of circumstantial evidence, is any likely to emerge.

For this reason I have, in part, used the technique of psychological profilers, in an attempt to fathom the criminal mentality of this Victorian sociopath. However, the study as a whole is not based on dramatic representation, but solidly researched documentary records, which are clearly set out in the text and can be corroborated. Licence has only been employed to illustrate, for instance, how Cream's elaborate scam might have been contrived. Whether or not it was so contrived must be judged from the information provided, and which I believe, taken as a whole, will convince the reader that Thomas Neill Cream, as he himself confessed, was indeed Jack the Ripper.

SHIRLEY VAN EYSSEN ( nee Goulden) ©2006

'He had busied himself throughout the day writing the biography of himself which it is said will only be given to the world when he is no more.'

# PART 1

*'I, Thomas Neill Cream, being at present sound of mind and body....'*

He paused, grinned wryly, observing, (even without the gold-rimmed spectacles of which he had been deprived in order apparently to prevent their ingestion), that the condemned cell's spy-hole had again become obscured by the application of an inquisitive eye to its outer circumference.

*Intrusive bastards!* Would they not, as promised, respect a man's last wish for an hour or so's privacy during what might well be his remaining days on Earth? Particularly since, even before granting even that small privilege the swipes had searched every nook and cranny of the cell, and indeed his own person, to ensure he had no means of doing himself in.

Shouldn't the fools jump though if they knew he had craftily concealed in the heel of his shoe a small metal spoon, finely honed on the unyielding brick of Holloway Gaol, the vigorous application of which, if he chose, could at any given time deprive the vultures of their prey. Had not the American bank-robber Oliver Perry, according to recent newspaper accounts, carved his way through a foot of mortar and out of Auburn Gaol with precisely such an implement? In Cream's case, however, lacking as he did any hope of a worthwhile future, another escape would have been a futile exercise; and as for taking his own life he had reached the somber conclusion that, should the worst come to the worst, the hangman Billington might just as well be permitted to save him the inconvenience and make a swift end of it all.

Last evening, though, he had been in higher spirits after the visit from his solicitor, Waters, who, capital fellow that he was, had managed to achieve a temporary stay of execution while awaiting certain affidavits from America. On the strength of this, despite Waters' obvious reluctance to raise false hopes, Cream had persuaded himself that all was not lost by a long chalk! As it happened, he had been equally cocksure in Holloway towards the trial's end -- and before the verdict had gone against him -- singing loudly and capering exultantly about his cell. Now, at Newgate, and a stone's throw from the hanging shed, his unnatural euphoria carried him throughout a sleepless night; but dawn's stark light filtering through the high barred window of the bleak stronghold revealed him slumped at his table, in a contrasting mood of deep despondency. It was then that Cream had begun to write, if for no better purpose than to distract him from his troubles.

'...do now readily confess to such deeds of which I have been accused and stand condemned; together with several earlier transgressions. These I had perpetrated in a resolute effort to deliver society, so far as is in one man's power, from the scourge of certain females -- by false sentiment termed "unfortunates" -- who have themselves brought untold misfortune to the world, corrupting all that is noble in mankind with their evil ways and foul temptations. "How oft is the candle of the wicked put out! And how oft cometh their destruction upon them!" Ideally suited, by virtue of my qualifications as physician and surgeon, to undertake such a crusade, I commenced operations (as it were) in 1888. I was known as Jack the Ripper.

I am tempted to tell one or two of the keepers as much, if only to liven the place up a little; since there is no chance that the police, if informed of my claims, will actually believe them to be genuine. Those buffoons have never been capable of recognising the truth, even when directly confronted by it, any more than they did back in June when first suspecting me in the Stamford Street poisonings. "The Chronicle", to my clear recollection, then pointedly observed: "...it is not beyond the bounds of possibility that The Stamford Street case may indirectly be the means of throwing light on the terrible Jack the Ripper murders." I was for a while a good deal disturbed by the comment, since until then

*Scotland Yard apparently had not even sufficient evidence to arrest me on the Lambeth poisonings. Now I feared I should be brought to book on all counts. Had I but been aware that, as a result of word from America, and in their infinite wisdom, the Bosses deemed me perfectly innocent in the Ripper affair -- being wholly convinced that I was at the time still languishing in the Illinois pen and poverty, and it was her sublime faith in the first and dread of the second that had caused her to urge Papa, a poorly paid Glasgow bank clerk, to seek more favourable opportunities in the New World. Having already uprooted to Scotland from his native Ire-land and failed to improve his lot, Papa was no doubt dubious at the prospect of starting up yet again in far-flung Canada, but there was no gainsaying Mama. Her maiden name had, appropriately, been Elder, and, our family settling in a rural suburb of Quebec, she soon became as much a driving force among the church elders as in my father's future career. Not that Papa, once he got himself started, was to prove anything but shrewd when it came to business, though his smooth brand of Irish blarney sure fooled many a rival.*

*As a result of Mama's early influence I have throughout my lifetime experienced sporadic bouts of religion; but being by nature intemperate in all senses, veered all too often from rectitude to recklessness. On a memorable Sunday during adolescence, I laid up with some mild ailment and assuming all the family to be at kirk, succeeded in inducing the hired-help to join me in bed. My unpredictable and for the most part irreverent Papa, though, had decided to go horse-back riding instead, and returning before the service was over found me aping his sport astride the slut. Prompted less, I suspected, by genuine disapproval than what he knew to be Mama's hidebound perception of paternal duty, he soundly whipped my upturned rear, predicting the while, alas only too accurately, that such base tendencies would be the end of me. The skivvy, on the other hand, was neither reprimanded nor turned away, since Papa had always been soft on women, in more ways than one no doubt, as a consequence of his ill-matched alliance to my cold and unbending mama. Under dire threat of peaching to "The Holy One" if I were caught again at the same game -- a far more daunting prospect as he well knew than a beating from him --I was from then onwards obliged to confine my activities to the barn; except for those infrequent occasions when, being dismissed early from school, I returned to find Mama out serving the community and Papa his employers.*

*Even now I recall, during intimacy with the unwholesome wench, her stale emanation of rotting vegetation which both repelled and curiously attracted me as we continued to compound our sin. The slut remained with us until my eighteenth year, when the family being conveniently away on holiday, I was able at last to use her without restraint.*

*Such was the handsome young humbug who sang with fervour in the church choir, presided over weekly Sunday school classes and conducted himself with respectful decorum among the pretty young ladies at Messrs. Baldwin and Company, Timber Merchants, where by way of a favour to his father he had been apprenticed at a minimum wage. The prim little virgins at Baldwin's were, as it happened, of scant temptation to a strapping lad who had already developed a preference for loose women -- one which, regrettably, he was rarely in a financial position to indulge.*

*Yet there was to be an upsurge of family fortune within the next two years as would considerably improve my prospects. Papa, elevated by Mama's determination, some passing experience in the trade and the luck of the Irish, managed to found his own timber firm which shortly began to flourish quite beyond his expectations. Reaching my majority it was naturally assumed that as the eldest son, I would wish to enter the rapidly expanding business; but my own most earnest ambition by then was to become a surgeon. My father at last agreeing, albeit reluctantly, to fund my training, I, accompanied by my constant companion, Andersmann, who had likewise opted for medical school, entered McGill University, in the fall of 1872.*

*I spent over three years in the fine city of Montreal, studying, (in various ways), human anatomy. In early '76, nearing graduation, I again encountered, in one of the low bars I was wont to frequent, my cousin Neill Thomas Elder, whom, in childhood, I had cordially detested. 'Squint-a-pipes!', he would taunt me, referring to that unfortunate affliction of eyesight with which I had been born. It was not until the commencement of my medical training that I learned, by the constant application of exercise, to control the condition, it later becoming manifest only in moments of extreme fatigue or stress. During those early years, as the helpless target of such unkind shafts I became increasingly more withdrawn and resentful. Not until I was a thickset lad of fourteen or so was I able to wreak vengeance upon my tormenters by means of a gashed eye (for an eye!) a bloody nose, or, even more satisfactorily, by bending an arm to breaking point or the twisted insertion of a penknife blade in a tender rump. I became increasingly less hesitant to employ such means of asserting myself, even to the extent, in time, of frequently taking offence where it was not necessarily meant, merely for an excuse to exact punishment.*

*Thus I was able to command a certain amount of respect but never the warmth of true friendship, and fell to associating with the only Jew boy in our community. Andersmann, not so much persecuted for his singularity as totally disregarded by the others, was drawn eventually into my company. His attitude I found obsequious and his Teutonic accent absurd, but nevertheless we shared an astute mind.*

*A year or so later I was to form an even more unlikely alliance, and that with none other than cousin Neill. Despite our childhood antipathy, we found ourselves now mutually attracted by the manifestation of a common trait, that of headstrong waywardness.*

*The son of my mother's brother, Murdoch Elder, Neill's family had immigrated to Canada at the same time as my own. Reaching adolescence it was generally remarked upon that the two of us had developed a more than passing resemblance to the portrait in our parlour of great grandfather Thomas Neill, whose name we had both inherited, together with a massive jaw, a fondness for liquor and a streak of perversity which, it was rumoured, had brought about great grandpapa's untimely demise at the end of a yardarm. Nonetheless he was referred to reverentially by Mama as 'The Captain', she holding firmly to the illusion that he had been something of a naval hero.*

*Neill and I had grown equal in physical but not mental prowess and my superiority soon won me leadership in the campaign of wrong doing upon which the two of us were presently to embark. Andersmann, finding me less dependent upon his company, and -- being something of a rotten little prig, disapproving of our proposed activities -- obligingly made himself scarce; though my young brother Danny, who considered me a mighty fine fellow and invariably dogged my footsteps, was anxious to be included in our escapades.*

*Evading detection for the most part was simple, the representative of law and order in our tiny homestead, (my family had not as yet become affluent enough to set up in the big city), being but a single dim-witted constable. More than once, however, an observant farmer whose orchards and hen-coops we were in process of raiding for saleable produce, confronted us with a shotgun, But Neill, less adept than myself in the art of deception, acted invariably as the scapegoat for our crimes, receiving a sound thrashing; while I, protesting histrionically that it was my reprobate cousin who had led me astray, thus gaining the sympathy of an impressionable farmer's wife or daughter, invariably escaped with a warning. Neill, displaying a curious quirk in his character which I was never to comprehend, readily shouldered the blame, accepting his punishment with not so much an air of resignation as a kind of careless bravado that, despite certain misgivings as to the true generosity of his nature, gained my unwilling respect.*

*Uncle Murdoch did not share my own father's business acumen. Over-indulgent in his drinking habits and failing after fourteen years to better himself and his family in the New World, he shipped them lock stock and whisky barrel back to Glasgow. Cousin Neill was left behind, and not of his own free will, having progressed from our minor misdemeanours to a more serious infringement of the law, which resulted in his eventual imprisonment. Thus had I not set eyes upon him for several years until that chance meeting in Montreal. I had made few friends at the University, sharing long hours of study with the equally solitary Andersmann, as a result of which we had both taken to wearing spectacles, our lenses heavily opaque.*

*So that although my cousin, upon his release, cut a pathetic enough figure in the shabby outfit provided by the penny-pinching authorities, I was delighted to see the unfortunate chap, assuring him I should willingly enough have provided him with a decent suit of clothes and a flower for his button-hole; but that my quite liberal quarterly allowance had all but been expended upon the hire of a stylish carriage essential to the escorting of ladies during the weekend, one or two new outfits, together with a distinctive horseshoe tie pin and an impressive watch and chain to wear for my forthcoming graduation photograph. After paying the rent in advance for lodgings, I now found myself embarrassingly short of funds. Cousin Neill, however, appeared, doubtless as a result of a less than formal education at the hands of his fellow convicts, to have developed a degree of cunning and sharpness of wit notably lacking in his earlier years. Indeed it was he who devised and encouraged the commission of my first professional crime, the perpetration of which, while causing no direct injury to certain of the college hierarchy against whom I had developed a grievance, served somehow to ease my oppressions.*

*On learning that I owned a policy in the sum of one thousand dollars, to cover personal effects, Neill proposed that given his assistance I might without difficulty, and little risk to myself, defraud the insurance company of that eminently advantageous sum, which, if the plan were to succeed, we should then divide between us. I was merely to hand him the keys of my rooms and soon afterwards, bearing with me as many of my possessions as I was able, make for an hotel in the township of Waterloo owned by the well-to-do parents of a young lady whose acquaintance I had recently made; after which Neill was to enter the premises at Mansfield Street and start afire. The idea at once appealed to me, particularly since there appeared to be no possibility of the deed being traced to myself. Accordingly I supplied him with all the necessary information as to the layout of the building, the landlady's usual hour of retirement for the night, and the keys of my rooms -- taking good care, I may add, (in order to avoid one of his exasperating lectures on the sins of dishonesty), to keep Andersmann in the dark. Growing ever more sanctimonious of late, I wondered if he might not have been better suited to the study of religion rather than medicine, and 'christened' him "The Rabbi".*

*All should surely have passed according to plan but for my skeleton, acquired for the purpose of studying anatomy, which, to avoid damage, I had been accustomed to place upon the bed during my absence. The room being illumed through the casement by a dimly flickering street-lamp, my cousin on entering was so startled by Mr. Bones as to almost completely lose his nerve, only managing by great force of will, so he declared, to suppress a yell which would doubtless have aroused the entire household. As it was, having hastily ignited some papers in the interior of my bureau, he left considerably less stealthily than he had entered, clattering frantically down the stairs and making off, without troubling to ensure that his work had taken effect. The result obviously was to alert that prim old witch of a landlady, with her narrow prohibitions, before she was burned in her bed --the flames being brought into control with little damage except to the bureau and a few sticks of furniture. Nevertheless, ever sanguine, I did not hesitate to pursue my claim with the insurance company, confident in the expectation that before long we should each benefit most conveniently by upwards of five hundred dollars.*

**FROM A REPORT BY INSPECTOR FREDERICK JARVIS OF THE METROPOLITAN POLICE, Montreal, July 7th, 1892.**

At McGill College he effected a fire insurance policy in his personal goods, wearing apparel, &c. for one thousand dollars with the Commercial Union Insurance Company, 1731 Notre Dame Street, Montreal, the policy being dated 15 September 1874 and numbered 176528, his address being 106, Mansfield St. Montreal, the householder being a Miss Jane Porter. A fire occurred in Cream's room on 18th April 1876 and was confined to a Bureau. Cream sent in a detailed claim for $978.40c. but the Company refused to pay, strongly suspecting incendiarism. In the end the matter was referred to arbitration and the claim was settled for $350.

*Judging it prudent to lie low some sixty miles or so away in an hotel at Waterloo -- attended, whenever possible, by the owner's daughter, Flora Brooks -- I was soon to find myself unwillingly engaged to be married. Back in Montreal at last and restored to solvency less by my half portion of the meagre sum received from the insurance company than by a further allowance from home, I bid farewell to cousin Neill, who with his share had decided to try his luck in Australia. With what unaccustomed diligence did I now resume my studies of the past four years, in order not only to avoid the cloying passions of Flora, who had begun unutterably to bore me, but that I might soon achieve the title of Doctor of Medicine and Master of Surgery.*

*Once obtaining our degrees Andersmann and I took our leave of one another, for my part with conflicting feelings of relief and regret. Over the years we had become inseparable but at McGill his Talmudic sermonising and money grubbing had irritated the bejesus out of me; particularly so since in deprecating his Hebrew ways, I was occasionally driven to reflect upon my own shortcomings.*

**MCGILL UNIVERSITY MEDICAL SCHOOL, CALENDAR OF 1873:**

...The Dissecting Room....Under direct supervision of Professor of Anatomy...to superintend and examine Students engaged in dissection. Abundance of fresh material for dissection will be provided.

PRACTICE OF MEDICINE. - (Prof. Campbell) - Surgical Anatomy and Operative surgery...various surgical instruments and apparatus exhibited, and their uses and applications explained...

MIDWIFERY. - (Prof. McCallum). Including ...humid preparations, by models in wax ... and by cases in the wards of the Lying-in Hospital.

MEDICAL JURISPRUDENCE - (Prof. Fenwick) includes toxicology, the mode of testing for poisons are exhibited, and post mortem appearances illustrated by plates.

CLINICAL SURGERY - (Prof. Fenwick)...lectures are in illustration of Surgical cases under observation in the Wards of the General Hospital. Bed-side instruction is followed up daily and all operations are performed in the presence of the class. The lectures are illustrated by cases under surgical treatment, by plates, surgical apparatus, morbid specimens...

FROM EXAMINATION PAPERS, 1876-7:

"Question 4. Describe the mode of death in hanging, strangulation, and suffocation respectively."

MCGILL UNIVERSITY MEDICAL SCHOOL, CALENDAR OF 1876.

The following gentlemen, 34 in number, have passed their Final Examinations for the degree of M.D., C.M. from this University. These examinations are both written and oral, and are on the following subjects: Principles and Practice of Surgery, Theory and Practice of Medicine, Obstetrics and Diseases of Women and Children, Medical Jurisprudence and Hygiene, - and also Clinical Examinations in Medicine and Surgery, conducted at the bedside in the Hospital, and a Thesis on some medical subject. The names of the successful candidates, their residences and the subjects of their thesis, are as follows....

...CREAM, Thomas N. Quebec, Q. "Thesis": CHLOROFORM...

*Having become entitled to style myself a doctor and a surgeon on home ground, I now sought qualifications further afield and before the year was out sailed for England. I had heard that St. Thomas's Hospital in London held excellent post-graduate courses, and that the streets were paved with whores. Even though I now wore spectacles most of the time and had already started to shed some of my handsome auburn hair, those exceptional physical powers with which, since the days of my youth I had been either cursed or blessed, were not to desert me; such powers as females appeared in some curious way to sense, and either shrank from or were drawn to according to their characters.*

*There were, I must own, even more pressing reasons than these for selecting far distant London as my temporary home. Having without undue difficulty succeeded in overcoming Flora's maidenly protestations of virtue, I had by summer suffered as much as I could endure of our spiritless association. Urged to appoint a wedding date, I declared myself unwilling to propose until my horizons were extended.*

*"By travelling to London I intend to broaden my experience, improve my skills, "I explained truthfully, "and by these means advance whatever hope I may have of obtaining your Papa's consent. Thus, sweet rose, though the very thought of it tears at my heartstrings, we must agree to part." I had inherited none of father's ways but for his persuasive manner and slight Irish-American brogue.*

*"Tom, my dear, how could you be so cruel as to talk of parting?" simpered the goose. "London may wait until I am made of an honest woman, and that as soon as is convenient; or we never can hope to receive Papa's approval."*

*I began to grow uneasy, for old man Brooks was reputed to have unerring aim with a shotgun, and had more than once conveyed the impression that he would not be loathe, with the smallest justification, to level it in my direction. Promising her that we should be wed before the year was out, I mentally noted there and then to book immediate passage to England, for an indefinite stay.*

*"Not to be wed until Christmas?" she whined, tossing her absurd yellow ringlets pettishly, and, confirming my worst presentiments. "Why,*

Tom, my dear, you are soon to be a papa yourself, don't you see?" Admittedly until then I had neglected to observe that my rose was becoming increasingly overblown, and wondered ruefully whether I should ever make a medical man. On that score I was soon put to the test.

During September Flora, now come to appreciate that it was prudent to postpone our marriage until I was in a more favourable position to support a family, agreed, though with some misgivings, to undergo a minor surgical operation. This was performed intrepidly by myself under her parent's roof -- a deft dose of chloroform ensuring that the silence of the night would not be shattered by her screams. While she was still under the influence of the anaesthetic I retreated to Montreal, suspecting the operation had been, with-out proper facilities, ill accomplished and not wishing to be held responsible if my dear fiancee failed to wake at all. I was to learn subsequently that Flora, recovering consciousness and finding herself alone and in considerable discomfort, had hollered fit to wake the entire hotel. The family physician, Dr. Phelan, was at once sent for, informing the parents in due course that an abortion had been performed upon their daughter, doubtless by the author of her predicament.

Old man Brooks, mad as a hare, took up his shotgun and pursuing me to Montreal, where under threat of instant annihilation I had no choice but to return to Waterloo and, as soon as could be arranged, wed Flora. The bride, continuing sickly and unappetising, nevertheless managed from the marital bed to extend a limp but eager hand in order to receive the wedding band, which, despite the presence of minister and parents, I jammed upon her finger with as much vindictiveness as I dared employ. My only solace in the otherwise joyless ssituation was the knowledge that, a day earlier I had, by means of threats and cajolement, secretly induced Flora to place her signature upon a marriage contract, which, should I chance to become a widower, would afford capital consolation.

By dawn on the following day I had left the sleepy township of Waterloo well behind, informing the blushing bride by means of a note that my departure was thus suddenly necessitated in order not only to spare ourselves the sadness of farewell but so that I might, by dint of hard *study and application, fulfil my intention to become a more worthy husband in the future. And as a token of touching concern, I enclosed in a separate paper a number of pills, trusting that she would take them regularly -- that I might soon return to find my delicate rose once again in bloom.*

*It was while I was in London that I heard without undue astonishment that Flora had died, the previous August, of a lingering illness. My sole regret was in discovering myself unable to obtain settlement on the marriage contract of more than a trifling two hundred dollars. This when it had been legally agreed that I was to receive ten times the sum -- what price justice?*

METROPOLITAN POLICE REPORT. 27th day of June 1892.

*Mr. William Buttle, Solicitor, 25, Basinghall Street E. C. called at this office and stated that having seen in Saturday's papers that Neale [sic] had been known as Dr. Cream, he thought perhaps he could give some information, as he knew in 1877 a young man named Thomas N. Cream who was staying at Gough Square, Fleet Street, a Medical Student and a native of Canada. This man Cream was paying his attention to the landlady's daughter and about March 1877 this young lady received a letter from a friend, a Miss Charlotte Louisa Botteril of 15, Plateau Street Montreal telling her that Dr. Cream was a married man, that he had got into some trouble with a respectable girl out there and had to marry her, and that on the first day he left her and came to England, and that her friends found her on the floor of the room in an unconscious state.*

*This letter by some mysterious means found its way from the young lady's pocket into the hands of Dr. Cream, who threatened an action for Libel against the writer, Miss Botteril, and demanded an apology and ten pounds for costs through his Solicitor Mr. N. P. Thomas, 1, New Inn, Strand. An apology was tendered by Miss Botteril through Mr. Buttle on the understanding that Dr. Cream gave up the letter in question and which was to be held sealed by Mr. Buttle till required to be produced in Court on any future occasion.*

*Mr. Buttle also has some letters (and one in particular) dated 31stMarch 1877 from St. Thomas's Hospital signed by Thomas N. Cream, M.D.*

*Mr. Buttle will be pleased to let Inspr. Tunbridge see all letters and papers in his possession, if of any service, by making an appointment any morning between 10 a.m. and 12.30 p.m.*

*George Bush, Sergt.*

# PART 2

His counsel having petitioned for a reprieve, Cream's execution date had been advanced to the 15th and now two warders attended the death cell around the clock. Each pair sat on a bench affording the prisoner relentless supervision, the avoidance of their expressionless gaze resulting in Cream absorbing himself even more in his work, pausing for the most part only to recall a particular incident or a train of events. Scarcely able to sleep, red and overstrained eyes reverting, without spectacles, to a grotesque squint, his once precise handwriting degenerating into an untidy scrawl, still the man plied his pen with almost manic rapidity.

In absence of word from the Home Secretary, and with the distinct likelihood that he would before long be brought to a higher judgment, the completion of the confession was, as he saw it, a necessary expedient -- an insurance policy, so to speak, on his soul. This was one policy however that Cream was in no hurry to redeem.

*Whitehall, November 11.*

*Gentlemen,*

*With reference to your further letters of the 9th and 10th inst., I am directed by the Secretary of State to inform you that, after the most careful consideration of the affidavits submitted by you on behalf of Thomas Neill, now lying under sentence of death in Newgate prison, and of all the circumstances of the case, he has been unable to discover any sufficient grounds to justify him, consistently with his public duty, in advising her Majesty to interfere with the due course of the law.*

*I am, Gentlemen, your obedient servant,*

*Godfrey Lushington.*

*Messrs. Waters and Bryan, Solicitors, 13, Temple-chambers, Temple-avenue, E.G.*

Cream raised his bleary eyes from the Home Secretary's letter, presented to him with due diffidence by Merrick, the chaplain, who had undertaken the task at the request of the Governor of both Newgate and Holloway jails, Colonel Milman. Milman had already experienced first hand, at Holloway back in October, an example of Cream's unbridled and offensive attitude, to which he had no intention of deliberately re-exposing himself. Before the court verdict, the prisoner had declared flamboyantly that, noted for his impeccable appearance, he was unwilling to be seen in public without a new suit. Permission to order one being denied, the Governor had then been subjected to so revolting a flow of foul-mouthed invective as never before in his career. Yet, on this of all occasions Milman would have been astounded at Cream's equanimity. It seemed he was finally for the drop, but the sods should not hear him whine. He accepted calmly the grim news that there was to be no reprieve, merely shrugging and remarking, as casually as possible, that he supposed it could not be helped. The chaplain offered the customary words of solace and took his leave.

Cream slowly tore up the letter and dropped the pieces one by one on the floor.

"Pick 'em up", rapped a warder. Cream made no move to obey but proferred an ingratiating smile.

"Why, my dear fellow, I do urge you to show some respect, if not for the Lambeth Poisoner, then at least for Jack the Ripper!" Much entertained by their expression of shocked bewilderment he broke into raucous laughter, the warders exchanging such glances as signified, in view of the man's obvious instability, their intention to avoid further confrontation.

Call themselves officers of the law -- from the Bosses downwards the simpletons literally never had a clue, though to be sure he had done his best to provide them with one or two real gems. And now, with nothing to lose, he was actually admitting, straight out, that he was the Ripper, only to be dismissed as a braggart, or even, (though the Home Secretary could unfortunately not be persuaded to this view), a madman. Though he had counted on being disbelieved, it seemed ironic that he was to be denied the credit for Jolly Jack's exploits until the publication of his memoirs, when he would no longer be present to enjoy the notoriety. Sighing, he again took up his pen.

*Arriving in London, England for the first time in October of 1876, I found that the city more than lived up to its expectations. If a man were not too particular, street walkers could be had for as little as a shilling a time, and did my appetite for study equal a constant ravening for such drabs, I should indeed have been a model student.*

*Fearing eventually to contract a disease, and a dalliance with my landlady's wholesome but dreary daughter having been brought to an end, I was thrown more into the company of my own sex; frequenting low bars and getting acquainted with an odd assortment of fellow tipplers, including many members of the criminal fraternity, whose robust accounts of their lawless escapades held me in thrall, and from whom I learned much.*

*One, an Australian adventurer, John Fordyce, was like myself, of average height and not dissimilar in colouring -- though I could then boast a striking copper mane, while his was a vulgar carroty thatch. Offering me a drink, Fordyce observed that we might well pass for one another at a pinch, which in certain circumstances could well work to our mutual advantage. He, as it emerged, though hardly older than myself, was already an accomplished trickster who specialized in using his wiles to fleece elderly widows of their mite; when however there was a scarcity of ewes for the shearing Fordyce would subsidise his income by staging, with apparent immunity from prosecution, an occasional robbery. The paternal allowance being never enough, bored with swatting and game for a lark, I was soon persuaded to join him in the pursuit of easy money; working separately but on a profit-sharing basis --and on the mutual understanding that where necessary we would provide one another with an alibi. Since the police have always lacked positive means of identification, it was a dodge which was to come in mighty handy on more than one occasion.*

*Fordyce, considerably more experienced than myself in the commission of crime knew pretty much how to stay out of trouble, and it was I, Tom Cream, Amateur Cracksman, who was obliged before long to fall back* upon our contingency plan. Emerging at dead of night from an empty office carrying a bag of notes in one hand and a jemmy in the other, I ran straight into an armed night watchman. This was no time for a display of heroics on my part, for the watchman at once blew a piercing blast on his whistle, bringing several policemen speedily to the scene. Though in a blue funk, I managed to stammer that my name was John Fordyce, a visitor to England, at present residing in the Rendlesham Hotel, Marylebone and, despite appearances being against me, should shortly be in a position to prove my innocence. Conveyed to the local police station, I passed a most uncomfortable night. However, the following morning, having developed quite a talent for bluffing my way out of a sticky situation, and sufficient money to stake myself, I was released pending trial.

Meanwhile, according to our prearranged plan, Fordyce himself had been getting noisily drunk in a public house where he was well known to the landlord and many of his patrons. When the case came before the magistrate several weeks later I had made myself conveniently scarce while my confederate put in a brief court appearance. Several unimpeachable witnesses testified as to his whereabouts on the night of the burglary, and the case was dismissed on grounds of mistaken identity. If I was cock-a-hoop over the success of our scheme, not so Fordyce; for the police, having a faint suspicion (though no evidence) that they had been taken in, began to display an undue interest in his movements, shadowing him everywhere. This soon drove the poor fellow to the conclusion that there was after all no place like home; and to our mutual regret he returned to Sydney. We promised however to remain in touch, and should the occasion arise, use our capital dodge again. I, for one, was to be profoundly thankful for that in future years.

If as is metaphorically stated, the arm of the law is long, it's leg must assuredly be longer, for had I not succeeded in yanking it to full stretch? The police may have been on to Fordyce but had let me go scot free. Thus did I reflect upon the amazing gullibility of those employed in the administration of justice, the ease with which they could be deceived, and the fun inherent in continuing so to do. The way matters stood, though, I had reached the threshold of what promised to be a *distinguished medical career, and came eventually to the realization that had luck turned against me in the Fordyce affair I should have been utterly disgraced. Facing this, a not uncharacteristic nervous reaction set in; and failing to pass my examinations at St. Thomas's, I retreated again to Edinburgh for the purpose of re-sitting them. There, for a while, much chastened, I came soberly to review my past indiscretions, agonizing night after restless night as to what heights I might now have ascended, had I not spurned Anderesmann's constant entreaties to follow the path of virtue. While from earliest development the Rabbi had with his avaricious Jewish ways predisposed my own tendency to covetousness, I knew over all that he did have my best interests at heart. To give the fellow his due, might not his advice, had I accepted it, have prevented my now teetering upon the very brink of ruin?*

*A course of reformation was clearly indicated, and rejoining the church I resumed my former practice of devoting Sundays to conducting a bible class, weekdays to revision and nights to indulging in but a solitary vice which, I am persuaded, did nothing to improve my vision. Alas, it soon became obvious that nature had not intended me for an ascetic. When in April of '78 I received double qualifications of the Royal College of Physicians and Surgeons at Edinburgh, I returned to Canada and before long had fallen once again into dissolute ways.*

*Entitled now to style myself impressively not only Doctor of Medicine and Master of Surgery, but to place the letters M.R.C.S. and M.R. C.P after my name, and having a background of practical experience in the post-mortem and obstetric departments of St. Thomas's, I had every expectation of becoming one of Canada's most prominent physicians. Alas such aspirations were doomed to disappointment. Deciding to specialise in obstetrics, I opened an office in the most fashionable section of London, Ontario. Though as a debonair bachelor, I managed to scrape an acquaintance with several females of wealthy and influential background, receiving occasional invitations to their grand soirees, it was with utmost mortification that I discovered myself unable to bring even one of the haughty bitches either to my examining couch or my bed. Urgently requiring income I was obliged presently to remove to less salubrious premises contained in a decaying edifice which stood, as I discovered, bordering an area much frequented by those women who were likely to require the attentions of an unscrupulous doctor.*

*Having attempted and failed to become a respected member of the community, and finding myself in such reduced conditions as had scarcely been anticipated during my long exertions to achieve honour and distinction as a medical man, I turned for a living to abortion. Deprived of the position in society that was mine by rights and driven to ignominy, my rancor made of me a hardened misogynist.*

*If my services had been rejected by females of the upper class, I soon found myself in great demand among their not quite so fortunate sisters, experiencing on occasion a less than professional frisson while, with each deft turn of the blade, I rid the world of yet another misbegotten whelp. But it was not until I had the misfortune to encounter Kitty Gardner, a lodging-house chambermaid who attended assiduously both day and night to the requirements of several gentlemen boarders -- receiving from her myself an unpleasant and debilitating disease -- that the smouldering resentment I had up until then managed to contain burst into flames of fury.*

*Missing her courses the strumpet had arrived at Dundas Street, and on my confirming her to be with child claimed the culprit to be a wealthy dry goods merchant lodging at her place of work. I later discovered, with extreme indignation, that during his stay in town the tradesman, not hesitating to use his financial advantages to the full, had already an entree to those exclusive circles from which I, a doctor of medicine no less, had been excluded! Determined to fix the blackguard I arranged a meeting, acquainting him with such information concerning Miss Gardner as had come to my attention and undertaking that on receipt of a certain handsome sum my lips should ever be sealed upon the subject of his indiscretion.*

*His boorish reply was that, suspecting himself to be unwell as a result of his connection with the girl, he considered an offer to pay for the abortion more than generous in the circumstances; and so far as any further demands from myself were concerned, on that or any other count, I might go and be hanged!*

*Thus euchred, and defiled by an unclean affliction, my grudge against Kitty Gardner, the author of these humiliations, turned to violent animosity. The woman's body spread unconscious before me on the operating table, and easing my instrument up-wards, I experienced an almost uncontrollable urge to terminate for ever the reproduction of her loathsome kind. In what frenzy of excitement did I vividly imagine myself agreeably engaged in the act of wrenching out her guts!*

*Somehow caution prevailed over this dangerous compulsion, and I decided, with a great effort of will, to postpone the operation until I had regained some vestige of control. Attempting to repair what minor damage my trembling fingers had already inflicted upon the patient, she, stirring before all was accomplished, started to moan, requiring further application of a liberally soaked chloroform pad. The contrary cow for some reason struggling to remain conscious, I found myself employing the pad with greater force and for a good deal longer than was advisable. Eventually removing the cloth I discovered to my consternation that the facial skin was badly excoriated, lidless eyes staring reproachfully up at me like those of a dead fish.*

*Commendably calm, considering the circumstances, I waited until nightfall when, unobserved, I removed the corpse to an outside privy, propping it up against a wall with the empty chloroform bottle nearby, fervently hoping that all indications would point to suicide.*

*TORONTO 14July 1892.*

*I have this evening returned from London, Ontario where I saw the Chief of Police concerning Cream, he says he remembers his coming and setting up in practice at Hiscocks Building, Dundas Street, London, Ontario about the Autumn of 1878. He was never arrested but in the morning of 2ndMay 1879 the body of a woman named Kate Hutchinson Gardener was round in a water closet in the backyard of the premises occupied by Cream, a bottle was beside the body which was found to have contained chloroform. An inquest was held by the Coroner. Deceased had been a chambermaid at the principal hotel in London, was proved that she had visited Cream's surgery on several occasions also tha tshe was enceinte. On the night prior to her body being found a girl named Maggie Flemming was in her company and left her in Dundas Street, not far from Cream's premises but Flemming did not see where she went to. Cream was called as witness and testified that the deceased had tried to induce him to procure an abortion but that he had repeatedly declined, he said he had not seen her in the evening prior to her body being found and there was no evidence to disprove this. The medical testimony was that no abortion had been procured but that the deceased died from chloroform poisoning and not self administered, there being abrasions in the face showing that the chloroform had been held to the face for a considerable time, which would have been impossible for the deceased to have done as she would have become unconscious almost immediately and consequently unable to keep her hand to her face sufficiently long to have caused the abrasions. On 13May 1879 the Jury returned a verdict that deceased died from the effects of chloroform administered by some person unknown. Thus the matter ended but sufficient suspicion rested on Cream to cause his practice to drop off entirely and he soon after left for Chicago.*

*Fredk. Jarvis. Inspr.*

# PART 3

Unknown to the prisoner, Killington, the hangman, was now regularly at Newgate, his quarters being already allocated. With greatest attention to detail he had already selected in honour of Cream a new length of hemp, one inch wide in diameter, supplied according to the regulations by courtesy of Holloway Gaol. The prisoner's weight having been ascertained, the length of the drop was tested several times and with every intention of affording the condemned man a swift end, though despite a strategically placed knot in the rope, a hangman could offer no guarantees.

If Cream was aware of such preparations he showed little emotion. Though morose at mealtimes, he invariably bolted his food, declining gruffly the occasional cheap cigar proffered by one or other of the more compassionate warders, and continued unceasingly with his work. A proposed visit from the prison. chaplain, the Reverend Mr. Merrick was spurned, Cream making it abundantly clear that he resented any interruption; though he was afterwards observed at odd moments surreptitiously glancing at his Bible.

That his attention was so entirely taken up with the task he had set himself was in itself a mercy, for if he had once addressed the fact that his life was shortly to be extinguished, and at a rope's end, he may not have been able to maintain that strange unnatural composure.

*The police lacking sufficient evidence to nail me in the Gardner affair, I nevertheless found myself the butt of ignorant conjecture, as a result of which my practice entirely failed and I was obliged, sick and dispirited, to leave for the United States. Some weeks later, restored to health, and presently regaining my accustomed* sang froid, *I established a new office at 434 West Madison Street.*

*I found no lack of custom in Chicago, Madison Street being adjacent to the bordello district; and having formed many dubious relationships ranging from procuresses to politicians, from prostitutes to pimps, continued to engage lucratively in my former occupation. Not that gain alone had motivated my efforts. While relieving whores of their clap-infested offspring -- and on odd occasions, if the fancy took me, of their own worthless lives -- I was, of course, in accordance with my professional obligations, arresting the spread of their dirty pox; and thereby, so I considered, performing a salutary service to the human race.*

*This was not, however, the start of my campaign of purposeful annihilation -- that was to be conceived way in the future. So if only the blackbird had refrained from squawking, the Faulkner case, which was the result less of deliberation on my part than, I own, of inebriation, could never have been brought against me.*

*Hattie Mack cleaned my rooms, and for a few extra dollars, had been further induced to oblige me with her inept assistance at abortions, these taking place not at my own premises but where she lived. Such was an ideal arrangement, providing me with a perfect cover for my activities, or so I thought until the trial, when to save her dusky skin she blabbed -- swearing upon oath that I had performed no less than five hundred abortions in Canada! This unlikely assertion cast considerable doubt upon the witness's veracity, and the jury, choosing to accept my own smoothly expressed version of the incident, found me innocent.*

*TORONTO, 14 July 1892.*

*Particulars of the case of murder on which Cream was arrested in Chicago on 23 Aug. 1880 are as follows:*

*A Canadian girl named Julia Faulkner was under treatment by Cream ... at the house of a coloured woman named Hattie Mack, No. 1050 West Madison St. Chicago, an operation was performed by Cream in the presence of Mack in consequence of which Faulkner died. Mack became alarmed and left the house but before leaving she hung a white handkerchief in one of the windows which, as she afterwards stated in evidence, was a signal agreed on between herself and Cream that she had vacated the house, whereupon he was to burn the house and so destroy the body. However, before this could be done, Police Officer O'Hara on the beat, noticed the handkerchief and went to the house but failing to obtain admittance forced the door and there discovered the dead body of Faulkner. He made inquiry of neighbours and learnt that Cream had been visiting the house whereupon he went in search of him and arrested him, next day he traced the woman Mack and arrested her also. An inquest was held the result being that Cream and Mack were both committed for trial charged with murder. They were both indicted on 2nd. Oct. 1880 and the trial took place on 16th 17th and 18th November 1880 in the Criminal Court, Chicago before Judge Geary. The woman Mack gave evidence against Cream but the jury returned a verdict of "not guilty"...*

*Fredk. Jarvis, Inspr.*

*I may have left the court a free man, but was henceforth denied the liberty to resume my dutiful as well as profitable career (a chap must make his way in the world!) as a Chicago abortionist. Setting up in general practice, and the scant rewards of this occupation proving entirely insufficient to my needs, I schemed to augment them.*

*The following year a patient, one Miss Stack, had the misfortune to die under my prescribed medication; whereupon I suggested in writing to Frank Pyatt, the pharmacist who had prepared the dose, that he had made a most serious error, which however I was, in the goodness of my heart, prepared to conceal from the authorities on payment of a certain sum. Though I hardly knew the reason, Pyatt, an unsociable runt, had in the past repulsed all friendly overtures such as the offer of a select cigar or a drink, maintaining our relationship on a strictly business level. His reserve had rankled, and it was as much on this account as any other that I selected him as a candidate for my first serious attempt at blackmail.*

*For good measure, though I made no mention of this, I had ascertained that Pyatt was, f or those who could meet the cost, willing freely to supply drugs such as the liberal quantities of morphine frequently obtained by myself for the purpose of gratifying a pernicious habit. This*

*I had unfortunately developed while attempting to control the severe and disabling headaches which I now increasingly suffered. I was certain the cringing little bastard, scared witless by any investigation into his affairs, would pay up, and so he did.*

*I decided to specialise for a while in this satisfactory line of business, selecting mainly the recipients of my missives from among patients about whom I had personal knowledge, or, as in the case of Wyatt, those against whom I held a grudge. Always ensuring that the demands were no greater than the paying capacity of my victims, I proceeded to write letters hither and thither, the benefits of which, though on occasions trifling, combined of fectively to enlarge my income. Unfortunately however these activities eventually came to the attention of the police, and I again found myself under arrest.*

EXTRACT FROM "The Chicago Tribune", 19th June, 1881:

# "DR _" CREAM

## IN THE TOILS FOR SENDING SCURRILOUS POSTAL CARDS

Dr. Cream, who was tried once in the Criminal Court on an indictment charging him with abortion and acquitted, is in the toils again, with a prospect of being rewarded according to his desserts. His offense consists in the sending of the vilest sort of postal cards through the mails an offense for which the revised Statutes prescribe a fine of from one hundred dollars to five hundred dollars, with imprisonment from **one** to ten years. The recipient of his foul abuse is a man by the name of Joseph Martin, living at 129 West Thirteenth Street, engaged in the business of preparing furs for some of the wholesale and retail fur houses in this city. Cream had attended his family as a physician, and appears to have had some difficulty in regard to a bill. Martin claims that he paid the doctor all he owed him, while the latter, claiming that Martin was in his debt to the amount of twenty dollars, resorted to the despicable scheme of sending him scurrilous postal cards, in order, perhaps, to hasten matters and bring about a settlement of the alleged debt. The postals were preceded by a couple of letters, written in the same hand as the cards, signed "Thomas N. Cream," and valuable in the case as means of identifying the writing on the postal cards. In the first letter, the doctor very plainly informed Martin that his (Martin's) wife and children were suffering from diseases which, he said, they had contracted through Martin himself. He then proceeded to threaten him with an exposure of the matter unless his bill was paid, and to be more circumstantial, added that the proofs of his allegation consisted of certain prescriptions on file at one Knox's drug store. The second letter was similar in its tone, but wound up with the threat, "I will learn that damned vixen of a low wife of yours to speak ill of me" -- from which it might be inferred that Mrs. Martin had perhaps been somewhat free in the use of her tongue.

The postal cards are three in number, and were all sent day before yesterday. The postmarks show that they were mailed from the West Side station, one at 9 a.m. and the other two at 6 p.m. The first is signed "Dr. Cream," and the second with the doctor's initials, "T.N.C."

The second runs as follows:-

"You had better learn that low, vulgar wife of yours to keep her foul mouth shut, with her second-hand silk dohlmans and second-hand silk dresses, and not talk about others. Two can play at that game. I heard on very good authority that you had to leave England on account of a bastard child you left behind."

"T.N.C."

The third and last was evidently intended as a clincher. It reads as follows:-

"You had better learn that low, vulgar vixen woman of yours to keep a civil tongue in her head, and not talk about others. Two can play that game. Remember the bastard child you left in England."

"T.N.C."

Such abuse as this would have been bad enough even if it had been based on facts. It was all the worse, therefore, because, as Martin claims, infamously false. Whether true or false, however, the sender of such stuff committed an offense in the eyes of the law, and Mr. Martin is determined to get justice. A warrant for Cream's arrest was accordingly sworn out, and he was brought in quite late in the afternoon, naturally very wroth at the turn which the affair had taken, and held in twelve hundred dollars bail to await the preliminary examination on Monday.

This thing of sending scurrilous postal cards through the mails, and thereby attempting to blacken the reputation of people, has gone far enough. Cream has added the crowning infamy of attempting to blast that which every man holds dearest -- the fair name of his wife and children -- and the average husband and father will be pretty apt to conclude that even hanging would be too good for him should he be proved guilty.

Shortly to be placed on trial for the postal fiasco, and chary of quitting town minus twelve hundred dollars bail extorted by the Court, (acquired from some wealthy dame whose daughter I had earlier been courting), I took meanwhile to placing advertisements in the newspapers offering miraculous cures for all ills. Since the bottles I dispatched contained for most part a mild remedy for constipation, recovery from any other ailment would have indeed been a marvel. Even so, to my astonishment I received letters from many grateful sufferers who proclaimed themselves never to have been in better health since taking my nostrum! One of these, from an elderly man, Daniel Stott of Grand Prairie, Boone County, a compatriot of mine, was to the effect that his fits of epilepsy had ceased due, so he most positively believed, to the amazing properties of my elixir; and further that he intended to dispatch his wife forthwith to Chicago to collect large quantities of same, for whatever price I might name within reason.

Awaiting the appointed visit of Mrs. Julia Stott and anticipating an aging matron, I was pleasantly surprised to come upon a dainty housemaid of about three and thirty, whose studied air of respectability, as it quickly emerged, masked an avid desire to fornicate. Congenial as the situation was, I, declining upon medical grounds to supply her husband at any one time with large quantities of the miracle cure, thus ensured the continuance of her visits to Chicago. Confiding that her hapless union had been contracted solely for money, but that her thrice married spouse had proved mighty tight with a buck, she said:

"The worst of it is being obliged to submit, night after night, to that rank goat's impotent fumblings, all the while craving, as the soldier boys say, a show of strength, which Tom, no girl could deny, you do put up better'n most. "

"And could wish to perform more often", I observed. "Will you not consider, Julia, the taking of steps to obtain your freedom? I grow daily more impatient to ask for your hand, my love."

"Don't I believe you, so long as it's full of cash!" replied the astute bitch. There'll be no neat and tidy divorce settlement from the likes of Stott, though, if that's your expectation. Why, the old miser would part with *his life a sight more readily than he'd part with a dime! Nothing should please me better, I'm sure, than to see him taken off by one of those fits." She paused, flashed me an expressive glance, and, as if reading my mind, spoke meaningly:*

*"The way things stand between us, would you not agree, Tom, as to our having precious little to lose and a good deal to gain by setting up an insurance on his worthless life?"*

*My immediate response was to prescribe a permanent cure for Daniel Stott. She returning to Grand Prairie carried with her some pleasant tasting rhubarb pills and the usual nostrum, both of which customarily contained harmless doses of senna, but were now rendered rather less benign by the addition of a few grains of strychnine.*

*The news of Daniel Stott's sudden death was at first put down to his constitutional complaint, epilepsy. However, already accused of a criminal offence, and therefore open to mistrust, I sought to divert suspicion from myself towards the firm of pharmacists who had made up the original prescription. The culpability of Buck and Rayner, could it be established, might even, as I intimated to my mistress, afford us an additional bonus, of say four or five thousand dollars, were she to sue them for compensation in her sad loss. My next move was to telegraph the Coroner of Boone County:*

## "SUSPECT FOUL PLAY _ WILL WRITE IMMEDIATELY.

## DR. CREAM _"

*Incredibly enough this sage, in his infinite wisdom, saw fit to ignore my recommendation that the body be re-examined for the presence of strychnine. Confirmation of Stott's poisoning, would, I felt sure, result in the crediting of my own written accusation against the pharmacist and, as we had so ingeniously planned, render the firm liable to prosecution. What then was my mortification to discover that the telegram and letter were actually considered the work of a crank!*

*Burning with wrath and determined to uphold my dignity, I decided to place the entire matter before the State's Attorney. That gentleman, unlike the Coroner, had the decency, (or so I thought at the time), to favour me with his undivided attention -- arranging for the body to be exhumed post haste. On it being established that Stott was loaded, as I had so rightly insisted, with strychnine, and expecting at least a public apology, I was to receive instead, through the offices of this confounded weasel, a life term for murder!*

## "THE CHICAGO TRIBUNE", October 18th, 1881. [1]

Sheriff Ames will start for Joliet to-morrow with "Dr," Thomas N. Cream, yesterday sentenced by Judge Kellum to confinement in the penitentiary for life for the murder of Daniel Stott at Garden Prairie in June last. Mrs. Julia A. Stott, paramour of Dr. Cream and widow of the murdered man, remains in the county jail, her trial as an accomplice in the murder having been postponed until the next term of Court, which does not convene until the second Monday of February next. Your reporter this morning interviewed Senator Fuller, one of the counsels for the people, in regard to this case, and his views in regard to the probability of the Supreme Court granting a new trial in case the matter comes before it. The Senator says he believes there is as little error in the record of this case as in any criminal case he was ever connected with, and he does not believe it possible for the Supreme Court to find anything that can reverse the case. It is a case, he says, where there can be no possible doubt of the guilt of the defendant, and the crime is one that stands almost without a parallel in the annals of crime. Mr. Stott was deliberately poisoned by his physician and his faithless wife simply for the purpose of putting up a black mailing job on a reputable drug firm of Chicago. The jury which found the doctor guilty was composed of some of the best citizens of the county, men of sound judgment, conscientious and honest, and, if ever a man had a fair trial and an able defense, Mr. Cream is that man. The people of the county are well pleased and satisfied with the result of the trial and the conviction of Mrs. Stott in February next is confidently predicted.

---

(1)    There is a slight discrepancy in this report, since Cream, according to prison records, started his life sentence at Joliet Penetentiary on November 1st, 1881

# PART 4

*Any refinement of character to which, as a gentleman, I might formerly have laid claim was harshly repressed during my several years as a reluctant guest of the State of Illinois. At Joliet Penitentiary my living quarters consisted of a gloomy and dank stone cell measuring eight by four feet, containing two small cots with cornhusk mattresses, a few ragged blankets and little else except the necessary covered pail -- this requiring to be emptied every morning down an open cesspool, each convict providing his own contribution to the stink.*

*With the prospect of spending all of my natural life entombed in this dismal citadel of stone galleries, iron staircases, doors barred by guards with lead tipped canes, and the hewing of rock my sole occupation, I began to grow savage as any caged beast.*

*I received few visitors over the years. Of my friends only Anderesmann did not forsake me, arriving unexpectedly on several occasions, which I own was good of the Rabbi, since back home it seemed he was now quite the fashionable physician, specializing in disorders of the mind; and but for his calm counselling I should surely have lost control of my senses. He assured me that whenever in dire need I might call upon him and that he would come at once; and but for this I dare say that in my agony of deprivation and despair I might well have dashed out my brains against those adamantine walls.*

*As for the Cream family only Danny made regular trips to Joliet, and from him I divined that Mama, ever obdurate, had forbidden the mention of my name. As for Papa, I had long been persuaded that his liberality in the past was but a substitute for fondness; for during the interminable years of my imprisonment he failed to establish any contact with me. Raised as I was to eschew all ordinary instincts of kindness, their passing, soon after one another in the spring of 1887, left me pretty much unmoved.*

*I felt no cessation of bitterness towards my father even when it emerged that the old buzzard had in his last days sent for all my relatives, disclosing to them that upon my conviction he, determined to clear the name of Cream, had taken certain steps in order to procure a remittance of my sentence within the passage of ten years; and charging each and every one, on receiving their inheritance, to ensure the continuance of his efforts. Convinced that he had done so more in the interests of restoring the family reputation than f or my benefit, and without so much as troubling to alleviate my torment by a word of encouragement, I could cheerfully have danced upon his grave! How inordinately did my filia affection increase however when I learned that, under the terms of our father's will the sum of sixteen thousand dollars had been set aside for me.*

EXCERPT FROM "THE ILLUSTRATED POLICE NEWS",
November 19th, 1892.
NEILL'S CAREER IN CHICAGO:

Mr. A. C. Trude of Chicago, one of the most prominent criminal lawyers in America, who was Thomas Neill Cream's counsel when he was prosecuted for murder in 1882 and was sent to the State Penitentiary at Joliet for life, said, in an interview with Dalziel representative at Chicago, that Neill's release from prison was effected by a political influence obtained by a free use of money. After his conviction the prisoner's father raised 5,000 dollars, which he placed in the hands of a well-known politician. What took place thereafter Mr. Trude does not know, but as a result of a petition, first for commutation of sentence and then for pardon, the prisoner's term was first shortened by the Governor, and he was afterwards released unconditionally.

EXCERPT FROM POLICE REPORT BY INSPECTOR FREDERICK
JARVIS

*CHICAGO, 11th July, 1892.*

*...Cream on that day (17 Oct. 1881) sentenced to imprisonment for the term of his natural life. He remained in the custody of Sherriff Ames at Belvedere until November 1st 1881, when he conveyed him to the State Prison at Joliet and handed him over to the custody of Major Robert Wilson McClaughry, The Warder of the Prison... Major McClaughry, the then Warden Governor of the Prison, is now Chief of the Chicago Police. He remembers Cream well as he saw him almost daily for about eight years up to the time he*

relinquished the Prison appointment. He also had some correspondence with Cream's father before the latter died and received moneys from the deceased to be pgic4 to Cream should he ever regain his liberty.[1]

*I had for many years now been accorded the doubtful privilege of sharing my noxious cell with a variety of companions in misfortune. The latest to be inflicted upon me was an old lag whose continual wheezing cough had increased my insomnia to such a degree that I could hardly remain wakeful enough to perform those daily duties as infirmary aid to which I had long been assigned. Coveting this occupation as a prime alternative to smashing granite, its loss, as I was only too anxiously aware, would result in my being denied access to those precious mind-dulling drugs without which the hardships of prison life would have been unendurable. I should undoubtedly have been driven eventually to throttle the swine, had he not obligingly choked to death himself. After a few nights of heavy sleep, aided by my habitual dose of filched laudaum, I awoke to discover another cell-mate sprawled upon the second iron cot. Cropped near bald as suffering had now rendered me, I failed for a moment to recognise the now dissolute and prognathous countenance of my cousin Neill. When I had recovered from my astonishment we embraced each other with all the sincerity a pair of dedicated rogues could muster, and conversed eagerly until we were sent about our respective prison chores.*

*My cousin, having fled Canada penniless some while back, had now come to me less by a heaven-sent miracle than the thwarting of a pathetic attempt to rob an offertory box, resulting in his incarceration at the county gaol. That establishment becoming overpopulated, he had been transferred to Joliet for the completion of his sentence. News travels fast along the grape-vine; and aware that I had now been mouldering there for years, had recently gained access to a substantial inheritance -- and that not only among the convicts was corruption rife*

---

(1)    It is confirmed by this report that McClaughry left the prison round about the time a substitute must have replaced Cream. The new Warden, not personally familiar with Cream, would have no reason to suspect such substitution. That money was exchanged between McClaughry and Cream's father, and that the Warden was handed (or even bought) a promotion to Chief of Police all adds to the probability of a cover up.

*in Chicago -- cousin Elder persuaded my regular attendant, a slimy individual aptly named Palmer, to throw us together, on an assurance he should be well paid by me for his co-operation.*

*Neill, being early accustomed to the rigours of gaol, appeared curiously indifferent to his situation, seeming in fact to regard imprisonment as no more than a welcome respite from the exigencies of the outside world; but then my cousin had but four months left before the completion of his sentence, and I probably as many years. Having already served some six of a slow and grinding life sentence, there was not the slightest chance of lawful release until I had spent at least ten years behind bars. Neill's arrival at Joliet, could I but turn it to advantage, might well be the means, (such was my consuming hope), of providing me with a long awaited opportunity to expedite my freedom.*

*How in those dreary years past had I ached for that annual day of solitary confinement to which, supposedly as an added punishment, they had committed me, since it afforded an opportunity of indulging uninterrupted in a series of detailed phantasies as to the agonising method of despatching to hell that viper whom I had once taken to my bosom, indeed contemplated making my wife, Julia Stott! She, though equally responsible for the death of her senile spouse, had been induced, apparently with little persuasion, to give evidence against me, thereby ensuring her own freedom and my conviction for murder.*

*The name of Doctor Thomas N. Cream had, owing to her treachery, been reduced to a humiliating cipher -- ("4374, Cream, Sir!") -- he who was at his trial described as "very good and intelligent-looking", and had yet allowed himself to be outwitted by an ignorant little slut. Denying hotly that I had tampered with Stott's dose, and insisting that Julia herself had plotted to do him in without my connivance, that cunning vixen nevertheless, by her delicacy of appearance, her plain manner of speaking, had succeeded admirably in turning the jury against me. To save her own neck the Jezebel bore solemn witness to my adding those four minute grains of poison to the prepared prescription, her husband surviving not twenty minutes after receiving it. Further to incriminate me she had no qualms in repudiating my statement that we had not a criminal connection, admitting unblushingly that such a connection had taken place on the very day we met.*

*Hour by hour, day by day and year by wretched year my rage had risen to such a pitch that, determined somehow to regain access to the outside world, I vowed death and destruction not only to Julia Stott, but to all loose women of her kind who came my way. I should take and break as many as could be had; they should be mercilessly annihilated, either by the sword or by means of any slow and agonizing death I might devise. Oh, how I should make them squeal, with what inordinate pleasure should I contemplate their anguish!*

*Before that year of 1887 was out I had masterminded a neat scheme of escape, aided, I own, by benevolent Mother Nature, who had never employed her craft to better effect than when she created both my cousin and myself in the likeness of our ancestor, the notorious Captain Neill. My cousin Elder was to have completed his sentence on November first, and had serious misgivings as to the likelihood of surviving a freezing winter on the outside, with only a pittance of ten dollars provided by the authorities and a carpet-bag containing all his wordly possessions. Incredibly enough he had come to regard the inside of prison as a safe haven, welcoming the constrictions which I found so unbearable; so that my proposal to exchange identities, backed by a generous offer of hard cash and the assurance which I had recently received of a pardon within the next four years, appealed to him no end. The offer of a further gratuity to the villain Palmer ensured that on the appointed day of cousin Elder's release, it was he who assumed the persona of No, 4374 – Cream, (Sir!) and I who stepped blithely out of Joliet goal.*

Like a tiger sprung from its lair Cream made for Chicago where he intended to obtain sufficient funds to pay off Palmer, hunt down Julia Stott and disappear to England. However, discreet inquiries revealed, much to Cream's chagrin, that the lady had long since vanished. Haggard and unshaven, the ravages of prison life had left their mark. What little was left of the once handsome auburn hair had now darkened, though his beard was still of reddish tone. Lips tightened to a hard line, brows drawn together in a permanent frown, he seemed considerably older than his thirty-seven years. Only too aware of the deterioration in his appearance, and particularly of the ill-fitting suit and sloping shoes which had once belonged to cousin Neill, his only consolation was that there was small chance, at present, of being spotted as the dapper Doctor Cream.

Before the trial his bank account had contained upwards of eight thousand dollars, which despite the risk of detection, he intended to withdraw. Strolling into the bank he approached a young counter clerk. Disreputable though he looked, Cream nevertheless boldly applied for his money, stating that he was leaving the country and wished to close the account. Fortunately the assistant, preoccupied by his own affairs, paid him little attention and set about arranging the withdrawal. While the bills were being counted out a senior teller strolled by, noticed the large pile of cash that was about to be paid across, and favoured him with what Cream interpreted as a suspicious stare. Cream broke out in an anxious sweat as the teller whispered something to his trainee. Perhaps he had not, after all, changed quite beyond recognition? Here was a guy plenty old enough to remember the murder trial of six years ago, when that highly distinctive and -- damn it -- wholly memorable lantern jaw had been portrayed in practically every newspaper and periodical in the State of Illinois. He was preparing to abandon his money and make a desperate dash for the door, when the senior clerk turned away.

"Pardon me," ventured the younger one uncertainly. "My boss says it ain't customary to hand over such a large amount of bills."

Cream's steely control failed him. Smacking his fist hard down on the counter he barked: "Damn your boss! Do you imbeciles presume to question a man's right to his own money?" He shook with ire and apprehension.

"No offense, Sir," stammered the unfortunate clerk. "We thought maybe a banker's draft might suit."

"Don't trouble yourselves to think, boy, just hand over the cash, and pretty damned smart!" snapped Cream. The thoroughly intimidated clerk did so, and shoving the bills into cousin Neill's carpet bag, Cream promptly made his exit.

As a result of the scare Cream felt it advisable to sail for England as soon as could be arranged, and, Lord alone knew how frustratingly, postpone his exacting of vengeance on Julia Stott. Reluctant as he was to grant a her reprieve, there was nothing for it but to do so. Cream had, however, with commendable foresight conceived a contingency plan for the tracking down and killing of his quarry, one which might with greater facility be implemented on his intended return to the United States some four years later -- a month or so before his supposed release from Joliet was to be announced[2].

If in the future the police tried to get him for Stott's murder, what additional satisfaction might then be derived from showing the dim-wits up. No better alibi could a man wish for than one which had in the past already proved eminently successful -- namely that Doctor Thomas N. Cream (4374, Sir!) had been serving his last few weeks in gaol when Mrs. Julia Stott met her untimely end.

Only delaying further to keep a prearranged appointment with Palmer in a derelict basement, Cream handed the warder an ample pay-off for services rendered. He had already been obliged to square certain other considerably more illustrious persons than Palmer, and with far greater sums, to ensure the success of his escape, leaving himself with precious little left to set up on foreign shores. But better to be poor than to rot in gaol! Until he should be publicly free to claim his inheritance he would doubtless be able to make ends meet, as always, by fair means or foul.

Cream now gave Palmer a letter, signed by himself and addressed to the Pinkerton Detective Agency, purporting to be from Joliet Penitentiary and post-dated to December 1890. Certain instructions were attached for the benefit of Neill Elder, who at the time designated, was to mail from the prison this and any other documents Cream

---

(2)   When cream, on receiving a sixteen thousand dollar inheritance, bought his way out of jail prior to 1888, as is the thesis of this book, it must subsequently have dawned disconcertingly on the grafters, at both low and higher levels, that they were guilty of freeing a serial killer -- one who, possibly as a result of long confinement, had conceived a maniacal hatred of those he regarded as loose women -- culminating in a series of atrocities so sadistic as, until then, to have been unprecedented. Public exposure would have caused a major political scandal, fear of which undoubtedly engendered a conspiracy of silence – one perhaps still prevailing.

might later see fit to provide; and subsequently be prepared to conduct an interview with the Agency on Cream's behalf. Palmer glanced at the neatly inscribed papers.

"And for what purpose shall Pinkertons be sent for to visit with `Dr. Cream', if a gentleman might pardon my asking?" Palmer spoke with mock deference, noting that Cream had taken the trouble to attend the barber for a shave and deck himself out in a tasteful new outfit.

"Why, to cod the fools that I'm still in gaol, of course," said Cream succinctly, adding: "And also to enable me, in the future, to renew my acquaintance with Mrs. Julia Stott. "The snitch who sent you down? Keep way more'n a dingus length from her, man -- that gal sure spells trouble."

Cream's sole response was to intone: *"They went to bury her; but they found no more of her than the skull, and the feet, and the palms of her hands."*

Palmer noted this as merely another example of Cream's odd-ball personality, viewing his quirky humour, violent outbursts, periods of unbending virtue and frequent spouting of biblical verses as eccentricities common to many "lifers".

Reluctantly Cream erased from his mind the pleasing miasma his utterance had evoked, and returned to the business in hand.

"Now see here, Palmer. Your fortune shall be increased only upon relaying to me, when next we meet, any information Elder can get from Pinkertons as to Julia Stott's whereabouts. As for now, my immediate plans are to take a long vacation."

"And not a moment too soon," opined Palmer phlegmatically. "Particular as on your freedom depends my own. If I get ripped, you do, and t'other way about." Always was cold and slippery as an eel -- they'll never catch the cuss", Palmer mentally reassured himself. As Cream started up the steep flight of stairs, the warder's continuum of thought became associated with that most improving and enviable foreign contraption, a prison treadmill. The name as well as the game was fitting enough for Cream.

"Watch your ass, Jack the Slipper³," he called after him. Cream turned, acknowledged the salutation with a curt nod, and went on his way, his predilection for a twisted phrase having inspired a future alias.

*Delivered at last from purgatory, the painful necessity of handing over several thousand dollars and certain other arrangements concerning Palmer having been successfully negotiated, I took passage for London, England. I had already remained in Chicago considerably longer than was safe in the hope of tracing Julia Stott, and failing to do so my frustration knew no bounds. That potent urge to inflict upon the loathsome female a slow and agonizing death, the exquisite details of which had for so long obsessed me, were even then, and for an indefinite period, to be thwarted. An angry volcano threatened to erupt within me, which red hot larva of emotion I was obliged to contain with an outward show of indifference. The pressure becoming intolerable I took to my hotel room until it should be time to board ship, unable to sleep and plagued by the fearful headaches to which I had from childhood been subject.*

*If I had not in this dark hour sent for Anderesmann, I should surely have gone mad; and as to his coming without delay I was undoubtedly in his debt. Even so -- more of this later -- I was to discover that the devious little Yid was not above letting me down quite deplorably. I must own though that he first made every attempt to sooth my tumultuous rage, persuading me to the utmost of his abilities to eschew the sanguine course upon which I was bent. "I pray you, Tom, most earnestly, to abandon these wicked schemes. Such a terrible undertaking as you have in mind can lead only to self destruction. "Doubtless he had my interests at heart, but continuing to sermonize monotonously as to my proposed reformation, I became stubbornly deaf to his entreaties. In view of this, Anderesmann, the turncoat son-of-a-bitch, became deaf to mine.*

*The fever subsiding only a day before my ship was to sail, and awaking from a confused sleep to find myself alone, I struggled to regain command of my senses. Blessed with a brawny build and strong constitution, it*

---

(3)    *For etymologists only -- "Jack the Slipper". A treadmill. c: from ca 1860. ob. From "The Penguin Dictionary of Historical Slang" by Eric Partridge. Abridged by Jacqueline Simpson*

was only a matter of hours though before I had summoned strength enough to pack my bags, hail a cab and reach the dockside as the gangplank was about to be raised.

Once at sea the tangy air greatly invigorated my spirits, and I began to enjoy the voyage, drinking freely with merrier company than that of Anderesmann and equally thankful for deliverance from the Rabbi's sermons as from gaol! To give the man his due, though excessively pious and mealy-mouthed, he had always seemed wholly devoted to my welfare; whereas in truth I, having never genuinely liked the fellow, and believing his moralistic preaching to be as much for the benefit of his own esteem as mine, had adopted the same attitude to him as to most women -- namely that Anderesmann existed only to fulfill my needs.

In Chicago I had become wary of recognition; but on later reflection concluded that an uncommon feat of memory indeed would be required in order to identify any man from inaccurate portraits and news items circulated so long ago as six years. For this reason when boarding ship I decided boldly to proffer my correct appellation, of which, in my own opinion, I still had some reason to be proud, rather than that of Neill Elder, of which I had none. It was as well perhaps that the shipping clerk misheard the name Cream -- doubtless because I was chewing tobacco at the time -- and entered upon the ticket slip "Thomas Coram". There seemed no point in deliberately drawing attention to myself on this account, and having been dubbed Thomas Coram more or less by an act of fate, I decided the alias should serve me, for a while, as well as another.

So it was the start of 1888 found me lying low in the east end of London under an assumed identity, to establish which I took a position during the weekdays as a factory clerk in a coconut warehouse in the name of Thomas Coram, with accommodation in Plumber's Row. During the nights and weekends I covertly practiced my true profession under the title of Dr Thomas Neill, from the ground floor back room at 16, Bath Gardens, Brady Street, across from the Hospital in Whitechapel Road. There were no requirements for doctors with foreign qualifications to be listed, so this frequent transformation of character was easy to sustain.

*I had tried but been unable to prevail upon the real Fordyce's co-operation during the Stott trial -- he being laid up in hospital at the time with a severe bout of malaria -- but we had corresponded regularly over the years. My old confederate had recently replied to a letter of mine, which, knowing he would never betray an old pal, I risked mailing to his Australian address on reaching London. Thus I learned that his good fortune had for once turned sour -- I being not due out of Joliet for several years at the time of Fordyce's trial and therefore unable to employ the dodge for his benefit -- and that as a result he had three months left to serve of an eighteen month sentence there for fraud.*

*Though I had been deadly serious in assuring Anderesmann of my determination to pursue what he had so virtuously termed "a wicked course", the fact was that, having been cooped up in gaol for so long, and bursting with rude energy I intended first to have myself a damned good time.*

*It was at the music halls in the guise of John Fordyce that I struck up the acquaintance of several ladies of the chorus whose capacity for high living matched mine. Being obliged to support their extravagant whims my funds were soon exhausted, yet I was loathe to surrender such privileges as I had become accustomed to enjoy.*

*Therefore I entered rashly upon a secret marriage ceremony with no less than seven of these delectable females, one for each night of the week, receiving their favours as of right and, without of course incurring any further expense. Even more agreeably I had contrived, so far as outlay of money was concerned, to turn the situation about, they being obliged to contribute to my financial welfare by whatever means I chose.*

*This happy state of affairs endured for several months and might well have prevailed indefinitely but for the misfortune of counting among my numerous brothers-in-law a member of the Metropolitan Police. His suspicions aroused by my frequent absences, and, as it emerged, an inexplicable distrust, I was placed under investigation. Charged with bigamy, as John Fordyce I once more put into effect the dodge. Brought to trial and positively identified in custody by each one of my outraged "wives", I should have found myself back behind bars but for the so-called Fordyce, myself in fact, having claimed I had been serving a jail sentence in Sydney during the period in which the bigamous marriages were alleged to have taken place. My aspiring young attorney, Marshall Hall, seizing upon this revelation, at once wired the Australian authorities who confirmed that a man named Fordyce, fitting my description, had indeed been an inmate of their penitentiary during the time in question. I can still see the mixture of perplexity and delight on Hall's face; and he sure as hell will never forget the expression of triumph on my grinning mug when the charges against me were dismissed!*

FROM "FAMOUS TRIALS OF MARSHALL HALL", by Sir Edward Marjoribanks.

`Marshall once defended at the Old Bailey, without knowing it at the time, one of the most famous criminals of modern times, Dr. Neil (sic) Cream. His method was to meet women of the unfortunate class; he gained their confidence and pre-scribed remedies for them, but if they were unwise enough to take his pills they died soon afterwards of convulsions. Some years before Cream was convicted and hung [sic], Marshall was briefed by Mr. Harry Wilson of Bow Street, to defend a man for bigamy. When he walked into court, he was aghast to find a whole bevy of young women who claimed to have been 'married' to the prisoner within the space of the last few months. The case seemed hopeless and Marshall advised his client to plead 'guilty'.'

"Nothing of the kind," said the prisoner indignantly; "this is a clear case of mistaken identity. Communicate with the gaol at Sydney, Australia, and you will find that I was there at the time I am supposed to have committed these offences."'

'A cable was despatched with the name and full description of the prisoner, and to the amazement of all concerned, except the prisoner, a reply came immediately confirming his statement: his alibi was perfect, and Marshall left the court musing on the narrow escape from gaol of an innocent man. Some years afterwards Marshall went into court to see Neil Cream on his trial, and he was astonished to recognise his client, the alleged bigamist. The mystery was never explained, but Marshall's theory was that Neil Cream had a 'double' in the under-world, and they went by the same name and used each other's terms of imprisonment as alibis for each other. There was a rumour current when Cream was executed that vengeance had at last overtaken Jack the Ripper...'

*The district abounded with noisome prostitutes forever enceinte, and worthily engaged in preventing the passage of disease from one generation to the next, I came again, as Anderesmann had hoped, into a mood of reformation, continually studying the Scriptures and interesting myself in the brotherhood of Freemasonry. I might even in time have entered into a new and more spiritually rewarding way of life but for a recurrence of that former disgusting affliction which again darkened my outlook and exacerbated to a dangerous degree the antipathy I felt towards Julia Stott and her kind. "They are all gone aside, they are all together become filthy; there is none that doeth good, no, not one.'*

*Indulging my proclivity for drink and drugs, and again ignoring Andersmann's advice, which, had I not rejected it, might even then have engendered in me some degree of restraint, I entered into a campaign of blood-letting lasting several months, for which I was arrested twice and released, thus proving at least to my own satisfaction that the* authorities were nothing but a bunch of idiots an in no way a match for myself. I took to taunting them on every possible occasion for their failure to catch me, even providing clues by means of subtly worded missives which, needless to say, they were too thick-headed to comprehend.

> I'm not a butcher,
> I'm not a Yid,
> Nor yet a foreign skipper,
> But I'm your own light-hearted friend,
> Yours truly, Jack the Ripper.
> Up and down the goddam town Policemen try to find me.
> But I ain't a chap yet to drown In drink, or Thames or sea.
> I've no time now to tell you how
> I came to be a killer.
> But you should know, as time will show,
> That I'm society's pillar.

How apt, four years later, did my little pun prove to be, when they changed my title to `The Lambeth Poisoner'. Had not then the ingenious Doctor Cream fulfilled his intention of becoming the very pillar of society?

Cream, regarding his weakness for puns a mark of outstanding wit, startled his keepers by barking out several times, as was his habit, "Ha,ha!" This expression, gleaned from the music-halls and invariably delivered without the least trace of a smile, was Cream's nearest approach to overt humour. He had in fact during his nightly prowls around London in his high hat and frock coat, immensely enjoyed assuming the theatrical role of villain; often affecting a false set of whiskers or flowing wig, which, though conveying a more than odd impression, had on many occasions proved an effective disguise.

The shuffling of boots on stone flags heralded the night shift, one of their number bearing a tin tray on which was Cream's supper, a bowl of bean soup, a suet pudding and a pint of beer. Cream paused, and forcing only enough of the revolting food down his throat as was strictly necessary for survival, swilled his beer with considerably more relish.

"Good evening, gentlemen." His mood was for the moment affable, and emboldened by it one of the younger warders proferred a wad of tobacco. Cream accepted it with a patronizing air, leaned back staring reflectively at the ceiling, and occasionally directing a spurt of brown fluid into his half empty soup bowl. Somewhere the dropping of a heavy weight reverberated inside the cell, discomforting all but Cream, who, with Anderesmann occupying his thoughts, seemed mercifully unaware of Billington's conscientious attempts to ensure his instant and painless departure.

EXCERPT FROM THE "ST. JAMES'S GAZETTE", October 24th, 1892, with regard to Thomas Cream, alias Neill..

# A STUDY OF HIS CRIMES BY ONE WHO KNEW HIM

### CHARACTERISTICS

He was evidently a very powerful fellow; but though his general features were good he had a very strong and protruding under-jaw and development of the back of the head, which betrayed the animal viciousness which he possessed so largely. This jaw was always at work either chewing gum, tobacco, cigars, or moving mechanically like a cow chewing the cud... He occasionally said "Ha, ha" in a hard stage-villain like fashion but no amount of good nature could construe it into an expression of geniality.

FROM THE "ILLUSTRATED POLICE NEWS"

Letter posted 28 September 1888 with a London East Central postmark:

*Dear Boss,*                                  *25 Sept. 1888.*

*I keep on hearing the police have caught me but they won't fix me just yet. I have laughed when they look so clever and talk about being on the right track. That joke about Leather Apron gave me real fits. I am down on whores and I shan't quit ripping them till I do get buckled. Grand work the last job was, I gave the lady no time to squeal. How can they catch me now, I love my work and want to start again. You will soon hear of me with my funny little games. I saved some of the proper red stuff in a ginger beer bottle over the last job to write with but it went thick like glue and I can't use it. Red ink is fit enough I hope ha ha The next job I do I shall clip the lady's ears off and send to the police officers just for jolly wouldn't you.*

*Keep this letter till I do a bit more work, then give it out straight. My knife is nice and sharp I want to get to work right away if I get a chance. Good luck.*

*Yours truly*
*JACK THE RIPPER*

*Don't mind me giving the trade name. Wasn't good enough to post this before I got all the red ink off my hands curse it. No luck yet. They say I am a doctor now, ha ha.*[4]

Concluding paragraph from: 'JACK THE RIPPER' -- THE HAND-WRITING ANALYSIS BY DEREK DAVIS, M.Sc.G., M. Inst. M.S.M. FROM "THE CRIMINOLOGIST", Vol. 9. 1974.

"After due consideration of the hundreds of calculations, I was able to offer the opinion that Dr. Thomas Neill Cream (known as Dr. Neill) whose authentic formal style of hand-writing I examined, also wrote the two letters 'Lusk' and 'Ripper' by using as much disguise as possible on each occasion.

D. DAVIS. 1974."

---

(4)    As actually underlined by `Jack the Ripper'.

## THOMAS NEIL CREAM

From a photograph by W. Armstead.

# PART 5

Early on the morning of Friday August 31st 1888, in that sleazy area of London which lay east of the Aldgate pump, a man respectably dressed in a dark twin-peaked cap, frock coat and tie, neatly secured with a horseshoe pin beneath a high starched collar emerged quietly from a house in Brady Street, off the Whitechapel Road, Carrying a black Gladstone bag, the pedestrian might have been taken for a doctor out on a night-call, which, in a manner of speaking, he was. Applying a red handkerchief fastidiously to his nostrils as he passed the Manure Works and quickening his step, the man turned right into Bucks Row, a narrow alley leading towards his rooms on the other side of Whitechapel Road. The passage was lit by the flickering light of a single gas lamp which advertised the presence of a small and solitary streetwalker. The man slowing to a halt inspected the woman keenly through gold-rimmed spectacles, noting her to be shabby and gin-sodden. Despite this she had, from a distance, the good fortune to appear several years younger than her forty-four years; but any illusion of youthful purity was instantly dispelled as, approaching, she accosted him with a gap-toothed and knowing leer. He, recognising the woman as an ex-patient called Nichols, and addressing her as Mary Ann, inquired solicitously, in his American accent with just a trace of soft Celtic brogue, as to how she did.

"Why, all the better, I'm sure, for the pleasure of your company, Doctor Fordyce. And how d'ye do, yourself? Feeling a bit on the warm side, I dare say, and who's to wonder, what with the weather being so close and not a breath of wind. Never mind, luv, I shall soon cool you down, and then you may call me Polly, as my friends do." Cream consulting his gold watch, and finding it to be past three a.m. decided that the time was as good as any for the slut to accommodate him. He treated her to his humourless smile.

"Well, Polly, you sure are hard to resist in that smart black bonnet of yours." Cream when he chose was a skillful flatterer. The drab brightened, less at the compliment than the prospect of retrieving the price of a night's lodging she had so rashly sacrificed on the straw monstrosity.

"Ain't nothing like a new 'at, as I always say, to bring a girl luck." She began a cheerful if slightly unsteady jig, steel-tipped boots clattering on the paving stones. Cream, already practised in what he was about to do, at once grabbed her shoulders, turned the woman about and propelled her towards a gateway between some buildings fronting a deserted stable yard.

"Shut your mouth, bitch!" Cream flung her with little ceremony against the gate. The woman, accustomed more to rough usage than she was to blandishment, retrieved her balance and began expressionlessly to lift her skirts.

"Move around" snapped Cream.

"Oh, you're another as likes it bottoms up, are you? Well, suits me, darlin', for I'll not be got in the family way again, not if I can 'elp it. Stony broke for weeks I was after you put me right the last time." Behind his opaque correctional lenses Cream's eyes narrowed with contempt. Philosophically the woman turned to face the wall, this time hauling the brown linsey frock and two workhouse gray flannel petticoats upwards towards her stays.

Meanwhile Cream, unimpressed by a pair of scrawny buttocks, was engaged in tearing open his medical bag and removing from an inner container a pad soaked in chloroform. Instantaneously he came behind the slightly stooping woman, grabbing her jaw firmly with his left hand, jerking the head towards him, and applied the pad determinedly to her mouth and nose. The woman already bemused with drink, flopped backwards without a sound. Cream immediately threw his cap inside the bag and donned instead a wide brimmed black felt hat and a rolled up mackintosh. Sweating both with anticipation and trapped body heat, the good doctor now lovingly withdrew a long-bladed keen-edged knife. This, nestling in its blue lined case, had been a precious souvenir of his post-mortem days at St. Thomas's; and with such speed and expertise as he had acquired there, Cream proceeded to cut the woman's throat through to the vertebrae. In a mounting frenzy of excitement he then began to inflict wild and jagged slashes from left to right and upwards towards the breastbone, utterly oblivious of blood, fatty deposits and other matter which, despite protective headgear, still spattered his face.

"For you, Julia, and for all whores," he muttered, pausing to savor his handiwork, and then for good measure delivering a couple of vicious jabs at the victim's private parts. Lust reaching its peak, he fell shuddering across the corpse and lay in a welter of gore until his paroxysms ceased.

The city was awakening, and already the rumbling of heavy carts on their way to market roused Cream to an awareness that nearby slaughter houses would soon be opening their doors to trade. His instinct for self-preservation rarely deserting him when sober, he rose, experiencing neither guilt nor horror at his deed, but rather the satisfaction of a master surgeon at the conclusion of a successful operation. Spent of all passion, he had become coldly incisive as the dripping steel which he now wiped carefully with his red handkerchief and replaced inside its case, together with the black hat and slimy raincoat neatly re-rolled between layers of newspaper. Hastily rinsing his hands and face at a nearby pump, removing a pair of galoshes and carefully wiping his spectacles, Cream calmly reassumed his favoured persona, one intended to render him entirely above suspicion, that of an eminently respectable physician.

The entire affair accomplished with ruthless rapidity, the worthy Doctor Fordyce was safely home and asleep when his victim's mangled form came to light.

*Until August of '88 I had received scant recognition from the authorities for my contribution to the sanitizing of their city. It was not until then that the surgical removal of the putrescence Nichols afforded me flattering coverage in the newspapers. It had been so simple to give them the slip that summer's night, as, considerably more innocent of blood than a new-born babe, I strolled calmly away from Buck's Row to my nearby lodgings in Plumber's Row, which lay between the Whitechapel and Commercial Roads. It was there that I had successfully established a new identity as Thomas Coram, working during the week as clerk* in a coconut factory. Unable to subsist on so modest a salary and Palmer & Co's greed having accounted for most of my savings, I sought to augment this income during the weekends by once more engaging in my proper profession. Practising illicitly as an abortionist had of course brought me into contact with all the right sort of people, namely those unwholesome denizens of the street from among whose number I proceeded to select several for immediate elimination.

I decided now to render myself all the more worthy of the honorary title Palmer had bestowed upon me and which I had now appropriately adapted to "Jack the Ripper" -- and amuse myself immensely into the bargain -- by throwing the Bosses into an even greater state of bamboozlement than they already were.

To add to the general confusion resulting from the Nichols inquiry I decided to despatch my next victim by rather more refined and esoteric means. Having, during my last months in gaol, acquired from the library a book about Freemasonry and believing the brotherhood to be founded on social and moral tenets not dissimilar to my own, I had f armed an ambition at some time in the future to join them. In London I obtained further literature from the organization, my mind becoming fixed upon a Masonic ritual into which an Entering Apprentice might expect to be initiated. While shaving I took to regaling my landlady and no doubt considerably mystifing the other residents of 67 Plumber's Row by a boisterous and, I venture to add, tuneful rendition of my own composition:

> Ha hum ho -- Jubela and Jubelo!
> Hum ha hum -- Not to mention Jubelum!

These fine fellows, according to Freemason lore, had all three attempted to top their victim from left to right, a method of throat-slitting which it had already occurred to me, just as a jolly, to try on Nichols; giving rise incidentally to the misleading rumour that the Ripper was left handed. Noting with fascination how the apprentices had themselves met their end, I now proposed, for my next little escapade, to adopt the same ritual, which, while bound to baffle the police even further, should also afford me the opportunity to pit my wits against, no less, their Commissioner, Sir Charles Warren. He, so I had heard, being a grand *panjandrum in the Freemasons, might be counted upon, particularly in consideration of the generous lead I offered, to represent at least one adversary of my own mettle. I had in truth begun to find the game of 'Bait the Bosses' almost equal in enjoyment to my work.*

FROM: Morgan's "FREEMASONRY EXPOSED".

`.,.they distinctly heard the voice of Jubelo exclaim, "0! that my breast had been torn open, and my heart and vitals taken from thence and thrown over my left shoulder."

...they heard the voice of Jubela exclaim," O! that my throat had been cut across, and my tongue torn out, and my body buried in the rough sands of the sea at low-water mark, where the tide ebbs and flows twice in twenty-four hours.

...they more distinctly heard the voice of Jubelum exclaim, "0! that my body had been severed in two in the midst, and divided to the North and the South, my bowels burned to ashes in the center, and the ashes scattered by the four winds of heaven[1]...'"

Cream stopped writing to greet one of his rare visitors, a moon-faced young journalist wearing a bowler hat which did not quite fit and a checked suit loudly proclaiming his lack of sartorial taste. Hardly of a sensitive disposition, Kennedy Jones on this occasion felt slightly nervous, for in all his five years as a cub reporter on a police gazette he had never undertaken so grotesque an assignment. The cub, by licking the hands that fed him had been recently lionized and was now in charge of his own column.

This promotion, though achieved mostly by opportunism rather than talent, was, to do him justice, also down to his unerring instinct for a scoop; and on the rumour that Cream was penning his memoirs he

---

(1)    It is on record that Emily Sleaper, the daughter of Cream's future landlady, (known to her as Doctor Thomas Neill), had "tried to join a masonic Lodge."

had been the first of his colleagues to apply for an interview with the notorious Lambeth Poisoner.

Jones shivered slightly as Cream shot him a penetrating look. Deprived of spectacles and with the additional strain to which his vision had recently been subjected, the left eye now swivelled completely inwards towards his nose, conveying a more than usually sinister impression.

Jones, forcing an air of jovial bonhomie extended a hand which was gripped with such unexpected vigor that he winced.

"Pleased to meet you, I'm sure, Doctor Neill. And hope to find you as well as could be expected in the circumstances, eh?"

"As well, I dare say, as a condemned man may be," Cream enjoyed Jones's obvious discomfort. "Now pray state your business sir." Though for the most part Cream spoke softly and with a pleasant Irish lilt, there was in his tone an indefinable note of menace. Jones blenched and backed closer to the warders. His voice, never particularly resonant, now, despite several clearings of the throat, rose on a note of almost feminine shrillness.

I understand sir, that you are engaged upon an account of your past experiences, that is to say, your ---"

"My career in crime?" Cream supplied, with as much an air of complacency as if he had been referring to his career in medicine. "Kindly address the point, sir, for time is running short"

Jones, gathering his wits with an effort, accepted Cream's nodded invitation to seat himself on the opposite side of the table, where he directed several furtive glances at the pile of written material lying between them.

"I wish sir, on behalf of my newspaper, to offer the sum of five hundred pounds for the commissioning of your biography, provided of course, sir, the work were to comprise certain details of your -- um -- former activities, such sir, as would serve to enlighten our readers with regard to the habits and mores of fallen women."

Buoyed by his own bombast Jones found himself nevertheless unable to return Cream's disconcerting boss-eyed stare, though noting him, surreptitiously, to have aged considerably since his last appearance in the dock. In a clumsy attempt to lighten the atmosphere he winked broadly and remarked: "I'll be a monkey's uncle, though, Doctor Neill, if you ain't a veritable wonder when it comes to the handling of a woman. Three or more of an evening, so they say, and all in the space of a few hours!" He raised his small bowler in admiration, revealing a thatch of greased-down carroty hair parted carefully in the centre and with a neatly formed curl nestling on his forehead.

"Sir, I have as little use for your approbation as, in my present straits, for your proposition." Even so Cream could not resist adding: "I may, however, be persuaded to reconsider the offer, were it raised to one thousand pounds."

"Steady on there, Doctor Neill, that's going a bit steep! Six-fifty is the most I can run to, and more than I ought, believe me." His heart missed several beats as Cream leaned across the table, confronting him head on, jaw to thrusting jaw; and with a distinct lapse of formality snarled: "Get out of here, you cheap sensation seeker, while you can still walk!" The reporter, only too eager to accommodate, jammed his hat on askew and scuttled for the exit. It was only when the hansom cab had conveyed him a considerable distance from Newgate that the thoroughly unnerved Mr. Kennedy Jones could stop shaking.

"ST. JAMES'S GAZETTE", October 24th, 1892.

> "...I believe he proposed to defray part of the expenses of his case by writing his life, which Mr. Kennedy Jones, a clever young journalist on a morning paper, arranged to buy for a large sum."

Cream stood before a small mirror attached to the wall, carefully trimming his moustache. He stepped back with an oath, his own reflection having been superimposed by the familiar face of Anderesmann. Turning he reassured himself, with utmost relief, that this was no crazy vision. It seemed that Anderesmann had been admitted to the cell while Cream's attention was occupied with his grooming.

"Darn me if it's not the Rabbi himself! This is indeed an unexpected pleasure, Anderesmann! In the absence of word and with an ocean between us I had begun to despair of seeing you again."

Drawn and wan, Anderesmann appeared exhausted by his transition. Without spectacles there was in those strange eyes an admiring, almost worshipful expression which not for the first time caused Cream to wonder uneasily if the man were normal. Oddly enough, while inwardly despising Anderesmann, Cream, basically a loner, did in fact share with him a unique empathy. Having little communication with the outside world nor another soul to turn to in his extremity, the advent of Anderesmann was more than welcome.

"Say, you old reprobate, it sure is great to have you here. Believe me, at a time like this a man learns to appreciate his friends."

Reprobate -- in truth the chap was practically Christ like in his willingness to sacrifice himself for the good of his fellow man. Why, he must have packed up and deserted his practice without a qualm as soon as Cream's plight had hit the American press! Cream, who currently possessed no friends, chose to overlook the fact that "The Rabbi" had not always appeared to him in quite so favourable a light -- indeed, on Cream's absconding from prison in the eighties and finding his mind still closed to any possibility of reformation, had withdrawn his support. Such uncalled for rejection had deepened Cream's smouldering animosity against not only the Jewish race as represented by Anderesmann but the human race in general and whores in particular. It seemed now though that Anderesmann had undergone a change of heart and Cream, desperately in need of an ally, decided magnanimously to forgive and forget. He raised his voice, distracting the attention of the two warders momentarily from their card-game: "They're going to hang me, you know, Anderesmann." His plea for sympathy apparently had effect for Anderesmann's eyes had moistened with pity; but he spoke firmly enough. "Come, Tom, you must not give way to despair. Remember that where there's life there's hope." (Platitudinous, point of nausea -- come to think of it the fellow was not unlike his late Mama, full of good intentions and a load of crap!).

Anderesmann continued on an optimistic note: "What do you say we get up a petition to Queen Victoria -- I hear she has the power to intervene?"

"I guess that might just be worth a shot -- at any rate what can I lose by trying? Well may you ask, old pal, how a man of my ability could have gotten himself in such a spot." Anderesmann had not asked, but Cream rambled on. "Sure would have made as fine and respected a physician as yourself, if only I had listened to your wisdom, eh, Anderesmann? Guess you were the only worthwhile influence in my life except for Laura Sabbatini. First decent woman I ever cared for, or came into contact with for the matter of that. Ought to have married the girl, despite her busybody of a mother who was always around; hardly gave us a moment's privacy, you know. But for her damned interfering ways I dare say I should have stayed out of trouble and made Laura a mighty fine husband into the bargain. They had a house in Berkhampstead with plenty of room and I a spot of money at my disposal -- enough to open a legitimate practice for once. Was I not, do you suppose, Anderesmann, more than entitled after the many privations I had endured, to benefit from the comfort of a well run home and the affections of a pleasing woman? Heaven knows I had already dedicated enough of my life unselfishly to the good of man, and it would then have been up to others to continue the crusade of purification I had taken upon myself."

"You always did have the makings of a philanthropist, Tom."

"Not to speak of a philanderer." Cream grinned. That he had courage enough to jest at a time like this was in a sense a tribute to Anderesmann, who, it must be said, always managed to bring out the best of his qualities.

"Seriously, though," (Then was Anderesmann anything but serious? Staunch friend that he was, there was no denying the poor guy always had been totally lacking in humour and deadly dull) "don't you see, Tom, it is precisely the philanthropic side of your character which the world must now be called upon to recognise before it is too late. I do believe that, should it be possible to acquaint the Queen with the true motivations for your actions, a reprieve could well be obtained, or better still an immediate par-don. With your consent I shall contact your Solicitor with a view to setting a petition before Her Majesty as soon as can be arranged. That way, Tom, you and Laura could still look forward to a happy future." It must be admitted that Anderesmann, with all his faults, was good for a word of encouragement, no matter how great the odds; but he was perhaps, though in a well-intentioned way, slightly underestimating Cream's problems.

"If I were a free man tomorrow, Laura would never have me -- even over her mother's dead body, ha, ha!" barked Cream, unsmiling. "Why, she has ceased her visits entirely over the past weeks, and what is more failed to respond to my letters." His bitterness increased as he told Anderesmann that he had willed her all of his estate -- though he had to admit that had mostly been dissipated in legal fees.

"Judging from the strong language in which you make known your disillusionment, my feeling is, Tom, that you are a good deal fonder of Laura than you care to admit." Anderesmann had as it happened touched on a tender spot. The sweetly submissive Laura Sabbatini was indeed the only person on earth successful in igniting the smallest spark affection in Cream. "It would ease your mind, Tom, would it not, to see her financially secure, should the worst occur. Is there no way you could raise more cash?"

"My memoirs are worth a good few hundred," Cream allowed. "But I don't intend to let that sneaky little bastard of a journalist get the better of me, for Laura or anyone else. Besides, these confessions were never intended for the prying eyes of the public you know, Anderesmann. Why, even if I were to be pardoned on the poisoning charges, those papers right over there on the table, should they ever appear in print, would put a noose around my neck pretty fucking fast, I can tell you! Publish and be *hanged*, you say? Not on your life, my friend!" He repeated his peculiar staccato laugh jarringly enough again to merit the warders' attention. One of them approached and removed the small moustache clipper thoughtfully from Cream's custody and returned to play his hand.

"If the confessions are to remain unpublished, then what on earth is your purpose in writing them?" asked Anderesmann.

Cream turned sanctimonious as a bishop: "I had less an earthly purpose than a spiritual one. It was as a devout Christian that I sought, by making a full admission of the crimes I had committed in the name of humanity, to gain credit for my actions upon a higher plane. I intend, upon completion to hand the sealed work to my legal representatives, to be retained in their care until my death, and thereafter destroyed."

"I beg of you to reconsider that decision. Sell your story for Laura's sake, Tom, urged Anderesmann. "Leave her something, at least, besides pain, to remember you by."

# PART 6

Back in 1888, on Saturday the eighth of September, a woman named Lyons, loitering along Flower and Dean Street, met a man swinging briskly out of Commercial Street, slowing to observe her intently from behind a pair of gold rimmed glasses. Uncommonly well turned out for a habitue of that neighborhood, she put him down for a clerk or maybe even a doctor, since he carried a black Gladstone bag and wore a high silk hat. Not being the first toff who had sought diversion from a frigid wife, she greeted him warmly. "Elio, darlin'. And what can I do for you then?"

Apparently the offer of her services was of interest, though the man snapped tersely: "Busy now. How about a drink later? Half after six, Queen's Head." Pleased at what promised to be a remunerative if uninviting conquest, Lyons went contentedly on her way. Investing in a new boa and a phial of cheap scent for the occasion, she began, as the day wore on, to regret her extravagance, fearing that he might not after all turn up. She was therefore relieved to find her prospective client waiting impatiently on the steps of the public house when she arrived promptly at six-thirty. Ushering her inside and without troubling to inquire as to any preference, he ordered a cheap jug of wine. Tossing down the liquor Lyons warmed to the business of entertaining the client, who for the most part responded dourly to her facetiousness, slowly sipping his drink with a curious expression which she, proud in her new boa, mistook for admiration. Abruptly her host slammed down his glass, startling the woman to silence.

"You are about the same style of woman as the one that's murdered". The contempt was now unmistakable.

"Now what would a nice respectable gentleman like yourself know about such a thing?" she humoured.

"You are beginning to smell a rat," he rapped. "Foxes hunt geese, but they don't always find 'em." Realising he had said too much the man rose to leave, Eccentric he might seem but Lyons did not intend to relinquish her chance of earning a shilling or two. Attempting to follow, she was unable however to keep pace with the man, who strode quickly on past the cemetery of Spitalfields Church and out of sight. Collapsing breathlessly on a grave-stone the prostitute roundly cursed her ill luck; for she had intended at least to get something on account. It was as well for her that she failed to do so.

Earlier in the week a drinking partner of Lyons, one Amelia Farmer had her nose in a tankard of beer at "The Ringers" when her friend Annie Chapman entered, clutching her chest and sporting a black eye, which, though it had been bestowed by another street woman might have done credit to John L. Sullivan.

"Cor blimey, Annie!" exclaimed Amelia. "blot cove laid on that shin er, dearie? Must 'ave been the Siffey swine -- just 'is style, ain't it?'

"Naw. Weren't no cove; Liza dun it, Liza Cooper that is, 'er what dosses sometimes along of us in Dorset Street. I made a good enough account of meself though -- whacked 'er across the chops once or twice, and lucky for the cow she can still chew 'er cud. Always were a tough egg, that Liza, particular wiv' a pint or two inside 'er. Quarrelled we did over a rotten bit of soap, though the two of us been friends nigh on fifteen year."

"One day your wicked ways will be the death of you, Dark Annie," observed Amelia crossing herself with mock reverence and bringing the faintest quiver of a smile to Annie Chapman's bruised lips.

"Gawd, Amelia, you always was a card. Ought to be on the 'ails, you ought! Come on, buy me a drink, there's a good girl, for I need one bad, and ain't got a penny to me name."

"'Ere's two of 'em, but a cup of tea would do you just as nicely." Amelia could afford to be generous, since she was the better preserved of the two and came by work more easily. Annie, who with her luminous blue eyes and abundant black curls had once held claim to beauty, was now past forty, drink-sodden and showing unmistakable signs of over-use. Feeling desperately ill she took Amelia's advice to rest up in a casual ward for a day or two. Discharged from the infirmary on

Friday, good-natured Amelia noted with concern that Annie looked, if anything, worse than before. But she told Amelia: "It's no use my giving way. I must pull myself together and go out and get some money, or I shall have no lodgings."

"I'd stake you again, me old darlin', but what with a few rainy nights, trade's fallen off something chronic since you bin laid up. Take yourself orf to Dorset Street for a night's rest. Donovan's a decent bloke who'd give you free run of the kitchen."

"Cheerio, then, duck." For tragic Annie it was to be a permanent farewell. Some time after six the following morning she was found not half mile from Bucks Row, in Danbury Street, with her throat cut through to the spine, a gaping wound traversing almost the entire length of her body from which the uterus had been neatly detached and removed, and the contents of her abdomen flung savagely over the left shoulder; while a pair of brass rings representing the only two long-term relationships she might boast, and her sole sad claim to respectability, had been dragged off and laid ceremoniously at her feet.

Deeply absorbed in the newspaper, Kennedy Jones, his po-faced wife and their two offspring were at breakfast. The harmonious crunching of toast and preserves, the tinkling percussion of spoon on bowl was shortly interrupted by several sharp raps at the door, proclaiming the arrival of a messenger with a sealed letter, addressed in an educated hand, to Jones. Transferring his attention reluctantly to the missive Jones discovered it to be from none other than Doctor Thomas Neill, care of Her Majesty's Pris on, Newgate, and containing such word as he had abandoned all hope of receiving. He emitted a whoop of triumph, splattering the napkin tucked under his chin with a liberal quantity of porridge and black treacle. Kennedy Jones the younger, aged three years and five months, promptly mimicked his father's breach of etiquette by ejecting the contents of his own mouth unerringly in the baby's eye; provoking an indignant roar from the unfortunate infant and a waspish glance directed at Kennedy Jones by his spouse.

"I should be most obliged, Mr. Jones, if you would endeavor to display some measure of decorum before the children," snapped Mrs. Kennedy Jones. Some years senior to her husband and the daughter of a dancing master, she held strong views on most subjects and particularly on the issue of decorum. She endeavoured to impose these views on her children and, alas with little effect, on Kennedy Jones himself, with an air of such haughty superiority as to convey a distinct impression that she had, by the greatest misfortune, contrived to marry beneath her. The Newgate messenger stood uncomfortably twisting his cap, awaiting a reply. Kennedy Jones removed a pencil from his ear, where it was invariably perched, a notepad from his breast-pocket and jotted a request to the Governor for a second interview with the prisoner Neill; this he sent the messenger hurrying to deliver. Cream wrote that he had carefully reconsidered the offer of Mr. Kennedy Jones and was now prepared, for the aforementioned sum of six hundred and fifty pounds, to provide Jones's employers with the exclusive rights of his memoirs, if and when they were completed. In order to expedite the work, it was by special request of the writer that Mr. Kennedy Jones might without delay supply certain items from the newspapers concerning the Whitechapel Murders and dating back to 1888.

Kennedy Jones waited but to bestow a withering glance at dearest Clara and both howling offspring, (the baby having retaliated by upturning his porringer on big brother's head), and left in haste for the newspaper library. Later that day he arrived at the prison, fighting again to combat his claustrophobic dread as huge bolts were drawn grating from their sockets, a giant key revolved laboriously in an outsize lock and the studded iron door of Newgate's condemned cell pivoted inwards on its axis. Jones passed beneath a high stone arch and into the cell's foetid interior, bearing a large file of data. The journalist's qualms on entering were to some extent alleviated by his preoccupation with a certain intriguing question -- why would a condemned murderer engaged on his own biography seek access to material on the Whitechapel slayings? Jones had first assumed Cream's purpose was to form an undoubtedly odious comparison between his own ruthless technique for killing prostitutes and that of a celebrated arch rival in sadism, one who as yet, four years after the perpetration of his atrocious crimes, had not been caught. *Or had he?* Jones was struck forcibly by the thought -- could it be that Thomas Neill, alias Thomas Neill Cream, actually held claim to a third alias, that of the infamous Jack the Ripper? It was certainly an astounding supposition and one which, if substantiated in Cream's memoirs by a detailed confession, would be the very making of the Gazette's young marvel, Kennedy Jones! Sustained by this agreeable prospect, and the comforting presence at close quarters of two hefty warders, he stepped forward to greet Cream with rather more aplomb than he had demonstrated on the last interview. Even so he found himself studiously avoiding the man's swivelled stare, experiencing now, worse than dread, a sense of utter revulsion as their palms met. Cream for his part seemed a deal more affable than at their last meeting, welcoming his visitor as if he had been a lifelong friend.

"My dear fellow, how good of you to come so soon. Delighted to see you I'm sure."

"Likewise." Kennedy Jones, usually loquacious, found himself momentarily lost for words, as he pictured the urbane doctor flaying the flesh of some pathetic drab with a similar expression of delight.

Handing the file to Cream he seated himself facing the prisoner, who under the strain of confinement had aged noticeably. Observing his worn appearance and ague-like trembling of the limbs, Jones prayed fervently that the condemned man would last long enough to complete any such confession as might be forthcoming, before his appointment with the hangman. If Cream had shrunk to a shadow of his former self, his writings, since Jones's last visit, were grown remarkably prolific, piled up in several stacks across the table's length. Jones shot furtive glances at them in the hope of determining for certain whether this blear-eyed balding monster did in fact incorporate the personae both of the malevolent Lambeth Poisoner and the brutal Jack the Ripper. Cream seemed amused by Jones's obvious attempts to decipher the inverted script, handing a page over with a patronizing air. "It is thought nowadays that a man's character may be judged by his handwriting," he remarked. "Though in my view, only when sober, Mr. Kennedy Jones, only when sober!" He had offered Jones the draft copy of a letter, composed and penned, with obvious deliberation, in the crudest hand:

*From Hell.*

Letter 'from hell' sent with a piece of 'ginny kidney'
to Mr Lusk of the Vigilance Committee

*Mr Lusk*

*Sir I send you half the Kidne I took from one woman prasarved it for you tother piece I fried and ate it was very nise I may send you the bloody knif that took it out if you only wate a whil longer signed*

*Catch me when you can Mishter Lusk'*

"One of the Ripper letters, I believe; and with an unusual sort of signature, should you not say, Mr. Jones?"

Kennedy Jones now entertaining a horrific mental vision of Cream thoroughly relishing a meal of fried whore's kidney, was again inarticulate.

"You may perhaps recollect, Mr. Jones, that the Ripper always signed his letters, and this one is no exception." Jones cleared his throat. "Begging your pardon, Doctor, I see no signature here at all."

"Seek and ye shall find, Mr. Jones. Be assured that 'Catch me when you can Mishter Lusk' does incorporate a signature." Cream spoke softly in his Irish-American lilt. "A *catchy* little phrase as one might say, ha,ha.

Jones, transfixed as he was by the conversation and eager for it's continuance, still could not suppress a grimace at Cream's penchant for paranomesia. Cream, without spectacles, interpreted it as a smile of appreciation for his wit.

Now whose signature do you suppose might be incorporated in such a phrase? Almost anyone's? Oh, no, Mr. Jones. Using each letter only once, and taking your own name for instance, we should be missing a 'J', not to speak of a pair of 'D''s and a third 'N'. At random, neither would Queen Victoria suit our purpose, she being minus a 'V' to start. Charles Dickens, Edgar Allan Poe, Gilbert or even Sullivan, not a chance. Well, if we pursued the problem I daresay we might find some names that would fit. But what's in a name, Mr. Jones? Or more to the point, what name is in the phrase? Take my own customary signature, for instance, Thomas N. Cream. Do you think that might suit the case, now, Mr. Kennedy Jones?"

Jones wondered suddenly whether or not he could be dreaming. It was almost beyond the bounds of credibility that he was actually at that moment sitting in the condemned cell at Newgate, engaged in a word game with Jack the Ripper! He watched in startled amazement as Cream took up a piece of blank paper and inscribed on it in large letters, the following, which he then passed to Jones:

```
T      from caTch
H      from wHen
O      from yOu
M      from Me
A      from cAn
S      from LuSk

N      from wheN
C      from catCh
R      from mishteR
E      from mE
A      from cAtch
M      from Mishter
```

Jones wavered between relief and disappointment. "Oh, come now Doctor, that 'aint exactly an anagram, is it now?"

"Why of course not. I might just as well have given myself up to the police as provide that sort of evidence, you benighted imbecile!"

"Quite so, Doctor Cream, quite so." A wintry draught swept through the slatted vent above the cell door, chilling the journalist to the bone. He had met Cream's gaze at last; it was a look almost bestial in its ferocity, an expression either of insanity or unequivocal evil.

Back home, Jones began work immediately on some copy. So intense was his concentration that neither the irritable complaints of his shrewish wife nor the unrestrained boisterous of his sons were permitted to disturb his thought. The supper hour came and went, a pair of lamb-chops with which he had rather condescendingly been served lying neglected and congealed on the board; still Kennedy Jones wrote on, checking from time to time various notes he had assembled for his own use at the newspaper library. It was not until the early hours of next day that his contribution was complete. Heaving a deep sigh of satisfaction, he remarked out loud:

"'Says I to me, `Kennedy Jones my good fellow, I must allow you have made a worthwhile point or two here. That devil in Newgate gaol is the Ripper, and no mistake.' Says me to I, 'Believe you me, he is. And if the world don't *see* the truth of it one fine day, why, we'll eat our ruddy hat!"

FROM ST. JAMES'S GAZETTE, October 21st, 1892

| THE WHITECHAPEL MURDERS. | THE LAMBETH POISONING CASES. |
|---|---|
| The crimes were all committed in the same district. | The crimes were all committed in the same district. |
| The victims were all women. | The victims were all women. |
| They all belonged to the lowest order of a certain class. | They all belonged to the lowest order of a certain class. |
| They were supposed to be the work of a foreigner. | Neill was an American. |
| There were certain marked periods between the murders which seemed to point the murderer taking voyages. | Neill travelled backwards and forwards to America. |
| "Jack the Ripper" had a predilection for writing letters about the murders. | Neill wrote several letters about the deaths of Clover, Shrivell, Marsh, etc., to various persons. |

| | |
|---|---|
| "Jack the Ripper" was described by the only person who has described him, as wearing a slouch hat. | Neill wore a slouch hat when when arrested. |
| The Whitechapel murders were remarkable for being, unlike all other murders, apparently devoid of any motive. | There is really no adequate motive for the Lambeth poisoning cases. |
| The murders were not accompanied by robbery. "Jack the Ripper" is believed to be a person suffering from a horrible disease. | The murders were not accompanied by robbery. Neill is supposed to be suffering from the same disease. |
| "Jack the Ripper" was evidently a very powerful person. | Neill is a very powerful person |

*Typical of their general ignorance, the Bosses never really rumbled that the Chapman job had been done by a man possessed of surgical skill, though their Divisional Surgeon, Bagster Phillips told them as much at the inquest, and I quote: "Obviously the work was that of an expert -- or one, at least, who had such knowledge of anatomical or pathological examinations as to be enabled to secure the pelvic organs with one sweep of the knife." It was further observed that it must have been someone accustomed to the post-mortem room, and that the murderer had a special method of arresting consciousness in his victim. Had I not back at McGill written a complicated thesis upon the art of administering chloroform? One might have thought, with the indications I had so thoughtfully provided that the numbskulls would have confined their search exclusively to highly trained members of my own profession. But no, in their efforts to appease the public, suspicion was invariably directed at those too clumsy and incapable of performing anything but the crudest butchery.*

*In figuring that it was a lunatic who did for Chapman, the police were, as usual, only fooling themselves. Though the des-patching of the woman and her like was strictly a matter of principle, as a businessman I invariably sought whenever possible to bring some degree of financial gain to my various undertakings.*

*Sometime before the Chapman incident I had read in a medical journal that as much as a hundred dollars each might be raised in America for human organs, transported there well pre-served in glycerine to keep them flaccid, for purposes of experimentation. Visiting a pathological museum attached to a medical school, and representing myself as the American publisher of the journal, I had offered to purchase certain organs for the sum of twenty pounds apiece -- unable to resist adding for further effect that as a promotional effort I intended to give one away with each purchased copy. This was a mistake, for the sub-curator, an insignificant tow-headed chap with an oatmeal complexion, took exception to my offer, and suggested quite unpleasantly that I apply elsewhere. I did so with similar result, and then realized that, in the course of other more highly motivated activities, I might myself obtain, in the very pink of condition, some highly saleable goods. Henceforth when free from the factory and able to engage in more fitting work, I carried about inside my bag a bottle of preserving f laid into which, whenever the opportunity arose, I placed whatever organs might be expected to raise the best market price on my return to the United States. Thus Chapman's uterus, being so expertly detached, occupied a place of honour among the other trophies adorning my mantleshelf.*

EXCERPTS FROM THE INQUEST ON ANNIE CHAPMAN.

On 26 September Dr. Wynne E. Baxter summed up the evidence:

Two things missing from the body, Chapman's rings, which had not been found, and the uterus, which had been taken from the abdomen. The body had not been dissected but the injuries had been made by somebody with considerable anatomical skill and knowledge. No meaningless cuts...An unskilled person could not have performed such a deed, nor a mere slaughterer of animals; it must have been someone accustomed to the post-mortem, room ... an internal organ which it had taken a skilled person at least a quarter of an hour to remove.® object of the attack was the abstraction of the viscera, and the stealing of the rings a thinly concealed attempt to disguise the fact

It was not necessary to assume that the murderer was a lunatic, because there was in fact a market for such organs. After the earlier medical evidence had been published in the newspapers, the sub-curator of the pathological museum attached to one of the great medical schools had informed (Dr. Baxter) of an incident that could have a bearing on the case. Some months previously an American had asked him to procure a number of specimens of the missing organ, and for these he was willing to pay twenty pounds each. He planned to issue an actual specimen with each copy of a publication on which he was then engaged. Even though he was told his request was impossible, the American had persisted in his demands, explaining that he wanted them preserved in glycerine to keep them flaccid. He had afterwards made the same request to a similar institution.

The murderer had a special method of arresting consciousness in his victim and was possessed of surgical skill.

# PART 7

On Sunday the 30th of September 1888 London's horde of prostitutes found themselves caught up in what seemed like a waking nightmare. For at dawn came news of not one, but two more of their number, not half a mile apart -- both with throats slashed from ear to ear, the second adroitly degutted. The double event struck stark terror in the golden hearts of every whore east and west of the city, including those fashionable areas where demimondaines managed to enjoy a similar, if considerably more advantageous life-style to that of their less fortunate sisters.

The public were outraged and the police, under intense criticism, pushed to extremes in their desperate search for the Ripper. Every Tom Dick and Harry who aroused the least suspicion was taken in, questioned --and in the case of one Tom in particular, erroneously released...

At about twelve thirty a.m. on the following Monday, 282 H, Constable Joseph Drage was on point duty in Whitechapel Road when, not far down an otherwise deserted side street, he managed to distinguish the outline of a man stooping in the doorway of a laundry. The constable was physically slow and ponderous but capable when called upon of surprising agility. The man, his attention wholly absorbed in an object lying on the bottom step, spun round as the constable loomed out of the darkness. With great presence of mind he beckoned Drage closer.

"Policeman, there is a knife down here. The sight of it makes my blood run cold. Nowadays one hears of such funny things."

Drage spotlighted a long-bladed rust-stained knife on the step. A strip of white cotton muffler blotched with crimson was bound clumsily round the handle with string, and from cursory examination appeared, like the blade, to be bloodstained. The policeman raised his light to the man's face.

"Now then, speak up. How how did you come by this here weapon?" The man, dazzled by the light's beam, delayed momentarily to remove his spectacles, carefully wiping the lenses with a clean pocket handkerchief. Drage noted that his eyes were strangely expressionless and not quite plumb.

"I was returning home from a visit to some friends in Bath Gardens, and passing through -- Great Garden Street, is it not? --" he peered vaguely at a sign above their heads -- "yes, yes, Great Garden Street, to be sure --

when, glancing downwards, it being a fine clear night, I happened to spot something white. Like many another responsible citizen in these murderous times, I have resolved to assist the police as best I might by means of keeping a sharp look out for suspicious objects. Accordingly, I struck a match, clearly illuminating the knife in question. which, on your approach, constable, I at once drew to your attention."

"Odd sort of customer," thought Drage, "though by the cut of his jib not exactly your ruthless killer; mild spoken and respectably turned out --city clerk more than like, weary of sitting at a desk and looking about for a comfortable pension. There had been several sizeable rewards offered for information leading to the arrest of the Ripper for which a member of the force was ineligible. Drage, who had pounded a beat in all kinds of weather for the last twenty years, knew full well that, had he himself ever the good fortune to lay hands on the Ripper, the only reward he might expect would be a commendation, or at best a minor promotion. At any rate, most things considered this was almost certainly not his man, particularly since he knew well enough that the knife, incriminating as it seemed, might possibly have been discarded by a butcher from one of the nearby abbattoires. He was not the bloke, like some of his colleagues, to make a fool of himself by pressing charges which could not be substantiated. Nevertheless he was required by law to complete his interrogation.

"What are you doing out so late?"

"I have been to a friend's in Bath Gardens."

Drage brought out his notebook. "Your name and address?"

"Coram --'Thomas Coram. 67, Plumber's Row," the man muttered.

Drage licked his pencil and wrote laboriously "'Thos." -- he looked up. "Did you say Cream?" For some reason the man for a moment looked strangely startled, and then replied:

"No! Coram. Thomas C-0-R-A-M."

Drage finished writing: 'Thos. Coram, 67, Plummer's-road, Mile End.' I think sir as you'd better come along with me to the station at Leman Street."

"Am I under arrest, officer?"

"Certainly not, Sir, nothing of the kind. Just a formality," Drage assured him. This trusting attitude was, it seems, also the order of the day down at the station, from whence the singularly suspect but extremely glib Mr. Thomas Coram was after brief questioning summarily freed to go about his business -- to the future misfortune of, (to name but three), Elizabeth Stride, Catherine Eddowes and Mademoiselle Marie Jeanette Kelly,

"The Times" 4 October, 1888.

Thomas Coram said at the inquest on Elizabeth Stride:

"I live at 67 Plummer's-road Mile-end[1], and an employed at a cocanut warehouse. On Sunday night I was coming away from a friends at 16, Bath-gardens, Brady-street. I was walking on the right hand side of the Whitechapel-road towards Aldgate. When opposite No 253 I crossed over, and saw a knife lying on the doorstep. No 253 was a laundry business, and there were two steps leading to the front door. I found the knife on the bottom step. That is the knife I found (witness being shown a long-bladed knife). The handkerchief produced was wrapped round the handle.

---

(1)  This was a common mis-spelling of 'Plumber's Row', London East 1., a street within close radius of all the Ripper crimes and leading across the Whitechapel Road directly into Berners Street --some two minutes walk from where Elizabeth Stride was killed. Bath Gardens, Brady Street was just over a minute's walk from Bucks Row (renamed Durward Street) where Mary Ann Nichols was killed. (See Map following).

It was folded, and then twisted round the handle. The handkerchief was blood-stained. A policeman came towards me and I called his attention to them[2].

THE CORONER: The blade of the knife is dagger shaped and is sharpened on one side. The blade is about 9 in. or 10 in. long, I should say.

WITNESS: The policeman took the knife to the Leman-street Police-station, and I went with him.

THE CORONER: Were there many people passing at the time?

WITNESS: I should think I passed about a dozen between Brady-street and where I found the knife.

TEE CORONER: Could it easily be seen?

WITNESS: Yes; and it was light.

THE CORONER: Did you pass a policeman before you got to the spot?

WITNESS: Yes, I passed three. It was about half-past 12 at night.

CONSTABLE JOSEPH DRAGE, 282 H, stated: At 12:30 on Monday morning I was on fixed-point duty in the Whitechapel-road, opposite Great Garden-street. I saw the last witness stooping down at a doorway opposite No. 253. I was going towards him when he rose up and beckoned me with his finger. He then said "Policeman, there is a knife down here". I turned on my light and saw a long-bladed knife lying on the doorstep. I picked up the knife and found it was smothered with blood. The blood was dry. There was a handkerchief bound round the handle and tied with string. The handkerchief also had blood-stains on it. I asked the last witness how he came to see it. He said, "I was looking down, when I saw something white." I then asked him what he did out so late, and he replied "I have been to a friend's in Bath-Gardens." He then gave me his name and address, and we went to the police-station together. The knife and handkerchief produced are the same.

THE CORONER: Was the last witness sober?

WITNESS: Yes. His manner was natural, and he said when he saw the knife it made his blood run cold, and added that nowadays they heard of such funny things. When I passed

(2)   Thomas Coram was by no means the only man ever to be caught "red handed" by the police with a knife and released, as is evident from a contemporary report in "The Sunday Times"19 April 1892. Andrei Chikalito, on trial in Russia for a series of bestial murders and dubbed "The Rostoff Ripper" "was… arrested twice but released both times even though, on the second occasion, he was found to be carrying a knife in his briefcase."

I should have undoubtedly seen the knife. I was passing there continually. Some little time before a horse fell down opposite the place where the knife was found. I assisted in getting the horse up, and during that time a person might have laid the knife on the step. I would not be positive that the knife was not there quarter of an hour previously, but I think not. About an hour previously the landlady let out some woman, and the knife was not there then. I handed the knife to Dr. Phillips on Monday afternoon. It was then sealed and secured.

*After the excitement had died down in the Chapman affair, and determined that on no account should Jack be considered a dull boy, my mind was constantly taken up with new ways and means of focusing public attention upon my work, as well as further discrediting the dam fool police. To this end I had taken to dropping the pinheads a few taunting lines now and again; and in a sporting effort to tip them off, had recently promised to provide on my next venture a delectable pair of ears! How then to go about it with anything like an original approach, one which would serve also to relieve my intense boredom, obliged as I was to lead the stultifying life of Thomas Coram during the weekdays? I had begun to long for the weekends when released from Coram's tiresome occupation at the factory and climbing into a decent set of clothes I could slip sprucely into the role of Doctor John Fordyce. It was under that singularly useful cognomen that on a Saturday night in the fall of '88, I dropped by Gatti's music hall for some lively entertainment; and there had myself one whale of an inspiration! The very first act happened to feature a droll young freak from Siam who actually sported two drooping heads, each regarding the other with the same incredulous expression as did their audience.*

"LADIES AND GENTLEMEN, "*the Master of Ceremonies had bawled,* "MAY WE PRESENT -- FOR THE VERY TIME IN LONDON -- INDEED THROUGHOUT THE CIVILIZED WORLD -- OUR AMAZING -- FANTASTIC -- IN SHORT, ABOLUTELY EXTRAORDINARY -- DOUBLE EVENT!"

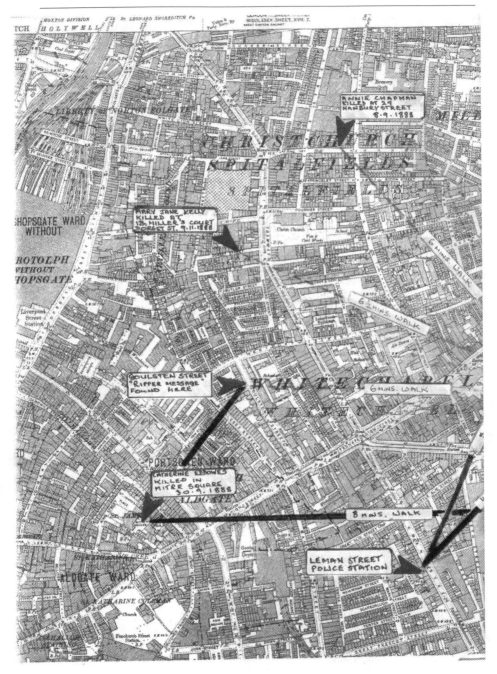

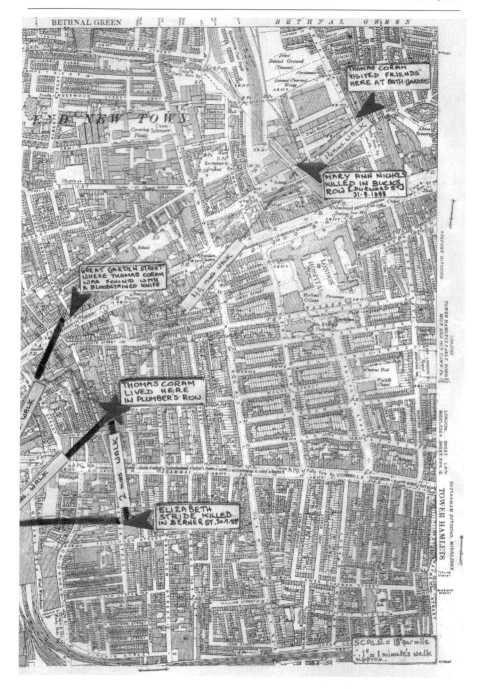

A nice turn of phrase, in my opinion, and one which provided me with a great idea. I had always been partial to mixed doubles. My next whore-culling should also be a 'double event'. Kill two birds with one stone, as the saying went -- a neat coup, if only I could pull it off!

I had my eye on a Swedish whore called Stride who regularly plied her trade in Berner Street, just down the way from my lodgings and outside the International Workers' Educational Club -- a penny-ante organization patronized by a load of lousy Yids, who, despite their grasping ways, had the gall to call themselves socialists. That this whore, Stride, was degenerate enough to offer her services to a bunch of kikes rendered her all the more deserving, in my opinion, of the fate I had in store. Whitechapel abounded with Hebrews, against whom, as it happened, I bore a strong grudge. This was mainly on account of Anderesmann, or rather the absence of Anderesmann.

Never a Jew lover, the relationship I had struck up with "the Rabbi" was, to say the least of it, an unlikely one, and yet endured; that is, up until the period four years ago, when I had the disillusionment of learning that good old irreproachable Anderesmann was capable as the next man of letting a pal down. To give him his due at the present time it is to Anderesmann's eternal credit that, suspecting no doubt my days are numbered, he has at last returned to my support, and for this I am truly grateful; but had he only shown equal compassion then, who knows but I might not now be confronting the gallows! It may be remembered that, when still in Chicago after breaking gaol, I was, due to my prolonged suffering, close to a nervous collapse, and begged Andersmann to accompany me to England until I had recovered my health. Of this he would not hear, and instead of his companionship proffered a load of puritanical recommendations as to my behaviour when I reached London, which I conveyed in no uncertain terms were unacceptable. The Judas then went on sourly to suggest that if I chose to take his advice so lightly it might be better if we saw less of one another for a while! Incensed by his refusal to stand by me, I found myself, on reaching London, filled with considerable antipathy towards Anderesmann -- and that went for the rest of his craven race too. As The Ripper I made it my practice whenever the opportunity arose to cast suspicion in their direction, and, I might add, with no small *success. The forthcoming double event should not, if I could avoid it, be an exception.*

*I still had to endure a dreary week at the factory before the last weekend of the month when I should be free to follow my keener interests. On Saturday night, September 29th, 1888 Doctor John Fordyce, with his fine silk hat and alpaca trimmed coat was not to be found in his accustomed Sunday night haunts. It was Thomas Coram, dressed in a shabby black cap and deplorably ill-fitting jacket who set out with every intention of tickling the ladies' fancy.*

*Certain they did not have the wit nor the ability to catch me, I had not at the time of the Chapman operation so much as troubled to clean up the knife, tossing it carelessly back in my bag where it had remained since, bloodstained and bound in a handkerchief. Around midnight, after a preparatory sniff of cocaine my confidence was such that I merely rolled the still soiled bundle inside a newspaper, stuffed it in a hip-pocket and made my way intrepidly towards Whitechapel Road. In order to pull off a double that night I was above all aware that speed was of the essence, my strategy being to strike first at random and without elaboration in the near vicinity of my lodgings at Plumber's Row; returning to clean up if necessary and collect the equipment for a rather more leisured operation on the woman Stride. Unfortunately however, these arrangements did not go quite according to plan, for nearing the upper end of Plumber's Row a little before half past twelve and crossing the Whitechapel Road at Great Garden Street -- a prolific hunting ground -- I withdrew the knife from my pocket and, as a drink-sodden drab approached, began to remove its binding. She should have been croaked in a moment and good riddance but that a huge policeman emerged quite unexpectedly from a sidestreet and to my dismay, advanced towards me. Discovered well after midnight in possession of a bloodstained weapon, I quickly threw the knife down on the nearest doorstep as the cop came up close and shone his light on it, and then at myself. Prompted by sheer desperation I managed to concoct a cock-and-bull tale to the effect that I had by chance noticed a white object lying on the doorstep, which to my absolute horror, on closer inspection, had proved to be a wrapped up knife. I was of course aware as I spoke that so weak an excuse would fail to deceive a cretin.*

*Incredibly, however, greatly to my relief, it was accepted. The policeman,
though he made some show of taking me in for further questioning,
was clearly convinced in his own simple way of my innocence, even
exchanging with me one or two jovial quips during our five minute
walk to Leman Street. At the station his colleagues touchingly adopted
the same trusting attitude; and on inspecting the knife declared the
instrument unsuitable for the purpose I had on more than one occasion
put it to. They decided as a precaution to keep the knife in custody,
but summarily to release Thomas Coram without so much as a spot
on his character. Crowing inwardly at my narrow escape that night, I
was nevertheless in due course to be a trifle less cocksure when, called
as an honest witness at Stride's inquest, I heard the Coroner describe
the knife they had nabbed me with as long and dagger shaped -- in
effect, contrary to police opinion, an ideal slut-gutter. At this point I
fully expected suspicion would now revert to me as the possessor of such
a weapon, and that I was completely done for. Not so, though; even
with the knife, Exhibit No. 1, pointing positively at me, my lodgings at
Plumber's Row not a stone's throw from where Stride was killed, and
-- a small additional clue I had in a rash moment tossed sportingly in
their direction -- that I was also an habitue of Brady Street, a further
stone's throw from Buck's Row where Nicholls had been ripped --the
Bosses, true to form still failed to spot the obvious.*

*Freed with little delay from the police-station that September night
and and warmly congratulating myself on my quick thinking, I found
that there was yet some ten minutes to spare before one o'clock, time in
which, if I moved with despatch, to promote Stride first on the agenda.
Younger then by four years and always an athletic man, I was able to
cover the short distance back to Plumber's Row in a matter of minutes.
There I hastily collected my bag of tricks and proceeded immediately
across the way to Berner Street, where to my relief I found Stride had
not yet deserted her post. I posted myself a short distance down on the
opposite side of the street, regained my wind and lit up Coram's pipe
(with a rather less exclusive brand of tobacco than that in which Doctor
Fordyce was wont to indulge) while sizing up the situation. Long Liz
Stride was a raw-boned Scandinavian, handsome once maybe, with
curls darkened by grease straggling from a ragged straw bonnet. I had
before my abortive trip to Whitechapel Road strolled down the street*

*in order to open a conversation with the slut. Gallantly offering a kiss and a red floral buttonhole, in the next moment I had coldly rejected her suggestion to copulate the entire night for the price of a shilling. You would say anything but your prayers," I admonished the abandoned bitch sternly.*

*Now ten or so minutes past the hour of one it seemed that everyone, with the exception of myself and Long Liz, were safely home in bed. Heavy cloud threatened a downpour and from the roomy recesses of my bag I withdrew my rolled up raincoat and wide-brimmed felt hat, replacing it with the peaked cap I had hitherto been wearing. Checking the selection of knives I had brought along, that my bottle of spirits was safely corked and that my dark lantern was in workable order, I snapped shut the bag and prepared to make my move.*

*It was then that some drunken lout came tottering down the street, paused by Stride, probably without a dime to his name, yet evidently accosted her. She must have turned him down for I could hear their voices raised in noisy altercation. "Whore, get in the fucking gutter where you belong!" They began to struggle and he threw her down on the sidewalk, raising a few indignant sqwawks. This scene suited my purpose admirably, particularly as a flamboyantly turned out Yid had just passed into Berner Street and witnessed the whole incident. He chose to ignore the brawl, scuttling by timid as a mouse while muttering in some outlandish tongue and casting a nervous glance at me. "Lipski," the drunk jeered after him, in reference to another of his sort who, the scoundrel, had the baseness to poison a respectable young lady! The drunk now reeled away and the flashy Yid quickly walked on. I followed at a casual pace, intending to ensure his departure, he peering uneasily back over his shoulder at me and my little black bag and calling out several times something sounding like 'Oy, hey'! Whether it was I he was hailing I doubt, for the fellow all at once broke into a run, making off as if the devil were at his heels. I pursued him as far as the nearby railway arch, and satisfied that he was not likely to return, doubled quickly back along the now almost empty street. All this had taken but a few minutes and Stride was still lying on the sidewalk in a dazed condition. I assisted her courteously to rise, she recognising me with apparent relief as the rather eccentric but kindly fellow who had earlier* than evening provided her buttonhole. Assuming, I suppose, I had reconsidered her offer, she willingly accompanied me inside the gates of Dutfield's yard. There in the gloom I came behind the snatch, gripping her hard by the shoulders, then jerking the head towards me by means of a checked scarf she wore, exposed her scraggy throat to the slash of my biting blade. All was accomplished in the space of seconds, without need of chloroform, and with the minimum of squeals. My patient now very sound asleep I lit the lantern and attending first specifically to the proposed removal of an ear, I prepared to fulfil my recent promise to the police. While absorbed in selecting the correct instrument for this task, to my utter consternation there came a rumbling of wheels down Berner Street! I had time only to extinguish the lantern and hurl it and the rest of my belongings back in the bag before a cart creaked through the wooden gates of Dutfield's yard, the wheels practically brushing the brim of my hat! If the driver had spotted me and cried out, what with the neighbours, the police and an outraged mob of Vigilanties led by a character called George Lusk, all eager to nab Jack the Ripper, I should surely have been a goner, As the pony reared before Stride's dead body, I leaped nimbly behind the cart and out into Berner Street, heart thudding fit to split my ribs, Placing as much distance between myself and Dutfield's Yard as was expedient, I found an empty alley, quickly divested myself of raincoat and hat (both practically unsoiled since I was growing more skillful at my work, and had by standing behind the whore been successful in directing the first heavy jets of arterial blood away from me), rolled up these garments and replaced them in the bag. I then sank to the kerb in order to restore my nerve -- this being accomplished with the assistance of a heavy draught of brandy from a flask which I invariably carried about me. The alcohol went rapidly to my head as did a top-up of cocaine: and under these influences, as always, I felt rapidly reassured in my invincibility. Had I not so far outsmarted the Bosses every inch of the way? Why, none of them had the brains to catch me, that was for sure! I should delay no further but proceed boldly with the second event. Far from sober I may have been, but as it rapidly emerged, no less effective when it came to slashing a slut!

Looking about me I realised that I was in Church Passage, leading into Mitre Square, which according to my information was regularly *patrolled every fifteen minutes or so by the police. I realized that there was no time to waste if I were to succeed in accomplishing the second event that night. It was then that along came Eddowes, singing raucously. I crept up behind the whore and managed by the aforementioned methods to silence her instantly and forever, applying with a surgeon's skill the Ripper's obligatory trademark -- some finely wrought etching. Expertly enough also, notwithstanding my condition, I removed a kidney from it's mesenteric attachment within the woman's gaping guts and placed it with the uterus in my spirits jar. It occurred to me with some amusement that a section of that prime juicy kidney delivered to a news agency, or better still to the celebrated Mr. Lusk himself, accompanied by a spoof letter, might in fact create a greater public sensation than a couple of grubby ears received by the police... At any rate I had my work cut out (no pun intended for once!), to finish before they all showed up; and so contented myself with slicing through one of the ears almost completely, in the hope of making the mortician's work even more disagreeable than usual when it fell in his lap! The shock was on me, though, when, with a parting glance at the whore I saw that the woman had been tattood on the arm with my initials, T.C.[3] Here was an astounding revelation, no mere co-incidence but a heavenly sign which clearly indicated to me that my campaign of elimination had all along been inspired not, as I had supposed, solely by my own profound sense of justice and decency, but by an even loftier motivation. With new clarity I could now see that this miserable sinner, this dirty disease-spreading whore had by supernatural means, been marked out for punishment at my hands -- and by no less than the Almighty Himself! I now knew for certain that my mission to smite the ungodly was a holy one, and must never, as long as there was life left in me, be forsaken.*

*In the grip of this astounding revelation my instinct for self-preservation still held sway. I had as before managed to protect my clothes from bloodstain, rolling shirtsleeves carefully to the elbow before operating. Both hands and arms were however smeared with the foul contents of Eddowes' guts, which had in in the heat of the moment been of no*

---

(3)   *Curiously enough, Catherine Eddowes had in fact been tattood on the arm with the initials T.C. -- though probably in honour of her lover, Thomas Conway.*

*consequence, but now caused me to retch. I had fortunately troubled to become well acquainted with the area, and now headed hastily north from Mitre Square towards some public washing facilities a few minutes away near Goulsten Street. Fortunately at that hour the remote passages were quite deserted; locating the place I had soon rinsed off the offensive filth and re-donning my hat and raincoat, did, so I trusted, present once more a fairly respectable figure. It was however to my renewed disgust on reaching Goulsten Street that I discovered a filthy piece of*

*Eddowes' apron which during the excitement had become detached, and, covered in blood and faeces, now adhered to my shoe. Tearing it off with agrimace I took yet another stiff swig of liquor. Now pretty darn drunk, I waxed maudlin with selfpity. Those who in a more enlightened age might have discerned in my actions the most praise worthy of motivations did in fact regard me as no better than a common murderer and would hang me ingloriously if they could. Commanded as I was to serve society as the Lord ordained, it was for this bunch of ingrates that I had sacrificed any hope of enjoying a rewarding life. My f ate henceforth was to be always on the run, hunted like a common criminal, with no safe haven. It was of course Anderesmann more than anyone else who was responsible for my situation. Had only the fellow come to London as I had begged him, he might well, by his steadying influence, have persuaded me to handle matters in a way less inimical to myself. My grievance against him and his sort had welled to such a pitch that, finding a piece of chalk in the gutter I clumsily, and, as was my wont when under the influence, with scant regard f or literacy, scrawled a meaningless message on the wall; this being, in retrospect, I suppose, a befuddled attempt to cast suspicion on the Jews for my own unlawful enterprise.*

**The   Juwes   are**
**The   men   That**
**      Will   not**
**Be  Blamed**
**     for   nothing**

POSTCARD MAILED ON 1 OCTOBER 1888, ADDRESSED
TO THE CENTRAL NEWS AGENCY.

*I was not codding dear old Boss when I gave you the tip. You'll hear*
*about Saucy Jack's work tomorrow. Double event this time. Number*
*one squealed a bit. Couldn't finish straight off. Had not time to get ears*
*for police. Thanks for keeping last letter back till I got to work again.*

*JACK THE RIPPER*

CONTAINED IN A REPORT BY CHIEF INSPECTOR DONALD
SWANSON dated 19<sup>TH</sup> OCTOBER 1888 TO THE HOME OFFICE.

*Israel Schwartsz of 22 Helen Street, Backchurch Lane, stated*
*that at this hour, on turning into Berner Street from Commercial*
*Street, and having got as far as the gateway where the murder*
*was committed, he saw a man stop and speak to a woman, who*
*was standing in the gateway. The man tried to pull the woman*
*into the street but he turned her round and threw her down*
*on the footway and the woman screamed three times, but not*
*very loudly. On crossing to the opposite side of the street, he*
*saw a second man standing lighting his pipe*[4]. *The man who*
*threw the woman called out, apparently to the man on the*
*opposite side of the road, 'Lipski', and then Schwartz walked*
*away, but finding that he was followed by the second man, he*
*ran as far as the railway arch, but the man did not follow as*
*far. Schwartsz cannot say whether the two men were together*
*or known to each other. Upon being taken to the mortuary*
*Schwartsz identified the body of the woman he had seen...*

*When sufficiently full of intoxicants I experienced no fear, conducting*
*my work with incredible bravado and the same clinical detachment*

---

(4)    This second man was described by Schwartsz as aged thirtyfive,
       five foot eleven inches in height, with fresh complexion, light
       brown hair and brown moustache. He was wearing a dark overcoat
       and old black hard felt hat with a wide brim. In 1888 Thomas
       Neill Cream would have been thirtyeight, approximately five
       foot nine or ten inches tall, invariably wore a moustache and
       probably still retained some of his reddish brown hair.

*which I had been used to apply on a professional level. With sobriety, however, realization of the appalling danger to which I continually subjected myself came increasingly to cause me the utmost anxiety. Only another drinking bout or the re-introduction of a heavy dose of drugs enabled me to overcome a series of terrible dreams in which, as a disembodied soul, I witnessing my former self, tongue lolling idiotically sideways, face hideously swollen and black, eyes bulging hideously from their sockets, being hurled into a pit of lime. Without these stimulants, despite the new found conviction that I was in the main performing my work according to God's holy ordinance, I believe I might not have had the courage to continue as long as I did. Cocaine, in particular, filled me with a masterful sense of power, an assurance that I might without difficulty overcome any opposition to the accomplishment of the task I had undertaken, that I was unconquerable and, in short, that I was equipped to beat the Bosses at their own game with the greatest of ease. Much as I enjoyed the challenge of outsmarting those fools, I never for a moment, after the Eddowes incident, allowed myself to forget that my mission was a holy one.*

Perceiving the presence of Anderesmann Cream paused to greet him. Anderesmann, more solicitous than ever nowadays of Cream's welfare, had recently taken to arriving at all hours. The condemned man had now been accorded the privilege of brief but unlimited access to those he wished to see; yet of Laura Sabbatini, the one person, other than Anderesmann, whom Cream had hoped would stand by him, nothing was heard. There had been no response to his letter informing her that she was now appointed not only the sole beneficiary to what little remained of his estate but also, in the event of his death, the sum of six hundred and fifty pounds payable through Jones. Having only agreed to the arrangement with Jones at Anderesmann's instigation, Cream now blamed him for Laura's dereliction.

"I should never have gotten caught up with a cringing little slimebag like Jones, as well you know Anderesmann, but for your urging me to take care of Laura. Without the slightest gesture of appreciation from the girl, darned if I feel disposed to pursue the deal."

"Patience Tom. You'll hear from her by and by. Stay with the good work and see the woman right -- it's the least you can do. The poor soul is innocent of any wrongdoing, and yet she must be suffering quite as much as you."

"Laura is hardly the innocent I may, as a gentleman, have led you to believe, Anderesmann, though my first impression of her was that of a dull unworldly little spinster, dominated by her crabby old mother. To a man like me, past forty and hardened in his ways, it was that very quality of wide-eyed ingenuousness I found appealing. Yet for all her artless airs, I regret that she was not above being too impulsive in her inclinations."

"Knowing you as I do, Tom, I should have thought that would suit you fine."

"On the contrary, Anderesmann. Our attitudes alter as we grow older, do they not? I had hoped by wedding Laura finally to set up an agreeable life-style for myself, become revered in my profession, start a family perhaps. To that purpose I required above everything a wife of flawless virtue. I told the girl straight, though in not so many words, that if I wanted a whore I knew where to find one. I must say for Laura that she accepted the rebuke with proper humility, praying that she had not sacrificed my respect and assuring me no such incident would occur again until we were married."

"My dear fellow, pray be open with yourself while there is still time. I still believe, despite your strictures, or perhaps because of them, that you do have some feeling for the girl. Why not let her know it?"

Cream's irritation flared again: "Confound it, man, have I not offered to marry her? What more proof of fondness could a woman expect? Where is the evidence of Laura's devotion to me, I should like to know, Anderesmann?" Temper rising to an hysterical pitch, he began to rant, "The two-timing bitch had better show up, she'd better show up, before it's too damn late!"

"Enough of that!" snapped one of the guards. "Stow it, Cream!"

"They shall never hang you, Tom," soothed Anderesmann. "Told them as much at the trial, did you not?" Cream wished he could share Anderesmann's optimism, now that a thorough search of his personal effects had resulted in the confiscation of that hidden weapon which might well have provided him at the final count with the means, one way or another, of escaping so ignoble a fate. The appointment with Killington drew hourly nearer with, as Anderesmann had to own, a dismaying absence of response from Queen Victoria to the appeal for clemency he had submitted on Cream's behalf. Anderesmann, though, refused to abandon hope, and continued to assure him that not only would there be a last minute stay of execution but that his sweetheart should visit before long. These reassurances partially mollified Cream, and with nothing to lose as matters stood by honouring his commitment with the newspaper, he resolved to do so -- though Anderesmann, if not Jones, was wholly aware that this was dependent entirely on the advent of Miss Laura Sabbatini.

WERE THESE FURTHER EXAMPLES OF CREAM'S "SPOOF" LETTERS, AND IF SO WAS THE WORD "PRACTICAL" A PUN ON MEDICAL PRACTICE?

LETTER FROM POLICE FILES, PUBLIC RECORDS OFFICE, KEW

*To Whitechapel Police, dated 9th October 1888.*

*Dear boss*

*I am going to do another job right under the very nose of the damned old Charley Warren. You had me once but like fools let me go.*

*Jack the ripper."*

NOTE: Police thought this handwriting was similar to other Ripper letters.

LETTER FROM POLICE FILES. PUBLIC RECORDS OFFICE, KEW.

On noteheading of the Central News Ltd, 5, New Bridge Street, London. 6 Nov. 1888.

*Dear Mr.Williamson,*

*At 5 minutes to 9 oclock tonight we received the following letter the envelope of which I enclose by which you will see it is in the same handwriting of the previous communications.*

*5 Oct. 1888. Dear Friend,*

*In the name of God hear me I swear I did not kill the female whose body was found at Whitehall. If she was an honest woman I will hunt down and destroy her murderer. If she was a whore God will bless the hand that slew her, for the women of Moab and Midian shall die and their blood shall mingle with the dust. I never harm any others or the Divine power that protects and helps me in any grand work would quit for ever. Do as I do and the light of glory shall shine upon you. I must get to work tomorrow treble event this time yes yes three must be ripped --will send you a bit of face by post I promise this dear old Boss -- The police now reckon my work a practical joke, well well Jack, a very practical joker ha ha ha. Keep this back till three are wiped out and you can show the cold meat.*

*Yours truly*
*Jack the Ripper*

# PART 8

It was 3:30 on the morning of November 9th 1888 when Mrs. Elizabeth Prater of Room 20, 27 Dorset Street, Whitechapel was disturbed from her uneasy slumbers by a sharp stab in the neck. She gave a mighty shriek, which was promptly smothered, for the fifth night running, by Mr. William Prater with the aid of a few loud curses and a down pillow -- her husband assuming that she was again dreaming that Jack the Ripper's blade was at her throat. The real culprit, a tiny black kitten which had curled itself affectionately around Mrs. Prater's neck in the dark, inflicted a final alarmed scratch and leaped from cover. Mrs. Prater flung the pillow aside indignantly:

"I'm sure I don't know why I ever took you back, Bill Prater, brute that you are! Done well enough all on me lonesome, I have, over the last five years, wiv' a proper room -- none of yer cheap dosses for the likes of me -- and one or two regulars to provide a nice bit of cash on the side. Pm indeblooming-pendent these days, I am, so for all that bothers me you can sling yer blasted 'ook!"

"I'm staying put," growled Prater. "And shall have a proper sleep for once, if I have to murder for it!". Somewhere outside in Miller's Court a voice echoed "MURDER!" Prater sat bolt upright and listened in vain for the cry to be repeated. ;hosing to dismiss the incident as nothing more than a neighbour's squabble he slumped down again with a pillow over his own head.

"Get up, you good-for-nothing bugger and find out what's going on out there!"

"Not on your bloody life, or anyone else's for the matter of that," replied her caring spouse.

Earlier that night Doctor Thomas Neill Cream, alias John Fordyce, stood before the dressing mirror inspecting his appearance with some satisfaction. Weekends were always welcome since they brought freedom from his onerous occupation at the factory in the guise of Thomas Coram, clerk. At such periods in recent weeks he had, as Doctor Fordyce, been taking the opportunity of attending "night calls" to various patients. On that Saturday, November 9th, 1888 he had made a late appointment to visit one of the girls who had come to his office earlier in the day seeking an abortion, a pretty enough piece she was for a slut. Always willing to oblige, Cream had promised to perform the operation where the utmost privacy might be obtained, namely in her lodgings at Miller's Court. Smartly apparalled, as befitted a man of his profession, in white linen shirt, light waistcoat, dark suit adorned with red silk handkerchief and astrakhan collar, boots gathered with pearlised buttons, he looked the very epitome of high class respectability.

The worthy physician ceremoniously donned the watch and thick gold chain without which his business ensemble was never complete, speared his tie with a distinctive horseshoe pin and stood back to admire himself. The Gladstone bag was in process of being washed out and aired so he gathered together his instruments and wrapped them carefully in an oil-cloth carrier, together with the spirit jar for preserving purposes, securing all with a strap. Wearing his slouch hat low over the forehead he left in good time to attend the assignment.

Cream marched briskly into Thrawl Street, practically bowling down his patient, Mary Jane Kelly. Still in her early twenties and comparatively new to the game, Kelly, thanks to the dewy Welsh mists of her adoptive home rather than to her wayward habits, had retained a fresh complexion; though a profusion of chestnut hair framing an elfin face was more attributable to Irish ancestry. Cream's burly form loomed towards her through the fog. Mary Jane recoiled in panic. At closer quarters she was immensely relieved to recognise her physician.

"My word, though, you didn't half give me start, Doctor Neill!"

"Did you take me for Jack the Ripper, then, young lady?".

"The very idea, Doctor Neill -- you being a medical gentleman and all!" The two of them proceeded to enjoy a good laugh at the absurdity of such an assumption. Mary Jane's merriment was dampened, though, on recalling the purpose of their meeting. The truth was she had not yet been able to earn enough cash to pay for the abortion, and would therefore have to postpone it -- unless of course the kind doctor would be willing to take his fee out in trade at some later date. It appeared that the kind doctor was not in the least averse to this suggestion -- in consideration of certain special requirements, the details of which he whispered in her ear, provoking further hilarity. Convulsed with mirth, she accepted the gallant loan of Cream's red silk handkerchief, dabbing elegantly at her face in quite the Parisienne manner -- having once spent a week or so on the other side of the Atlantic and considering herself in consequence the very mistress of Gallic airs and graces. To maintain the air of pleasantry Cream treated Mary Jane, already the worse for several pints of beer, to a swig of the brandy flask in his hip pocket, she returning the favour with a loud and untuneful rendition of "A violet I plucked from my mother's grave." Cream, a virtuoso on the autoharp, grimaced, silenced her with what she took for a good-natured shove and proceeded with his own particular line of entertainment -- a series of crude jokes and depraved suggestions unbecoming to say the least in a man of medicine. As they neared Kelly's lodgings in Miller's Court, Cream removed his kid gloves thoughtfully. "My proposition appeals to you then, my dear?"

"Yes."

"Then it's a deal. A sovereign on account of future services and the removing tonight of your little problem into the bargain. You'll be all right for what I have told you, that I promise."

"Mary Jane, or Marie Jeannette as she preferred to be known professionally, was entirely agreeable. "It's a good man you are, doctor, and I swear shan't regret helping a poor unfortunate girl with her troubles. Rest assured, me old darlin' I'll make it up to you when I'm well, and in every way you fancy." She giggled, treating him to a cheeky wink. "Now as for the job at hand, let's get it over and done with. Come along, my dear, I've left a nice fire burning in the grate, so you will be quite comfortable at your work."

The winter's night may have been cold but Cream, in eager anticipation of what was to occur, felt distinctly overheated. He slapped his hand down none too gently on her shoulder, devouring full young lips with a hard and hungry kiss. They passed through an arch into the narrow court of houses, stopping by the door of Number 13. Mary Jane slid her hand through the broken pane of an adjacent window, drew the bolt, and ushered Cream into a room so small as to contain only basic necessities in the way of furnishings -- a single chair, two ricketty tables and a bed. She carefully rearranged a man's jacket, a pair of shabby trousers and a grubby shirt which had been hanging inside the door. Removing her outer garments she placed them carefully on the chair, in tidy contrast to a large bundle of old clothes dumped by friends and strewn carelessly about the floor in place of rugs. Jaunty hat topping a bedknob and boots placed carefully side by side against the hearth, Mary Jane stood pale as her milk white shift.

Cream, highly stimulated, was tempted to make perfunctory use of the girl first, but decided reluctantly that business must precede pleasure --particularly since he took so great a pleasure in this particular form of business. He steadied himself to perform the preliminaries, carefully rolled back the bedsheet. "Now my dear, just lie down and let me have a look at you. shall be through in no time. "As the girl resignedly prepared herself for his examination, reclining on the bed, shift raised, knees agape, Cream removed his tools of trade, laid them with slow deliberation on the bedside table, washed his hands in a bowl, and began to explore her body. Dexterous at first, in accordance with obstetrical training, his thrusts became increasingly more rough, causing the girl to gasp.

Cream selected an instrument "Quietly now, my dear -- we shall soon make an end of it all." His smooth reassurances did little to alleviate the agony of such violent probing as now brought tears to the eyes of his victim, though for fear of arousing the neighbours she bore in stoic silence the indignity and pain. As the girl stifled her moans Cream's excitement reached a peak, sweat beading from his naked scalp to trickle slowly down his forehead. Regretfully he was obliged to desist in order to wipe his spectacles; and took the opportunity to stoke the fire with anything that would serve to provide more light for his work than was presently available from the guttering candle in its broken wineglass. He would happily have prolonged the poor girl's torture even more, but for the probability that as a result of further 'treatment' without anaesthetic she might be constrained to scream far too loudly for his liking. Reluctantly he produced the chloroform pad.

"Now, my dear, this will not hurt in the least. Soon you will be fast asleep and know nothing. Easy now, knees well spread, that's the way. All will be over presently."

In her last moment of consciousness his horrified victim was aware of Cream leaning towards her with a long sharp knife. Peering closely into her face, outthrust jaw, teeth bared in a bestial snarl, the absence of spectacles accentuating his villanous squint, the man's expression was positively maniacal. "Oh, dear Jesus save me, 'tis the devil himself -- MURDER!" she yelled in an agony of terror. Cream promptly slammed her silent with the chloroform pad, and soon, mercifully, Mary Jane Kelly was beyond all pain.

In the privacy of those four walls and with little danger of discovery, Cream's sadistic compulsion drove him berserk. The room became a charnel house, a welter of gore, his body slick with grume as he flayed, lacerated, amputated in a hellish orgy of decimation. Pieces of flesh were slashed away, flung upon picture hooks, breasts hacked off and thrown aside, skin flayed and, as a final act of degradation, one of his victim's hands forced into her gaping belly.

"Jezebel, Jezebel, you dirty snatch, I'll rip out your fucking liver!" Revolting obscenities spurted as relentlessly from his lips as gouts of life's-blood pumping through severed arteries to spray the walls crimson. His uncontrollable desire to destroy, expressed in this monstrous display of barbaric butchery continued until the furnace he had built in the hearth with all the coals available, and constantly refuelled with various items of clothing, slowly waned; as, transiently, did his murderous lust. He now felt drained of all purpose, the remains of what was once a human being, reduced to lumps of torn meat, evoking in Cream, now that his frenzy had subsided, a complete absence of emotion. Though even he had not prepared himself for such a blood-bath, having intended, allowing for the convenience afforded by Kelly's room, merely to despatch the baggage and her disgusting spawn methodically and tidily. Instead he had become, in an excess of passion, completely out of control, was drenched with blood and perspiration, requiring urgently to clean himself up before venturing out into the night.

Cream stripped, rinsed off in the wash-basin, discarded the bloodstained water and changed into the shabby outfit hanging on the door by which they had entered. The clothes stank and fitted him badly, but would do well enough until he reached home. His own perfectly tailored costume, with the exception of jewelry and shoes, were consigned regretfully to the glowing embers which, stimulated by a splash or two from his brandy flask, sent up a huge sheet of consuming flame. As an after thought he tossed Kelly's pathetic sailor hat with it's trailing blue cords into the blaze, though her other clothes, unlike their owner, were spared.

For obvious reasons it was now vital for Cream to make himself scarce in London, and arrangements were already underway for his return to the United States. Always the business man he did not hesitate therefore to enlarge his sales stock; preparing immediately afterwards to leave without a backward glance at the hideous remains of his victim. As a man of God, however, it did occur to him that, provided with this unique opportunity for privacy, a few parting words delivered by himself, might not go amiss. He therefore returned to the bedside, rearranged one or two gruesome items on the side table, the better to create a satisfactory sensation when they should be discovered, and began to drone expressionlessly:

*"Thou shalt be filled with drunkenness and sorrow, with the cup of astonishment and desolation. Thou shalt even drink it and suck it out, and thou shalt break the sherds thereof, and pluck off thine own breasts: for I have spoken it, saith the Lord God."*

REPORT FROM THE METROPOLITAN POLICE C.I.D. dated November 12th, 1888.

*"An important statement has been made by a man called George Hutchinson which I forward herewith. I have interrogated him this evening and I am of the opinion his statement is true...Also that he was surprised to see a man so well dressed in her company which caused him to watch them."*

*F. G.ABBERLINE, Supt."*

`...She went away towards Thrawl Street. A man coming in the opposite direction to Kelly tapped her on the shoulder and said something to her. They both burst out laughing. I heard her say "Alright" to him and the man said: "You will be alright for what I have told you."*

*He then placed his right hand round her shoulders. He also had a kind of small parcel in his left hand with a kind of strap round it.*

*I stood against the lamp o the Queen's Head public house and watched him. They both then came past me and the man held down his head with his hat over his eyes. I stooped down and looked him in the face. He looked at me stern[1]. They both went into Dorset Street. I followed them. They both stood at the corner of the court for about three minutes. He said something to her. She said: "Alright, my dear. Come along. You will be comfortable."*

*He then placed his arm on her shoulder and she gave him a kiss. She said she had lost her handkerchief. He then pulled out out his handkerchief, a red one, and gave it to her. They both then went up the court together. I then went to the court to see if I could see them, but I could not. I stood there for about*

---

*three quarters of an hour to see if they came out. They did not, so I went away.'*

*Age about thirty four or thirty five, height five feet six inches, complexion pale. Dark eyes and eyelashes. Slight moustache curled up each end and hair dark. Very surly looking. Dress, long dark coat, collar and cuffs trimmed astrakhan and a dark jacket under, light waistcoat, dark trousers, dark felt hat turned down in the middle, button boots and gaiters with white buttons, wore a very thick gold chain with linen collar, black tie with horseshoe pin, respectable appearance, walked very sharp*

## THOMAS NEIL.L. CREAM WEARING HORSESHOE PIN

*Neill Cream at McGill University.*

Detail of photograph above showing horseshoe pin

**(Photographs courtesy Notman Photogaphic Archives,
McGill University, Montreal)**

NOTE: George Hutchinson's statement to the police varied in slight detail from a report published in "The Times" of November 14th, 1888, according to which the Ripper suspect had a dark complexion (as opposed to a pale complexion in his official statement) and dark moustache turned up at the ends. He was wearing a long dark coat trimmed with "astrachan", a white collar with black necktie, in which was affixed a horseshoe pin. He wore a pair of dark spats with light buttons over buttoned boots and displayed from his waistcoat a massive gold chain. His watch chain had a big seal with a red stone hanging from it.' Cream was known not only to possess a seal and thick gold chain, but undeniably the ubiquitous horseshoe pin which figures in all reported versions -- and which, as a young man, he is seen wearing above.

**ILLINOIS STATE PENITENTIARY Joliet, Illinois, U.S.A.**

```
DESCRIPTION OF CONVICT:
WHEN RECEIVED                 Nov. 1st, 1881.
REGISTERED NO.                4374.
NAME                          Thomas N. Cream.
ALIAS                         . . . . .
COUNTY                        Boone
TERM                          September
CRIME                         Murder
SENTENCE                      His natural life.
AGE WHEN RECEIVED             31
NATIVITY                      Scotland
LEGITIMATE OCCUPATION         Physician
HEIGHT                        5 feet 9 inches
COMPLEXION                    Medium dark.
COLOR OF HAIR                 Brown.
COLOR OF EYES                 Light gray.
SOCIAL STATE                  Widower.
HAS PARENTS                   Father.
CHILDREN                      None.
RELIGION                      None.
HABITS OF LIFE                Moderate.
MENTAL CULTURE                Good
TOBACCO                       Chew
FORMER IMPRISONMENT           . . . . .
NAME AND ADDRESS OF NEAREST RELATION Wm. Cream, Father,
                                     Quebec, Canada.
```

GENERAL REMARKS: Peculiarity of build and feature, Stout solid build, full face and forehead -- Hair quite thin on top and fore part of head -- Irish descent --complexion slightly florid -- Heavy massive jaws and chin -- Size of Boot worn, g. Weight 182 Scars and deformities -- Deep scar on left side of abdomen --says caused by surgical operation.

FROM "The Times", November 12th, 1888.

## THE WHITECHAPEL MURDER

'Great excitement was caused shortly before 10 o'clock last night by the arrest of a man with a blackened face who publicly proclaimed himself to be "Jack the Ripper." This was at the corner of Wentworth-street, Commercial-street, near the scene of the latest crime. Two young men, one a discharged soldier, immediately seized him, and the great crowd, which always on a Sunday night parades this neighbourhood, raised a cry of "Lynch him". Sticks were raised, the man was furiously attacked, and but for the timely arrival of the police he would have been seriously injured. The police took him to Leman-street station, when the prisoner proved to be a very remarkable person. He refused to give any name, but asserted that he was a doctor at St. George's Hospital. He is about 35 years of age, 5 ft. 7 in. in height, of dark complexion, with dark moustache, and was wearing spectacles. He wore no waistcoat, but had an ordinary jersey vest beneath his coat. In his pocket he had a double peaked light check cap, and at the time of his arrest was bareheaded® It took four constables and four other persons to take him to the station and protect him from the infuriated crowd. He is detained in custody, and it seems that the police attach importance to the arrest, as his appearance answers to the police description of the man who is wanted'

*As a result of my various activities, the Big Boss, Sir Charles Warren, was finally hurled from his pinnacle. Newsboys crying the event roused me from a deep torpor, brought on by those persistent headaches which were my constant affliction -- and had fallen into the desperate habit of treating with ever increasing doses of drugs and stimulants.*

*During those months leading up to November 1888, until the elimination of Mary Jane Kelly and her line, I had diligently pursued God's purpose with determination and the clinical detachment of a surgeon, Not so at Miller's Court. I could afterwards only ascribe the involuntary lack of control I had exhibited there to some sort of temporary aberration brought on by the overwhelming pressures of the task I had set myself.*

*I wonder now whether it was selfless dedication that even then prevented me from renouncing the noble cause to which I was sworn -- or had I reached that undefined borderline somewhere between reality and an illusory belief that I alone could continue to beat the odds? Was I indeed a holy crusader, or merely the victim of a delusion? Anderesmann, expert on the subject of unsound minds, and in whom I have confided all, maintains that I must have suffered some sort of brainstorm, and indeed has based his petition to Queen Victoria on that opinion. However I am dubious as to whether such a plea will succeed, since Waters has already tried and failed to win a reprieve on the grounds of insanity. The truth of the matter is, of course, that when unintoxicated I am sane as the next man, ("How sane is the next man?", counters. Anderesmann). My downfall is undoubtedly due to that one great weakness which preys upon even the stoutest of us --I refer to extreme over indulgence in the pleasurable things of life, such as, in my case women, drugs and drink. When heavily under the influence of all or either one, I was often, I admit, hardly accountable for my actions.*

*Conscious after the Miller's Court affair that any further manifestation of Jack the Ripper might prove more than ever inimical to my welfare -- the police, with or without their much vaunted bloodhounds, must soon be at my heels -- I began to contemplate making myself scarce for quite a while. I was in any case due to show up in North America round 1891 when my official release from gaol was to be announced; so that would be the obvious destination -- New York first, perhaps, where I might hide out, disguised and under yet another pseudonym until I could figure a way to get Stott, and then publicly re-emerge in Canada as Thomas Cream. There would doubtless be plenty of whores around New York deserving of my attention, I reasoned, plus a ready market for the select stock of pickled preserves laid up by me in recent months with a view to disposal at a modest profit. I had however little hope of being able to continue in that line of trade once my present supply was exhausted, for it was now abundantly clear that were I to remain free to pursue the cause, a new and safer method of extermination than that of surgical dissection had to be devised, one which would clearly require the use of rather more subtle and less overtly dangerous means.*

*My decision to leave London was greatly precipitated by a regrettable escapade, some three days after the Kelly incident, culminating in near disaster. Heady with triumph over that pompous ass Warren's dishonourable downfall, I was foolish enough to go out on the town to celebrate. The result within several hours was to render me sufficiently inebriated as again to become a total stranger to caution. Blissfully lighthearted, I became mischievous as a schoolboy on Hallowe'en; and proceeded to have fun by streaking my features with coal dust in an attempt to scare even more silly than they already were the uneasy citizens of Whitechapel. Sunday was now the only lively night of the week in the East End. Servants flocked exuberantly from garrets to enjoy a few hour's leave, thinking themselves -- like the sluts exchanging curses with police on their respective beats -- to be safe in a crowd. Squawling dogs, cats and equally mangy children scavenged the gutter for scraps, church army bands competed loudly and untunefully with organ grinders and their chattering monkeys, the hullabaloo being intensified by strident cries of sea food and hot pie vendors -- in short a typical cross-section of London's shabby, sinful and yet utterly fascinating east end.*

*Such was my lack of judgment and restraint when drunk that I found myself proclaiming loudly under a gas lamp that I was Jack the Ripper! To my momentary amusement several female passers-by, noting my sinisterly blackened face, set up the most frightful din, one fat old bitch in a checked cap and apron, puffing a clay pipe, dealing me a hard box on the ears from which I reeled. Had I not been so drunk I should have pushed her ugly face in. Soon I was surrounded by a veritable lynch mob of local toughs, and would have probably been done to death in an instant if a policeman had not come upon the scene and arrested me forthwith. Marched at a brisk pace once more to Leman Street police-*

*station on that chill November night and shocked to lucidity by the confounded scare, I put up a tremendous show of professional arrogance. Confronted fortunately by a different desk sergeant (though no less gullible) than the one who had previously questioned me as Thomas Foram, I brazened out the situation, adopting the immensely superior tone of an educated man and declaring myself to be a respectable doctor at St. George's Hospital out on a mercy call to an elderly patient in Whitechapel. I claimed that without realizing I had besmirched my face in the course of stoking a fire to aid the poor sufferer, thus inadvertently casting suspicion upon myself. Loftily I declined to supply a name on the grounds that I was a physician and a gentleman and that they had therefore no business to demand it. The desk sergeant and the policeman who had arrested me, somewhat impressed by my manner and speech, practically touched their forelocks with respect as they humbly apologised for any inconvenience or embarrassment caused to me as a result of my false arrest. Again I left Leman Street a free, and, I should add, considerably more sober man in every respect, at least for that night!*

*The end of November saw me back in the United States. Lying low for some weeks in Brooklyn, I eventually managed to set up practise there under another alias. As a result of the frightful dangers to which I had, in the course of performing my duties in London, become exposed, together with the physical damage I had unfortunately sustained as a result of drug dependence and too great a partiality for alcohol, I was for a time quite unable to employ that cool head and steady hand of which I had been proud, and which had carried me thus far successfully through my campaign. Though on arrival in America once more on the verge of a breakdown both physically and mentally, the thought of renouncing my holy vow -- namely to rid the world of as many whores as was in my power to annihilate -- never for a moment entered my mind. It was a question of regenerating all my strength and resources for the mounting of a fresh campaign -- this time meting out punishment in not quite so messy and inconvenient a manner. If I could hit on a better way of operating, I realized there would be for me the added advantage of further confusing, (on both sides of the Atlantic), the goddamned police -- whom I believed to be incapable of figuring that a guy might change his methods deliberately to fool them. After a great deal of deliberation I eventually managed to come up with an ideal option, one calculated to involve me no personal danger since my presence would not actually be required at the kill. As a physician I had it all along in my power to ensure that death should not, as in the past, be mercifully swift. Such detailed knowledge of their suffering as I now contemplated inflicting upon the loathsome cunts should provide an even more just and agonizing punishment--slower, sweeter and more pleasurable even to contemplate than a swift slash across the throat. Thus should I, God's servant, now smite the unrighteous -- no longer with the sword, but softly, more insidiously, with a piercing dose of strychnine.*

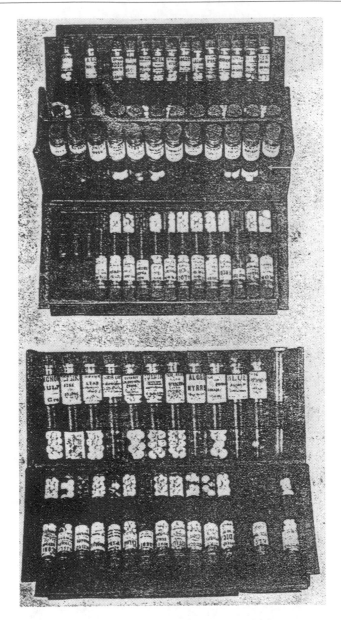

**Cream's "Sample" Case of Medicines.**

A.-Top view; the two sides fold up on the central double row of bottles. The empty bottle indicated by the arrow contained the strychnine pills mentioned at the trial.

B.-Side view.

*Eight little whores, with no hope of heaven,*
*Gladstone may save one, then there's be seven.*
*Seven little whores begging for a shilling,*
*One stays in Henage Court, then there's a killing.*
*Six little whores glad to be alive,*
*One sidles up to Jack, then there are five.*
*Four and whore rhyme aright,*
*So do three and me,*
*I'll set the* town *alight*
*Ere there are two.*
*Two little whores, shivering with fright,*
*Seek a cosy doorway in the middle of the night.*
*Jack's knife flashes, then there's but one,*
*And the last one's the ripest for Jack's idea of fun.*

# BOOK II - THE LAMBETH POISONER

## PART 1

### THE LONDON POISONINGS

### "POLICE CHRONICLE AND GUARDIAN,
### June 11th, 1892.

The Daily Chronicle's understands that the London police have obtained very remarkable evidence in reference to the poisoning of the two girls in Stanford Street. This evidence has just been put before the legal authorities at the Treasury and no doubt more will in due course be heard of it. To begin with, it is declared that the police have traced the letter found in the room where the girls were poisoned. It is added that no anxiety exists as to the difficulty of arresting the supposed murderer, and that in all likelihood the Stamford Street case will be found to be one of a series of similar crimes. Indeed, it is not beyond the bounds of possibility that the Stanford Street case may indirectly be the means of throwing light on the terrible Jack the Ripper murders.

Inside the condemned cell at Newgate Cream was hard at work ignoring even the presence of a gnome-like individual, who sat in a corner sketching him from all angles, and occasionally displaying courage way beyond the call of duty by darting forward, armed only with a pair of calipers, to check whatever were visible of Cream's personal statistics. These measurements he managed to obtain with an astonishing degree of accuracy, since Cream was so intend on sorting out papers that he was hardly aware of such proceedings. The famous waxworks exhibition at Madame Tussauds had honoured him with the offer of two hundred pounds for a suit of clothes and a prominent position in their Chamber of Horrors. It had amused him at the time to accept the offer, and he agreed to supply Tussaud's most gifted modeller with the opportunity to recapture in wax those infamous features -- on condition that the cash, which might usefully contribute to his welfare, at least for the time being, was paid over immediately.

● 113 ●

Not that he was entirely resigned, as the dreaded November 15th loomed inexorably near, to being, as he saw it, judicially murdered. If anything, he had come more to share Anderesmann's sublime belief that the Queen might at the last see her way to granting a stay of execution; certainly he and Anderesmann were of one mind as to the Prosecution having been able to offer precious little hard evidence against him. As for the so called incriminating fact, that he, by his own admission, had possessed pre-knowledge of, to quote but one instance, Donworth's murder by strychnine poisoning -- Cream himself had provided an ingenious answer for the Defence, which was not of course given proper consideration -- namely that as a medical man, he was able form a correct diagnosis from details of her death circulated by those in attendance at the time. All of this, he presumed, had been relayed accurately by Anderesmann to Palace sources, though still without any positive reaction. Yet Cream hung tenaciously to the notion that if anyone could contrive such a miracle it must be Anderesmann; and should he succeed, why Cream looked forward immensely to confounding Tussaud's every effort to regain their investment.

If, on the other hand, all attempts on the part of Anderesmann failed, at least Cream's full and frank confession; that testimonial of his outstanding service to mankind, would shortly ensure his immortality. He had, in effect, completed the composition, except for placing in chronological order and editing, diaries previously written in 1891, commencing with his return to London that year and detailing the Lambeth poisonings. It was ironically only on account of these crimes, committed four years after the Ripper had disappeared forever from the London scene, that he had been condemned. There was but one small comfort to be derived from the dreaded possibility that he might after all be hanged. His posthumous confessions, made public, would empower him even from beyond the grave to discredit the Bosses. The last laugh would be on them when word was out the Ripper had been topped after all -- but only by mistake! Pity he would not under those circumstances be able to share the joke, ha,ha! His bitter rasping laugh resounded throughout the condemned quarters, disconcerting the already hardened pair of attendants and prompting even the hitherto intrepid wax modeller to leave.

Cream finished dealing with the Ripper work and then turned his attention to the material which had arrived earlier in the day. Noting irritably that the yellow japanned box containing the Lambeth diaries had al-ready been broken into and inspected by the prison authorities -- certain of his personal effects having been removed as a precaution, such as the horsehoe pin -- his right of privacy had nevertheless been respected with regard to the sealed documents. Unlike notes of the Ripper murders which he had also made as far back as 1888, but decided to destroy just before his arrest -- only to reconstruct them in fuller detail at the behest of Kennedy Jones -- Cream had risked preserving the Lambeth diaries for the sake of posterity. The box had been wrapped in newspapers and buried at his re-quest in an obscure corner of Laura Sabbatini's garden at Berkhamstead --Cream at that stage confidently expecting to be found not guilty at his trial. After his release he planned to draw up a new Will, to remain sealed during his lifetime, indicating the whereabouts of this material. His expectations of freedom being now thoroughly dashed, he had sent a request to Laura for access to the diaries -- anticipating at this juncture that she would take the opportunity of bringing them to the prison in person. However, to his extreme displeasure the japanned box was duly returned by messenger, and without as much as a kindly note. He could have choked to death there and then simply from aggravation, forgoing Billington's assistance next Tuesday, but that the completion of his work was at hand. It was only in the afternoon that he had managed to gain control of his anger, and was able to concentrate in sorting through the rest of the material for collection by Kennedy Jones.

*Aboard the S.S. "Teutonic", Fall, 1891.*

*I had at various periods in my life been accustomed to keeping journals, some of which, however, from necessity, were either destroyed or hidden from-prying eyes. I begin this particular account at the commencement of my third voyage to England. **They shall no more offer their sacrifices unto devils, after whom they have gone a whoring** the Good Book tells us. And **There is no peace, saith the Lord, unto the wicked.** Jack the Ripper may have vanished forever but I, Doctor Thomas Neill*

*Cream am steaming towards London with every intention of resuming the one man crusade I had taken on two years ago, and valiantly continued to pursue in Brooklyn New York. There, after the last Ripper job, I had been hiding out from '88 until last July, when, as previously planned, the date of my (or in actual fact, Cousin Neill Elder's) official release from Joliet Penitentiary was announced. To tie in with this event it became imperative for me to show up again, first in Chicago and then Quebec. The trip to Canada was consequently engineered for the purpose of visiting some of my beloved friends and relatives -- with the sole intention of conveying the regrettably false impression that I had only recently been freed.*

*My visit to Chicago was for an entirely different purpose. I made it my business to meet up with Cousin Neill Elder, (alias 4374, Cream), shortly after the gates of Joliet Pen had cranked open to release him, last summer. As soon as we had celebrated our joint liberation over a magnum of champagne, I despatched him post haste to Murray, the Superintendent of Pinkerton's Chicago branch, whom previously, on my instructions, Cousin Neill had sent for in prison. Fortunately I had never personally encountered Murray, though he may have seen portraits published at the time of my trial. Whether or not this was so, Cousin Neill apparently experienced no difficulty in passing himself off as myself; indeed Murray was easily prevailed upon, as I had hoped, to put out an extensive search for Julia Stott -- the she-devil who had so treacherously played me double -- on the pretext that she might be persuaded to assist in obtaining a pardon for the unjustly convicted Doctor Cream. There was consequently no reason to suppose that Cousin Neill would not now be able successfully to repeat his impersonation, experienced as he had become in the role during the ensuing four years, and sporting our pronounced family resemblance. Here was my chance to collect such information as Murray had come by as to where she might be found, and, at long last, take revenge upon the slut! I could barely contain my impatience until Neill returned from Murray's office; but when at last he did show up, it was with exasperating tidings. Murray it seemed had turned out to be some lousy detective, who was not only fooled for a second time by Cousin Neill's simulation, but had, to my utter dismay, failed dismally to locate Stott.*

*Fleeing from the British police to Brooklyn, New York (on hindsight, with undue haste, judging from their continued bungling of the investigation over the past two years), a period of nervous exhaustion set in. Yet under the ministrations of a dumb but, it must be said, mighty loving relative, MaryAldous, who, I agreeably discovered was willing to die or lie for me, (in more ways than one!) I gradually regained my strength. To aid this effort at rehabilitation I had strictly, though with utmost difficulty, striven to deny myself the use of alchohol or drugs, except of course for medicinal use. In this new crisis of frustration I returned to my old, and as I now have good cause to appreciate, utterly disastrous ways. I was denied all prospect of bringing that wicked hussy to justice and thereby inflicting upon her the most agonizing death I could devise; and came again, from pent-up animosity, to a point of collapse. On reaching Canada, doubtless as a result of my nervous condition, brother Dan's wife, Jessie, objected to entertaining me as a guest in their house. Her ungraciousness embarrassed Dan and the rest of the family to such an extent that, no doubt considering me of unsound mind as a result of my prison experiences, they offered collectively to finance a restorative sea-voyage. This in itself had a cheering effect, for though I had now gained possession of a further legacy left to me by dear Papa, I had little objection to my devoted family electing to foot the bill for a trip I already anticipated taking; and two days out at sea, am reaping the benefit of their generosity in terms of immense relief at putting an ever increasing distance between myself and the good folk at home -- this reprieve corresponding with a distinct improvement in my mental outlook. Just as well I am normally of extremely robust constitution, with a capacity for speedy recuperation, for with God's work once more at hand, it is imperative that on our landing in Liverpool, scheduled for October 1st, I have all my wits about me. Vital as it is that I continue to perform my appointed task effectively, I pray that the Good Lord will grant me not only physical but also spiritual strength -- so that I may find it within myself to overcome the single, but perhaps fatal flaw in my character -- not, I hasten to add, that of excessive indulgence in women, which, as I have often reminded Anderesmann, is a man's God-given right, and damned good luck to a fellow, by Jove, if he can stand the pace -- but the aforementioned insatiable appetite for drink and drugs. Try as I will to conquer this one weakness for any length of time, my efforts are inevitably doomed to failure, as a result of which I sink deeper into addiction and perform acts that if were I sober would more than likely never enter my head. Lacking in these circumstances any sense of judgment, I pray that I may not eventually place my very life in jeopardy.*

**Thou shalt be filled with drunkenness and sorrow, with the cup of astonishment and desolation... for I have spoken saith the Lord God.**

Reviewing the foregoing had revived in Cream fond recollections of those two years spent in Brooklyn, after his getaway from London, a city which had become strictly out of bounds, at least until such time as the hue and cry over Jack the Ripper had subsided. Once in America, and making a serious effort to control his predilection for chemical and alcoholic stimulants, Cream had, on sober assessment of the peril in which he had recently placed himself, not for the first time become unnerved. Whether he actually was what used to be termed morally insane, Cream possessed a strong sense of justice, but only when applicable to others. As one ordained by divine decree to execute prostitutes, it would in his opinion have been a gross injustice were he condemned to hang for his pains. The very prospect of such a frightful miscarriage, whenever he was clear-headed enough to consider it, put him into a lather of anxiety. It was at this time that he reverted to a former method of operating, one which had proved effective enough in the past, and with the considerable advantage, as opposed to ripping, of ensuring he would not be found *in flagrante delicto"*. Strychnine, of which poison there was already some in his possession, might be relied upon once again to provide his victims with the most agonizing death possible -- and Cream intense satisfaction in the detailed knowledge of what appalling suffering he had so righteously inflicted.

He had chosen New York as an ideal place to recuperate, owing to the presence there of Cousin Mary Aldous, long one of his ardent admirers. Her father had founded a grocery store in Brooklyn, and on the death of both parents in a street accident Mary had inherited premises above the shop and a small income. Since the orphan was as yet only sixteen, a maiden aunt took over her supervision, exerting such unaccustomed disclipline as to induce Mary to contact her Uncle William in Quebec, cadging an invitation for the summer; and a long hot summer it proved to be. Deeply impressed with dashing Cousin Tom, on leave from McGill Medical, and aching to be relieved of her virginity, she became hopelessly infatuated with her obliging kinsman; and was returned at vacation's end to her aunt bearing a small keepsake of the visit. After the aunt's shocked departure and throughout Mary's strategic marriage to old Aldous the dairyman -- followed remarkably soon by a stillborn birth -- she sustained her romantic image of Cream. Even on reading of his arrest and imprisonment for the murder of Daniel Stott some years later, she had refused to believe his guilt, writing regularly and sympathetically to him at Joliet. Meanwhile just before Cream's appearance the obliged and obliging Aldous, having successfully enlarged his business with the aid of Mary's income, had died, leaving her adequate funds to maintain not only the matrimonial apartment in Brooklyn, but a flourishing dairy farm in New Jersey. Cream found her to be fortunately no less impressionable in her early thirties than at sweet sixteen, though, to his approval, considerably more accomplished than she had been. In the prime of womanhood, an excellent cook and housekeeper, and owning, to boot, out-of-town premises which might if necessary provide a safe haven (should Brooklyn become as dangerous to himself as to others), Mary would make an ideal landlady. She readily accepted the story that he had escaped from prison in order to prove his innocence of the Stott crime, and that in shielding him, her girlhood aspiration of marrying a real live doctor might just be fulfilled --when in 1891 he should be officially free to take up his own name and collect his rightful inheritance. She was, if questioned later, to deny emphatically ever having set eyes on him in Brooklyn prior to that time.

In the city or out on the farm with only the cows and Mary for company, and enjoying a steady diet of home comforts, Cream quickly recovered his nerve, if not his patience. He began shortly to make restless trips alone to Brooklyn leaving Mary contentedly occupied baking his favourite pies, mending his socks and generally indulging in an abandonment of domestic delight. Meanwhile, alone in Brooklyn Cream began to practise a little medicine.

## CONTAINED IN AN INVESTIGATIVE REPORT ON CREAM BY INSPECTOR FREDERICK JARVIS, FROM AMERICA.

### *New York City. 29th July 1892.*

*I beg further to report that since my arrival here I have made enquiries as to the Cousin who corresponded with Cream while in the Prison at Joliet and whom he is said to have visited after his liberation. The person in question I found to be Mrs. Mary Aldous, formerly Mary Cream, now residing at 1509 Atlantic Ave. Brooklyn. She states that Cream called upon her one afternoon in the middle of August last and stayed only about an hour, he said he was going to England and would probably make his home there, if he could get a satisfactory settlement of his deceased father's estate, as in consequence of his imprisonment he did not suppose he could do any good for himself in America or Canada...*

```
POLICE  CHRONICLE  AND  GUARDIAN
          June 8th, 1892.
```

The only fresh item worthy of record today is, says 'The Morning Leader', the fact that the officials of the Criminal Investigation Department have received a communication from the police authorities of New York, with reference to the individual who is believed to be the poisoner of the Stamford Street girls and many others. The communication is understood to be to the effect that a person answering the description of the supposed poisoner resided for some time, about two years ago, in Brooklyn, New

York, and that while he was there several girls of loose character were mysteriously poisoned. The American cases are said to bear a striking resemblance to those which have occurred in South London during the last twelve months... When, however, the mysterious poisonings in Stamford Street attracted the attention of the London police, and the details of the case were fully reported in the newspapers, the American authorities placed themselves in communication with the London police, with the result that there arrived in London the other day a long statement as to the poisoning cases which took place in and about New York over two years ago. Such importance is attached by the Scotland Yard officials to this statement that an officer acquainted with the whole of the details of the South London cases will be despatched almost immediately to New York, carrying with him several of the letters writ-ten by "Fred" to the Stamford Street girls, as well as a portrait of the suspected prisoner.

# PART 2

*Anderton's Hotel, Fleet Street, London. October 6th, 1891.*

*Ashore in Liverpool I spent a while there gratifying my re-pressed desire for physical relief, and thence to London and the commencement of more serious affairs. This city, despite the fog, is still the greatest, and right here on Fleet Street the perfect location for a man who enjoys night life. It is only a short jog either on foot or by cab down to Gatti's Royal Adelaide on Villiers Street, an old time favourite, or past the plush Cafe de Paris in the Strand to even more opulent palaces over on the west side. As a matter of fact, though, I should have found almost any place a welcome change from the stifling confines of "The Teutonic". I had remained for most of the voyage drinking unsociably in my cabin, the choice of companionship on board being limited to a party of male college students on an educational tour of Europe and a group of monks, bound it seemed, by a vow of silence. The only female, a surly old maid, spent most of the voyage closeted in the cabin next to mine, rapping ungratefully on the wall when I attempted on rare occasions to lighten the atmosphere with, I suppose, a slightly tipsy serenade on the autoharp. Regardless of her obvious lack of musical appreciation, I, ever the gentleman, despatched the steward with a peace offering. Alas, it was later reported to me that, having been sufficiently mollified to sample my glass of wine, her ill humor was later compounded by what appeared to be a particularly unpleasant bout of mal de mer ...*

*This bit of fun served, though, but temporarily to soothe my savage heart; I was for most of the voyage between deep depression and hot anger over my inexplicable failure, yet once again, to bring down heaven's wrath upon the Jezabel, Stott. Not until the very day we reached Liverpool did the truth occur -- that all along it was actually the Will of the Almighty which had **prevented me** from fulfilling what I had taken to be His purpose; but if I was not to kill Stott, then what indeed was that purpose? On this point I was sorely troubled and perplexed, until, as the ship came into harbour, the answer was sent to me, flooding my whole being with spiritual illumination. The Good Lord's purpose was simply to ensure that I should never waver in the carrying out of His* *holy work. That Stott had gone unpunished was now revealed to be of no account at all. Perceiving in each prostitute I destroyed only that whore of whores, and being denied the exacting of vengeance upon Stott herself, there had been created in me an unceasing urge to pursue to the last my policy of death to harlots. In continuing this campaign I should of course have the symbolic -- but no less profound -- satisfaction not only of performing my religious duty but of of having the opportunity in so doing to express, not once but repeatedly, that implacable hatred I bore for Stott. God surely does move in mysterious ways his wonders to perform.*

*Met a rather surly but beddable bitch called Eliza Masters this afternoon, and accompanying her across the river to Orient Buildings, Hercules Road in the Borough of Lambeth, where, in the course of exercising my still not inconsiderable charm &c for an hour or so, I learned that she had many acquaintances in the same line of business, many of whom lived in that area. Fleet Street having alas grown too expensive for my pocket, and Whitechapel too risky for my health, Lambeth would seem the ideal area to arrange lodgings, which I propose to do first thing tomorrow. Later repaired to Gatti's and met Eliza's room-mate, a fellow slut called Lizzie May. I am of a mind to turn this situation into another double event, and have informed the girls that I intend to contact them by mail, subject to finding suitable accommodation in the next few days. Meanwhile there exists an even more pressing demand on my energies, but one which l confidently expect to dispose of within the week.*

Tuesday night, the 13th October 1891 may have been lucky for some, but certainly not for nineteen year old Ellen Donworth, a.k.a Nellie Linnell, who collapsed on Waterloo Road, South Lambeth, and later died in the most painful and distressing circumstances, If Jim Styles, taking a breather between pints outside the Wellington public house across from the station had not been one of London's elite, a warm-hearted Cockney costermonger, he would have left the girl sprawled flat on her face. For a woman to pass out in that area abounding with seedy bars, and close to the notorious Morpeth Place where prostitutes were practically two a penny, was even before eight p.m. far from an uncommon occurrence, and one which generally evoked little sympathy. Styles was however charitable enough to offer his assistance. Dodging across the road between clattering cabs and horse-drawn omnibuses he assisted the girl to her feet with some difficulty. The stricken creature gasped: "Eight Duke Street, by Westminster Bridge Road.

For Gawd's sake get me 'ome there's a good chap before I croak. A tall gentleman it was, with cross eyes, a silk hat, and bushy whiskers gave me a drink twice out of a bottle with white stuff in it."

Styles became alarmed, for what was visible of the girl's face, contused and bloody from the fall, had taken on so ghastly a pallor as to convince him that if she had not actually reached death's door, her arrival there was imminent. She now commenced a violent fit of twitching and trembling, which amazingly enough hardly affected her command of speech, for she continued to proclaim loudly and insistently that she had been poisoned by some weird character in the street, On the strength of this Styles eventually managed to persuade a reluctant friend en route to the Lord Hill, by name of Adams, to assist him in half dragging, half carrying the screaming young woman to her lodgings. Together they propped her unsteadily against the lintel, down which she began to slide slowly toward the steps. Adams, al-ready regretting his involvement, hastily made himself scarce, leaving Styles to rap urgently at the door. It was opened by a blowsy charwoman, who, noting Donworth's condition, attempted at once to close it. Styles inserted a foot in the aperture, and then a burly right shoulder, over which he had slung Donworth's temporarily inanimate form. A slatternly female in a dirty cap and apron retreated before him into the dilapidated passage.

"Soddin' pissed again is she, that Nellie Linnell, or Donworth, or whatever she likes to call 'erself? A proper disgrace and 'er not twenty years of age. The two of yer had better be orf before the madam ear's of it. Raise the roof, she would, and stout enough to do it, the fat sow, if that Nell was to be brought indoors such a state.

"Steady on, old lady. This girl ain't drunk, you know. She's as sick as a bleedin' parrot."

"'Ere, not so much of the old, if you please. Missus Clements to you, Missus Annie Clements, that is."

Donworth rousing from her torpor began to retch, impelling Styles, if only for the sake of his Sunday best, to eschew further formality. Pushing Annie aside, he marched his burden hastily down the hallway in search of facilities. Annie, who in actual fact (when she could get away with it) disregarded her employer's instructions as a matter of general principal, decided now that she might as well be co-operative, "Get 'er upstairs smartish, then, me lad, before the madam finds out" The girl having managed somehow to contain her vomit until she been deposited on the bed and provided with a chamber pot, now lay back in exhaustion. Annie had the opportunity of observing her facial injuries more closely and said, not without admiration: "Sorted 'er out proper, didn't yer, me lad -- smack across the nose and a pair o' prime shiners -- no more than she deserves, though, the little trollop."

"Now see 'ere, I never done that girl no 'arm, so don't you go saying I 'ave", protested Styles, having not the least intention of being blamed for Donworth's condition, which at present seemed, at least to him if not Annie, so desperate as hardly to inspire hope for the girl's survival. "Better send for the doctor and fast if you know what's good for you, for she says as some rum cove gorn and poisoned 'en Now I'm orff, then, but just you remember in case she goes and dies, Missus Annie Clements, I've got a clear conscience I 'ave. The name's Jim Styles, and I'll not be afraid to answer to it if there's to be an inquiry."

No sooner had Styles left than the girl emitted a fearful cry, which brought 'the madam' waddling in from the next room as fast as her eighteen stone would permit. Donlan's back had contorted into a high arc, and she could neither be straightened nor held down by the combined, and not inconsiderable efforts of both women. Failing to ease the agony of her convulsions by application of a mustard poultice, and finding themselves unable during merciful intermissions to convince the terrified girl she was not dying, there was no alternative but to send for the doctor's assistant, Mr. Johnstone. He on hearing the patient's repeated assertions that she had been poisoned, pronounced her, with praiseworthy accuracy, to be undergoing fatal tetanic convulsions, such as would be caused by an over-dose of strychnine. Here, then, was a very grave matter indeed -- a matter, most like, of murder, he informed 'the madam'.

"Murder? Stuff and nonsense!" she gasped, her several chins quivering with indignation (or was it consternation?) at the unwelcome prospect of being drawn into a police investigation. "I shall obtain a second opinion from a *proper* doctor."

"There'll be no time for that, ma'am," said Johnstone with icy dignity. "This woman must be got to the hospital right away."

"Hospital? Poison? You must be mad as the girl, with her feverish ravings. It's plain to tell she has only a queasy stomach and shall be well enough by and by. Take it from me, Johnstone, Nell Donworth is a sensible clean-living young woman, and not at all the sort to go taking poison, or anything else for the matter of that, from a strange man in Waterloo Road. Indeed, I should be quite surprised if one so young and pure had the acquaintance of any gentlemen at all."

"Oh, but madam," put in Annie slyly, "surely you ain't forgot our Nell's admirer -- a proper nob too, sez she. Wrote 'er two letters, 'e did, one come this very day, which she read out to the lot of us, sayin' she wuz to meet 'im tonight at the York, and be sure to bring the letters wiv' 'er, And that's where she upped and gorn, as well you know, just after six,"

Annie received a baleful scowl from 'the madam' together with a few sharp words to the effect that she might hold her tongue or prepare to suffer the consequences -- these being drowned by the girl's deafening screams as she was assailed by an even more excruciating convulsion. Johnstone at this point swept aside all protestations and dispatched Annie at once for a policeman. Ellen Donworth, still suffering appalling agony, though sufficiently coherent at intervals to furnish the law with a further bizarre description of her poisoner, was conveyed in a cab to St. Thomas's Hospital. Sadly she did not survive the journey.

Today, in London, across from the Wellington public house in Water-loo Road, there happens to stand, at the very spot where, all those years ago, hapless Ellen Donworth leaned dying against the station wall, a small flower stall. It's fresh and vivid blooms, during their brief span, lend brilliance and vitality to the otherwise dismal thoroughfare; and may perhaps serve as a touching memorial to that pitiful young girl, whose own life was so ruthlessly cut short by one who, at her inquest on October 22nd 1891 could only be identified, like Jack the Ripper himself, as 'a person (or per-sons) unknown.'

*London, 5th November, 1891.*

*Mr. F. W. D. Smith,*
*c/o William H. Smith & Son, 186 Strand.*

*Sir,*

*On Tuesday night, 13th October (last month), a girl named Ellen Donworth, but sometimes calling herself Ellen Linnell, who lived at 8 Duke Street, Westminster Bridge Road, was poisoned with strychnine. After her death, among her effects were found two letters incriminating you, which, if they ever become public property, will surely convict you of the crime. I enclose you a copy of one of the letters which the girl received on the morning of 13th November (the day on which she died). Just read it, and then judge for yourself what hope you have of escape if the law officers ever get hold of these letters. Think of the shame and disgrace it will bring on your family if you are arrested and put in prison for this crime. My object in writing you is to ask if you will retain me at once as your counsellor and legal adviser. If you employ me at once to act for you in this matter, I will save you from all exposure and shame in the matter; but if you wait till arrested before retaining me, then I cannot act for you, as no lawyer can save you after the authorities get hold of these two letters. If you wish to retain me, just write a few lines on paper, saying, "Mr. Fred Smith wishes to see Mr. Bayne, the barrister, at once. "Paste this on one of your shop windows at 186 Strand next Tuesday morning, and when I see it I will drop in and have a private interview with you. I can save you if you retain me in time, but not otherwise.*

*Yours truly,*

*H. BAYNE.*

ENCLOSURE TO THE ABOVE LETTER:

*MISS ELLEN LINNELL,*

*I wrote and warned you once before that Frederick Smith, of W. H. Smith & Son, was going to poison you, and I am writing now to say that if you take any of the medicine he gave you for the purpose of bringing on your courses you will die. I saw Frederick Smith prepare that medicine he gave you, and I saw him put enough strychnine in the medicine he gave you to kill a horse. If you take any of it you will die.*

*(Signed) H.M.B.*

Orient Buildings fronting a mundane Lambeth thoroughfare known as Hercules Road, was hardly exotic as it's name implied, consisting merely of a small row of ricketty houses, occupied for the most part by those living on immoral earnings. Eliza Masters and her close friend Elizabeth May were in a state of great excitement; for Eliza had received anxiously expected word from a man she had picked up a few days earlier in Fleet Street, and who, it appeared, was one of those rich Americans with plenty of cash to indulge his preferences -- these being, so he smoothly indicated, for double assignments. Were she to produce an equally agreeable partner, both young ladies might confidently expect to receive their just reward. Eliza had sniffed unconvincingly that she had never been so insulted in all her life -- leaving the client in little doubt before he left that for the right price full co-operation might be obtained.

They had posted themselves as from the appointed hour of three onwards by the front window in eager anticipation of the man's arrival and exchanging lewd suggestions as to how he might best be entertained. Eventually down the street marched a high-blown dignitary wearing a silk top-hat, gold-rimmed spectacles and a smart cutaway jacket.

"'Ere he comes, luv. Better 'op down and let 'im in while I open the bottle of port. 'Ad to do 'im proud, didn't we then? Plain enough to see 'e's a bloke as is used to the best, my girl, and that's what e's goin' to get."

Lizzie, who had opposed Eliza's extravagance on grounds that it was the toff who should be providing the booze, now let out a snort of indignation. "Why, I do declare if that Matilda Clover as lives down the way 'ain't givin"im the eye. Buck-toothed bitch, turni$^{p}$' to grin at 'im bold as brass, she is!"

"Well, I never!", exclaimed Eliza. "The bugger can't take 'is eyes orf 'en Look, 'e's gorn and passed right by our place already,"

"And is doggin"er back 'ome, or I'm much mistook."

"Oh no you ain't", not at all", snapped Eliza. "Wot ever does the cheeky little fucker think she's up to?"

"That's just about the measure of it -- pinchin' our bloke, that's what she's about," replied Lizzie, "and neither one of us ain't standin' it. Come on Lize, let's get after 'em." The jilted pair marched furiously down towards the intersection of Lambeth Road, and would have elbowed young Miss Matilda Clover and her basket of clean washing straight into the gutter, where, so far as those two ladies were concerned, she belonged -- but for the fact that, as they came up to No. 27, Clover dodged nimbly inside the house, the gentleman close behind, and the door was slammed shut practically in Eliza's face. The two prostitutes waited in vain for them to emerge, and after a long while retired forlornly to Orient Buildings, their dreams of being set up in the style to which they were unaccustomed having been sadly shattered.

"There, now, didn't I say you was wastin' your money on a bottle of bloody port, Lize?"

"Bottle of bloody poison would 'ave been as much as 'e de-served," admitted Eliza gloomily. "But we'll do for the sod one day, so I tell yer. And as for that common Clover, she'll come to a bad end, she will, just you wait and see."

REPORT FROM INSPECTOR FREDERICK JARVIS

*Montreal*
*29th August, 1892.*

*Since my return to Montreal I have seen Miss Emily Turner...She states that she was in London from October last until January last and ... says that during November and December last she ... became acquainted with a gentleman who called himself Major Hamilton and said he was living at the Hotel Metropole, Northumberland Avenue; he took her to supper several times at Gatti's in Villiers Street, Strand and once to a Restaurant next door to Alhambra, Leicester Square, he was in the habit of sending his notes at the Aquarium (where she worked for a photographer) by Messengerboys, making appointments to meet. These notes she says she has destroyed. One evening while at supper he suggested she should live with him and that he would take some nice rooms for her in Lambeth Palace Road and allow her two pounds per week. To this she alleges she did not consent. On one occasion he remarked she had a cough, and said he would send her some-thing for it. Next day she received a parcel containing some under clothing and a box labelled "Starkie" Chemist, Quinine Pills, containing seven or eight long gelatine capsules containing a white powder. She took one of them and it made her very sick, burnt her tongue and caused a headache for days after-wards. She felt so ill that she went home to her sister's Mrs. Marshall and never went back to the Aquarium so never saw the man Hamilton again... She describes Major Hamilton as a man about 40, of medium height with a peculiarity about his eyes, he generally wore gold eyeglasses...*

# PART 3

*103, Lambeth Palace Road, London S.E.1*

*October 14th, 1891.*

*Have from last week been occupying a second floor front room under the new alias of Doctor Neill; this to guard against the British police taking an undue interest in yours truly Thomas Cream as a result of my imprisonment abroad. Passing again as Fordyce is out, since the last letter I mailed him from New York was returned unopened by a relative, together with news to the effect that the poor sod had stopped a bullet between the eyes from an enraged outback widow. As for Thomas Coram, humble clerk, he too is no more, and shall never be resurrected, the name having always born too great a similarity to my own for comfort. These and all other associations with Whitechapel are now at an end. I can never return there for obvious reasons -- not least of which is the possibility of running into that eagle-eyed swine Hutchinson, who could probably still identify me as the Ripper.*

*All in all Lambeth has turned out as good a place as any right now. The lodgings, one of the few respectable in the district, are owned by a Mrs. Sleaper, who, appropriately, passes her time either dreaming by the hearth, or in her bed, while management of the household has fallen into the charge of her daughter, Miss Emily. As a consequence of that young lady's slipshod housekeeping, the rooms are less than immaculate, and meals for the most part inedible. After breakfasting once on slightly rancid bacon, greasy fried bread and warm coffee, accompanied by a torrent of chatter from Miss Emily, I resolved in future to take only toast and milk or the occasional evening meal on the premises, and -- jokingly of course -- to prescribe Miss Sleaper a permanent cure for verbal diarrhoea if she does not keep her distance. To ensure privacy I have taken the precaution of purchasing a yellow japanned box equipped with a strong lock, in which I shall preserve these personal diaries and notes, plus a few other valuables such as my precious collection of randy photographs. The Sleapers may soon boast another medical man among their lodgers, one, Harper, who, according to Miss Emily, expects shortly to qualify from my old alma mater, St.Thomas's. Have seen him about the house and attempted to strike up a civil conversation, with little response. For a green young student, Harper, it would seem, holds far too high opinion of himself and ought perhaps to be brought down a trifle.*

*I have since arriving in London on the 5th, lost no time commencing business. Back in September 1888, I had visited the Lyceum theatre for a performance of "Doctor Jeckyll and Mr. Hyde" and thoroughly identified with the central figure (or figures) as depicted so realistically by that gifted actor Mr. Richard Mansfield. As a result of this play, the public had formed a strong association with Mr. Robert Louis Stevenson's wicked doctor and what they fancied to be the persona of the devilish Jack the Ripper -- so much so that Mansfield himself at one time came under suspicion. I, greatly impressed by his rendition and likewise possessing a marked histrionic streak, found myself imitating Mansfield's manner and gestures to the point where I stood in some danger of giving the game away. I was obviously obliged to curb this tendency at the time. Lately however I have begun to exercise my penchant for melodrama in a more practical direction. I had casually been cultivating a depraved young slut called Ellen Donworth, and arranged to meet her last night outside a public house near Water-loo Station. For the occasion I had purchased from a theatrical costumier a rather ludicrous, maybe, but nevertheless effectively concealing set of false whiskers; and in the deep dark disguise of my favourite and, some might think, most appropriate role, that of stage villain, accosted her outside a public house near Waterloo Station. To my glee the whore totally failed to recognise as myself the abundantly bearded chap who offered her a drink (though she had plainly already had at least one too many) from what looked like a harmless ginger wine bottle. Attempting to suppress my own accent, I addressed her as best I might in what was undoubtedly a far from authentic South London dialect -- the imperfections of which she however, was fortunately in no condition to detect.*

*"Looks like you've 'ad a bit too much of the booze, me old darlin'. Won't bring no joy tomorrow, only the devil of an 'eadache, and don't I know it! Now this 'ere drink is a bit of orlright, though -- takes them*

as merit's it on a regular trip to Paradise. Do yourself a good turn luv and 'ave a swig."

"Don't know as I ought take nothink from from a stranger", she replied dubiously. "Considering as I'm meeting a gentleman and must be on me best behavior."

"You won't ever be on better after a drop of this," I assured her. "It's only a spot of brandied milk with a dash of cocaine and morphine to lace it up a bit. Livens a girl up something chronic, that does -- puts 'er on top o' the world, I'd say!"

"What's in it for you, then?"

"Why, **you,** my girl, that's what's in it for me. Want a good time, I do, and can pay for one fair and square. Just you swallow this up, let on where you live, and scarper orf 'ome. I'll be round in a while, when the stuff's 'ad time to work."

"What about my gentleman, the one I was to meet at the York, then?"

"You don't want a gent, what you want is a real man, like me, darlin'. I could teach you a thing or two can't be learned from no nob." Young as she was the hardened strumpet shrieked with derisive mirth at the suggestion that there was something still left to experience of her stock in trade. I took the opportunity to pour my magical elixir into her open mouth, and while the stupid bitch now literally choked with laughter, added the empty bottle to a pile of floating debris in the gutter. Having downed the mixture not entirely of her own volition, but finding the brandied milk warming to the stomach, I was scolded with only mock severity for such "imperence". Despite my funny ways, the dirty snatch announced that being none too particular really as to which bloke received her favours, she was prepared to consider a firm offer from me on a first come first served basis. A suitable price being negotiated, she handed me a paper detailing her address and swayed tipsily off down the Waterloo Road. It was the last I saw -- but by no means the last I thought -- of her.

*In the past two years I have come to appreciate the advantages of slow execution. The never-to-be-forgotten thrill of instant blood-letting back in the Ripper days may have been a unique pleasure, but one, however, which might properly be described as short-lived; and the dissecting of corpses, to a man of my profession, hardly more stimulating than any clinical operation. The worst of it was that these operations, with only one exception, were of necessity performed right out in the open, under appallingly nerve-wracking circumstances, and so quickly as to permit those cunts a far more merciful end than they deserved. The beauty of a remotely controlled kill, apart from being considerably more safe, is that it permits me to enjoy at my leisure the company of younger and therefore more desirable whores, using them as I will, and envisioning their all too expressionless features contorting in agony at my whim. Of all poisons, it is strychnine that can be best relied upon to put these jezabels to the torture of the damned; and I need only visualize the prolonged suffering which, in the name of the Good Lord, I have and shall cause to be visited upon them, for my mind to explode in erotic images. Growing older I have come to appreciate that the imagination has far greater power to gratify a man's sexual instincts than his prick.*

The repetition of Cream's habitual and extremely unpleasant "ha-ha" had come to unnerve his keepers to such an extent that even though anticipating it, they still jumped visibly. Cream, interrupting his reading to observe the effect, neglected to explain the joke, revelling in their uneasiness. His own tension had been somewhat lessened by seeing Anderesmann earlier, who remained hopeful of a last minute reprieve. If Anderesmann's optimism was in reality unfounded, it still effectively supported Cream's attempt to convince himself that he would never hang. Not that Cream was altogether grateful for Anderesmann's revival of interest in his welfare, considering The Rabbi" merely to be sustaining that favourite 'holier than thou' role for his own self-aggrandisement.

Anderesmann had observed poignantly that the death-cell at New-gate was surely a far cry from Chalmers Sunday School in Quebec where he recalled Cream, as a promising young physician, teaching the word of God to a group of children with the intention of inspiring them to like achievements. How then had he come to this, given that in the old days Andersmann had been so sanguine of Cream's salvation; and indeed had for years made every effort to ensure his adherence to the straight and narrow? Cream turned the responsibility neatly back on Anderesmann, observing that his misfortunes were at least partially due to Anderesmann's own lack of consideration in absenting himself from Cream's life at the time he was most needed -- adding with increasing irascibility that in all conscience a fellow ought now to damn well do what he could for a friend without expecting to be canonized. As a result Andersmann, as usual taking the least line of resistance, left without a word; and Cream resolved impatiently to eliminate the fellow from his mind for the time being, on the grounds that, though a good enough sort, he was a source of constant aggravation.

*103, Lambeth Palace Road, London S.E.I.*
*October 18th, 1891.*

*One vice I cannot be accused of, particularly during this month of October, is idleness. Even before the Donworth job I had mailed the promised letter to Masters, with the usual instructions to retain it for collection until my proposed visit to Orient Buildings on the 9th; and taking the opportunity of roundly reproving the hypocritical bitch for pretending that a certain suggestion I had put forward at Gatti's with regard to herself and May had not only made her extremely cross, but, moreover, deeply shocked them both -- on the grounds, if you please, that even whores have principles! Aware as she that a show of cash would magically influence the bending of these principles, I felt sure a double event could be counted upon -- though I daresay hardly the sort Masters and May had in mind. Accordingly on the appointed day I donned a silk top-hat, well tailored black suit and a becoming new pair of gold-rimmed spectacles delivered that morning from Aitchison's and marched off to Hercules Road. Arriving there in quite a sprightly mood, I regrettably allowed myself to be diverted from the work on hand by a pretty girl with long brown hair, wearing a grey dress and strapped apron, carrying a basket of groceries. She smiled at me invitingly, revealing bright teeth, which though uneven and slightly protruding, somehow added to her undoubted allure. Though I am now past forty, my predilection for drugs and alchohol has done nothing to dull the edge of that always insatiable appetite for women -- nor, as yet, even more singularly, effected my outstanding ability to consummate it. So, as I hotly pursued temptation in the shapely form of a yet more buxom maid than either of those I had arranged to meet, the double event was perforce abandoned. Masters and May must have spotted me passing by the window of their shared lodgings, for shortly afterwards the hunter found himself hunted by a pair of furious, cursing whores who chased him in a most undignified way around the corner to Number 27, Lambeth Road. Only just in time the girl unlocked the door and stepped inside, I behind her, slamming it closed with such force as to almost knock off Master's impertinent nose. I now set about using the girl vigorously, and such was my pleasure that I decided to postpone ending it there and then. As a bee to honey I now anticipate indulging for a week or so in sucking the sweetness of Matilda Clover. Such a delightful relationship it promises to be, and cheap and the price, even if destined to be quite short lived.*

Some time during the days leading up to Tuesday October 20th 1892 Matilda Clover and her latest gentleman friend had entered Lilley's, the shoe shop in Westminster Bridge Road, resulting in a gift of some fetching high buttoned boots for the young woman. Matilda was thoroughly enjoying quite the best days of her rather uneventful life, accompanied about town by a proper gent -- one who had proved more than capable of showing a girl a good time in every possible respect. He had come across at first as a tender and considerate escort, addressing her respectfully as "Miss Clover", insisting that she visited Doctor Graham for treatment of a severe drinking problem and issuing written reproaches whenever she fell from grace; further demonstrating his caring attitude by commissioning a photograph of them both at Armsteads, each posing separately and with grave dignity for Mr. Armstead, in order to exchange fond mementos; all this thanks to good-natured Lucy Rose, her landlady's maid, who had agreed to take care of the child during Clover's frequent absences from home. As Matilda told Lucy on the night of the 20th, returning to 27, Lambeth Road rather the worse for wear after an exhaustive tour of the lowest dives in Lambeth, the bloody boots had begun to pinch, but that the gent who had paid for them insisted on her continuing to wear them, even in bed, on the grounds that he expected to receive his money's worth.

"Peculiar sort, but a great spender -- spends 'ere, there and every bloody where," she giggled, receiving a disapproving look from Lucy Rose, who, in her French maid's uniform and with a smattering of education, was employed to lend higher tone to the establishment.

"Better not let Mrs. Phillips hear you talking so coarse, Tilly," warned the maid. "She only takes on ladylike girls; for as well you know they raise the best prices."

"Wot's the use of being *like* a lady?" snorted Matilda. "It's only worthwhile *being* one, Lucy Rose. That kind marry dukes and raise higher prices than I ever could for spreading *their* legs. 'T'ain't 'really fair, is it?

"Talking of what's fair and what's not," said Lucy Rose, "I saw the man you brought in, and know that he's still upstairs. Mrs. P. don't let them stay the night, not unless they pay extra, as well you know; and it's more than my job is worth to look the other way while you go and break the rules."

"Keep yer 'air on, young Luce, I'm just orff to bring in a pint or two of Bass, then my Fred'll take 'is leave nice and polite like always. Said 'e's a proper gent, didn't I?"

"I believe you," said Lucy. "Spotted him as you brought him in, with his caped coat and high hat -- real silk and all I shouldn't wonder. Not much like Fred the coalman, as is supposed to be the nipper's dad, I'm sure."

After Clover had returned to her rooms and duly entertained the "proper gent", Lucy Rose supervised their farewells from the stairhead; and some while after her client had left, Clover prevailed once more upon her to mind the baby and went out again. The entire household had been settling for the night by the time Matilda came home -- and soon afterwards all terror broke loose at Number 27, Lambeth Road.

EXCERPT FROM REPORT ON THE DEATH OF
MATILDA CLOVER AT THE TOOTING VESTRY HALL
Wednesday 22nd JUNE 1892.

*Lucy Rose, a domestic servant, residing at 90 Merrow Street, Walworth Road, said that in September last she took a situation with Mrs. Phillips at 27 Lambeth Road. The young woman, Matilda Clover, occupied two rooms on the second floor with her little child. She used to bring men to the house. On the night before she died she remembered letting her into the house with a man. It was early in the evening. There was a lamp in the hall, but it did not show a very good light. The man was very tall and broad, and was about forty years of age. He had a very heavy moustache, but no whiskers. He was wearing a silk hat, but was not wearing glasses. He was in the house about an hour. While the man was in the house Clover went out for something, and later on he went out. The witness went to bed about ten o'clock and was wakened by hearing Clover screaming loudly as if she were in pain. She got up and called the landlady, and they went to Clover's room. Clover was lying across the foot of the bed with her head fixed between the bed and the wall. Her head was bent backward, and she was lying on her back. Clover said, "That wretch Fred has given me some pills, and they have made me ill." She also said that she was not in pain, but that she trembled so much that she was taken with convulsions. She said Fred had poisoned her. The witness lifted her up and put her on the pillows, when she said something seemed to be sticking in her throat. She vomited a great deal, and witness gave her some tea. She asked for drink several times. She told the witness that while she had gone Fred had made the pills and told her to take them before she went to bed. He gave her four pills.*

*In answer to the Coroner the witness said that the landlady knew that Clover had said she had been poisoned. Witness went on to say that during the time she was speaking to the de-ceased she did not appear to have attacks of pain, and was quite conscious. She had convulsive fits, which left her quite exhausted. She trembled all over and stretched out. While a fit was on she groaned; these occurred every two minutes, and while the attacks lasted she seemed in great agony. She said she thought she was going to die, and would like to see her baby. At that time the landlady had gone for the doctor. Clover asked that Dr. Graham should be sent for. Mrs. Phillips came back and said Dr. Graham was not in, and she went for Dr. Coppin, who came. Witness asked Mrs. Phillips if she had told the doctor about Clover having* taken pills, and she replied that Dr. Coppin had asked Clover what *pills they were. Clover told him, whereupon the doctor said that the man, meaning Fred, must either have been drunk or mad to have given them to her. Witness had never seen Dr. Coppin before. She remained with Clover from the time the doctor came until she died. That was about 9.15 a.m. In the after-noon Dr. Graham came, and Mrs. Phillips told him what had taken place. Witness told him what the deceased had said about being poisoned, and that pills had been given her. Upon hearing that he told her that he should not want her again. The deceased's box was still at Mrs. Phillips, so far as the witness knew. Witness had seen a letter addressed to Clover, which was as near as she could remember as follows: - 'Dear Miss Clover, -- Will you meet me outside the Canterbury at 7:30 tonight? Do you remember the night I bought your boots? You were too drunk to speak to me. Please bring this paper and envelope with you. – Yours, Fred.' Witness added that the deceased went out to keep the appointment, but did not take the letter with her. Witness could not find it after her death, however. Mrs. Phillips never told her not to say anything about the circumstances of the death. She had never seen any other man with the deceased; but Mrs. Phillips generally opened the door. She did not know Dr. Graham by sight. She did not know the character of the house before she went to it.*

*October 22nd, 1992.*
*103, Lambeth Palace Road, London S.E.I.*

*Having searched the newspapers in vain for news of Clover's death, curiosity has finally won over caution, and I asked vacuous Miss Emily this morning whether she would be so kind as to run over to Lambeth Road and inquire after a young lady there of my acquaintance, with a small child, whom rumour had it was poisoned. To this she agreed, and knowing her predilection for involving herself in the business of others, I looked forward to receiving titillating details of how the whore had died, and more importantly confirmation of same -- a circumstance which, however, I had little reason to doubt, since while she had gone to bring some beer, leaving me alone in her room I had taken the opportunity of pre-paring a capsule containing enough strychnine to kill a horse! On Clover's return I suggested she looked a little peaked, owing most likely to her having downed one or two beers on the way back, and ordered her to take the tonic before retiring.*

*Much as I had enjoyed my dalliance with Matilda, when she was sober enough to be of use, by last Tuesday the execution was already overdue and a further reprieve would have been a clear dereliction of duty. At the last, in accordance with my gallant custom established during the good old Ripper days -- the bestowing of a flower here, some cachous there, as an act of charity to the condemned -- I rewarded Matilda's services with pair of but-toned boots from Lilley's. Since she can now have no further use for them, I might not have been averse, having put out so much showing the whore a good time, to retrieving them in order to recoup at least some of my expenses. The fact of the matter is, though, that were I to call personally at 27 Lambeth Road upon a pretext and actually succeed in purloining the boots, there is always an outside chance that they might somehow, in the event of an inquiry, be the means of linking me with Clover -- maybe through the sales clerk at Lilley's. Deciding to content myself with whatever details Miss Emily could discover of the affair, it is with much irritation that I have just opened the door to the woman's knock, only to find that she has changed her mind about going over there. Unlikely as it is that she is smart enough to have caught on to me, I decided as a safety-measure to confuse the issue -- not too difficult in the case of that dizzy dame -- by suggesting that if there had, as I suspected, been any foul play at Lambeth Road, it was probably perpetrated by none other than the notorious Lord Russell, who is presently involved in a scandalous divorce, one which has lately occupied Miss Emily's wholehearted attention and recently been the subject of her continual gossip. So low an opinion has Miss Emily*

*formed of the gentleman in question that I am quite sure she will credit
him with any amount of wrongdoing and myself of absolutely none!*

*Though Matilda was nothing but a drunken whore, and received
precisely the punishment she deserved, I had begun to grow accustomed
to her companionship, and find myself, somewhat to my surprise,
missing it just a trifle; but having hit the bottle pretty hard all day, I wax
maudlin ... It is unwise to continue writing in such circumstances, since
when engaged in solitary drinking and craving the attention that has so
often been denied me, I am wont, as in days gone by, to compose and
despatch outrageous letters. Although signed only with a pseudonym,
my penchant for creating a sensation has of course always engendered
certain risks, and indeed once served to incriminate me. Entirely on
my guard when sober, the effect of over indulgence in alchohol, not to
speak of my latest pick-me-up, small doses of strychnine, morphine and
cocaine, are prone, I fear, to lower my awareness of danger; and yet I
grow ever more incapable of renouncing them.*

*This apart, I have always derived immense satisfaction from ruffling
the lofty complacency of those who persist in setting themselves up above
others, seizing the advantage of an over privilege existence entirely
unrelating to their own achievements. In earlier years I indulged in
the game of Blackmail more for financial gain than fun; but being
at present solvent, the situation is reversed. It is now with the sole
motive of causing such consternation as might be calculated to throw
the recipient into a permanent state of anxiety that I put forward
unfounded accusations--designed of course to divert suspicion from
myself-- as well as, just for jollies, demanding unrealistic sums of cash
which I should never be foolish enough to collect. The name of the game
has changed, I guess, to a jarring Postman's Knock.*

*London, 19th October, 1891.*

*G. P. Wyatt, Esq., Deputy Coroner, East Surrey.
I am writing to say that if you and your satellites fail to bring
the murderer of Ellen Donworth, alias Ellen Linnell, late of 8
Duke Street, Westminster Bridge Road, to justice, that I am
willing to give you such assistance as will bring the murderer*

*to justice, provided your Government is willing to pay me £300,
000 for my services. No pay if not successful.*

*A. O'BRIEN, Detective.*

*Dr. W.H. Broadbent*

*Sir,*

*Miss Clover, who, until a short time ago, lived at 27 Lambeth
Road, S.E., died at the above address on 20th October (last
month) through being poisoned with strychnine, After her
death a search of her effects was made, and evidence was
found which showed that you not only gave her the medicine
which caused her death, but that you had been hired for the
purpose of poisoning her. This evidence is in the hands of one
of our detectives, who will give the evidence either to you or to
the police authorities for the sum of £2500 two thousand five
hundred pounds sterling). You can have the evidence for £2500,
just put a personal in the Daily Chronicle, saying that you will
pay Malone £2500 for his services, and I will send a party to
settle this matter. If you do not want the evidence, of course,
it will be turned over to the police at once and published, and
your ruin will surely follow. Think well before you decide on
this matter. It is just this -- £2500 sterling on the one hand, and
ruin, shame, and disgrace on the other. Answer by personal on
the first page of the Daily Chronicle any time next week. I am
not humbugging you. I have evidence strong enough to ruin
you for ever.*

*M. MALONE[1]*

---

(1)  Extortionists Messrs. O'Brien and Malone never did come forward
to receive their due -- since they did not exist, and were only
two of the many aliases adopted by the sadistic and cunning
Doctor Thomas Neill Cream.

# PART 4

In late October 1891 Louisa Harris, more commonly known as Lou Harvey, finding no custom from one end of Piccadilly to the other on a damp and rainy night, and suffering from wet and swollen feet, plumped herself down at the bar of the Alhambra, a rather grander place than she was used to, and ordered a tot of gin. Undignified as it was for a girl to pay for her own liquor, there was always the chance, even though she was not dressed up for the occasion, of attracting one of the classy Johnnies that hung about that place, looking for a bit of rough. As she told her protector, Charles Harvey back in St. John's Wood the next afternoon:

"Before I'd as much as tossed back the mother's ruin, a cove all in black but for a nice gold watch, quality it was, set 'imself down beside me. Said 'e was a specialist in women's problems, and that 'e would see me orl right if I was to meet 'im later outside the St. James's 'All. Orff we went from St. James to a place in Berwick Street for the night, and a strange customer that one turned out to be, so I tell yer. 'Strewth, though bald as an egg on top, 'e was strong and 'airy as an ape, and, wiv'aht 'is specs, squiffeyed into the bargain. But as for looks, on a rainy night a girl can't be too partic'lar."

"No, nor on any other night, either, if she knows what's good for 'er," cautioned Harvey, puffing at a noxious stogie purchased with some of the profit and regarding Lou contemplatively. "I'll own you're not 'arf a bad looker, though, Lou, if a touch on the plump side. Wiv' a bit more paint and powder and a few flash togs, don't know as you might not do pretty well for yourself up west. Take the rich Yank last night -- fancied you quite a bit, didn't 'e?"

"No complaints, 'cept for a couple of spots on me forehead 'e didn't much like the look of. Wants to give me a bit of somethink tonight."

"Thought 'e did that last night," observed Harvey.

"Get away, Charlie! Somethink for the spots -- told you e's a doctor, didn't I?

"And I'm a bleedin' archdeacon," said Harvey. "Now don't you go takin' stuff from no stranger, Lou. "I 'eard there was a working girl poisoned to death down by the station not so long ago."

"Well, my gentleman's promised to take me to the Oxford Music 'All tonight, and there's no 'arm in that. Meeting 'im on the Embankment by Charing Cross tonight."

Since Harvey preferred his present trade to that of his former more taxing and less lucrative employment on the omnibuses, he had an invested interest in Lou's survival.

"Don't know as 'ow I won't toddle alongside then, just to see fair play."

He followed a discreet distance behind Lou as she duly kept her assignment with the the doctor, accompanied him to a public house for a glass of wine, and received the gift of a red rose. Harvey was waiting outside as the couple emerged, and shadowed them once again in the direction of the Thames Embankment. As Lou and her escort stopped under one of the infrequently spaced street lamps on the river side, Harvey, sauntering casually up and down on the opposite pavement, turned to see Lou holding out her hand to receive what were, unquestionably at so short a distance, a pair of long white capsules. There came a low and to Harvey, what with the noise of passing traffic, quite inaudible exchange of words, culminating, to his utter horror, in Lou apparently placing the capsules in her mouth. With a loud curse he attempted to charge across the road towards them but was impeded by the passing of a hansom cab which drew up in front of the street lamp, effectively blocking his view. An oncoming carriage-and-four then forced Harvey to give way or be downed by pounding hooves; so that when he could cross, the cab had pulled away, picking up speed rapidly as the driver applied his whip. The street-lamp now shone on to an empty pavement. Lou Harris, together with her medical adviser, had vanished into the murky darkness, and so far as Charles Harvey knew, might never be seen again.

*103, Lambeth Palace Road, London S.E.1.*
*23 October 1891.*

*Yet another bitch accounted for, one Lou Harris, an insignificant little whore with whom I spent the whole of one night and yet, as with most of them, should probably fail to recognise a week later. Whores may well be seen as "unfortunate" in the eyes of the world, but in my not inconsiderable experience they count them-selves as among the most fortunate of women when assessing their own charms. The overweening vanity of a slut as to her personal appearance has invariably, in my experience, far exceeded that of any respectable woman I have ever met; so much so that the whore invariably perceives in herself qualities of beauty and desirability where none exist; disregarding the fact that men are attracted to them for the sole purpose of sating their lust. Should they however be made conscious of even the smallest defect, these women will stop at nothing to conceal it. Thus it was in the case of Lou Harris, who when I had pointed out that her complexion was not quite flawless, readily ingested my cure-all remedy; of that I am certain, even though when intoxicated my memory has of late been known to play me false. If there are minor details of the Harris cull about which I am slightly hazy this morning, bar receipts confirm that the affair had all gone according to design, including my established custom, observed whenever possible, of maintaining the niceties of wining, dining and presenting the condemned with a gift of some kind, clothes, sweets, trinkets or flowers -- preferably a blood-red rose.*

*Of the actual execution I retain total recall, in that it took place on the Embankment at Charing Cross, that I told Lou Harris we should meet some time later in the evening at a music hall and that I gave her enough strychine to make sure she would provide better entertainment there than any on the bill! Adding the appropriate initials L.H. to those on the death-roll, and congratulating myself that in this month of October alone, three whores are al-ready accounted for, I feel that I am due for a long Sabbatical. Ever since I arrived back here I have, as in earlier days, performed my duties with unrelenting determination and vigour, the strain of which is once more telling upon my health. I can only handle frequent bouts of insomnia, quickened heartbeat and constant headaches by the use, or if I am to be honest with myself, abuse*

● 147 ●

*of drugs. As a physician I know that it is absolutely imperative during this self-prescribed respite to attempt once more to control these habits; most particular since further memory lapses in the future could well be inimical to my safety. With the aim of strengthening self control I plan to devote some of my well earned leisure to sorely neglected religious pursuits, and shall write to a family acquaintance, the Reverend Doctor Matthews up in Brondesbury, with a view to joining a few prayer meetings.*

*Who knows but that the Good Lord may now see f it to reward me with an honoured position in the society f or whose benefit l have fought -and shall continue to fight -- a lone crusade. When tam recovered I shall resume the practice of medicine, strive for eminence in my profession and even an element of outward respectability in my private life. Perhaps the time has come to consider taking another wife.*

In early November 1891 at the home of The Reverend Dr. Matthews in Christ Church-Road, Brondesbury, a prayer meeting was in session, attending by, among others, that devout personage, Doctor Thomas Neill of Lambeth. During the final hymn his resounding but not unmelodious baritone voice attracted the attention of all, including a petite young lady hovering against the wall at the back of the room in a rather drab brown costume relieved only by a touch of lace and pink ribbon at the wrists and throat. While Cream was still focussed on the hymn, she lifting her veil surreptitiously and cast a brief glance in his direction, impressed by what she saw. He was dressed, as usual, in the height of fashion -- dark cutaway jacket, neatly tied cravat centred by some sort of jewelled pin -- half-moon or horsehoe shaped, she thought. Although middle aged, bespectacled and almost bald, his general appearance was in keeping with the sort of man even her mother might find acceptable -- of which there had been few. Laura Sabbatini was nearing her thirtieth birthday now, and though passably pretty, the occupation of ladies' dressmaker was hardly conducive to meeting eligible suitors. Besides, as the only unmarried daughter of an elderly widow, hard of hearing and requiring extensive care, she had for years been obliged to sacrifice her own personal interests in favour of her mother. The perjorative term "spinster" had begun to hang over her like a pall, and she craved an emotional outlet.

The service was over, and Mrs. Matthews was bustling about with lemonade and cucumber sandwiches. Laura removed her hat and elected to assist, offering the tray of refreshments to every person in the room except Cream. Then, timing her approach to perfection, she walked towards him, smiling.

"Good evening, Sir. Will you take lemonade or tea? Please help yourself to the sandwiches. I believe also there is plum cake to be sliced in the kitchen, should you prefer something sweet"

"Why, thank you, ma'am, I should like that fine. Allow me to introduce myself: "At *your* service, Doctor Thomas Neill Cream" He appended his correct sir-name as an afterthought, since the Reverend Dr. Matthews from Quebec had known the family for years.

Laura was enchanted both by Cream's manner and status. A medical man -- how could mama disapprove?" Mama could, though, and did when Laura returned home to Berkampstead and confided hesitantly that during her short stay in London she had acquired an admirer -- one who was both charming and persistent in his attentions.

"I am aware of it, Laura, for you had, perhaps inadvertently, referred to the fact several times in your letters. Furthermore, though your acquaintance has been brief, I have already received a note from the man himself requesting permission to become engaged. Why, nothing is known of him but for his own claims. This proposal has, in my opinion, been advanced with quite improper haste and must be at once rejected. "

Laura's desperation lent her strength. "I beg you to reconsider, mama, for I care for Tom most awfully, and do intend to take him for my husband. Now please be a dear, kind mama and give us your blessings. Has he not after all, in seeking your approval without delay shown himself to be the perfect American gentleman?"

"An American -- Lord preserve us!" gasped the old lady, but in the face of Laura's new found determination there was nothing for it but to capitulate. With an air of pained resignation she penned a brief note of assent to Cream, and handing it to Laura remarked with foreboding: "Marry in haste, my girl, repent at leisure."

Laura had entered Cream's life at a vulnerable moment. Having temporarily discharged his duty, as he saw it, to rid the town of whores, including one of whom in different circumstances he might have been disposed to take on as a full time mistress, Cream was at a loose end. Laura was the first respectable woman he had ever been genuinely attracted to, and had proved a unexpectedly agreeable contrast to looser associates; sharing his interest in religion, music, and, even though she dare not admit it to herself, the facts of life. On one occasion, behind closed doors at Cream's lodgings Laura expressed a coy willingness to be taken advantage of -- just that once, mind; but to her profound humiliation the offer was rejected. If Laura felt shamed by her forwardness, Cream's reaction shamed her more. With the hypocrisy of his generation carried by him, like all else, to an extreme, Cream regarded every women as either pure or profligate. "Be so good as to remember, Laura, that you are a lady, and not a whore!" he railed.

Cream was now all for the sanctity of marriage. Apart from Laura's undoubted charms, he had reached his early forties and was still aiming for social acceptance, preferably by setting up home and practice in a genteel area -- Berkhamstead would suit the purpose ideally. Besides, Laura's worshipful attitude towards him was quite gratifying, her pliability a boost to his self esteem. Appealing as he found the situation, when Laura was safely home with mother Cream's lofty standards did not prevent him from sallying forth to meet prostitutes; but he still made frequent trips down to Berkhamstead, playing the attentive fiance, following up with several *billets doux*.

*103 Lambeth Palace Road, London S.E.I.*
*November 18th, 1891.*

*Received an unpleasant jolt a night or so ago. Although I am still resting up, went for a stroll down Piccadilly, and reaching the Circus stood for a while quite watching the girls pass by with no other motive than wishing to enjoy the view. Along came a whore, her hair piled up in an elaborate coif f beneath what looked to be an expensive if over decorated hat, more paint on her face than an omnibus, and a yellow silk dress that owed nothing to style. Atop this was a huge fluffy matching boa, wound twice around her neck so to as practically conceal her face from view. Had I not been on vacation I should have enjoyed taking her some place and winding it considerably tighter. This unfortunate choice of apparel, together with the slut's ungainly waddle, conveyed the impression more than anything of an outsized baby duck. Had nothing better to do just then, so offered her a drink at the Regent. No sooner had we become seated than she demanded to know if I remembered her. Needless to say I did not. It was then she made a claim that momentarily shattered my composure, to the effect she was, of all folk, none other than Lou Harris! I could hardly believe my ears as she continued on to inquire, brazen as could be, why I had neglected to meet her at the Oxford, as arranged. For a moment I thought I had seen a ghost, but recovered myself in an instant; since if this was a visitation from the world beyond, it certainly was anything but ethereal!*

*Being quite positive that Lou Harris had been dead by my hand for the best part of a month, I realised almost right away that this must be a "rip" -- one of the many whores in the pay of the police who, with their usual lack of principle, used them for the purpose of entrapment. The Yard must, I presumed, be conducting an inquiry into Lou Harris's sudden demise, either on the way to the Oxford, or, what now seemed to be more likely, inside it, where her death throes would have created precisely the furore I had intended. Since there had been no mention of such an incident in the Press, it was pretty obvious the police had decided to clam up until information from one of their agents put them on the right track. This I am aware, is common practice thoughout the force and designed expressly to trick some poor sap into incriminating himself. If the rip had hoped to wring a damaging admission from me, in that I had known Lou Harris, and could tell therefore that this was an imposter, the slut was doomed to disappointment. With a contemptuous glance I rose, not troubling to reply, and marched rapidly away.*

*Judging from this latest tomfoolery, it is clear the Bosses, over the past four years, have hardly succeeded in sharpening their intellect; which sure is fortunate for my future aspirations, and unf- ortunate for theirs. It so happens that earlier in the month I met and have gotten myself engaged to a young lady, Miss Laura Sabbatini. Settling down in Berkampstead as a doctor and respectable married man --some chance they will have of buckling me now!"*

EXCERPT FROM A STATEMENT TAKEN ON
SEPTEMBER 23rd 1892
BY INSPECTOR J.B. TUNBRIDGE
REPORT FROM THE CID NEW SCOTLAND YARD

*23rd day of September 1892.*

*I beg to report that on 26 inst, as approved, I proceeded to Berkhamstead with a view to procure a statement from Mrs. Sabatini, mother of Laura Sabitini, to whom Neill was engaged...*

*Mrs. Sabatini, 282 New Kent Road, S.E. says: -*

*I am a widow and mother of Laura Sabatini who was engaged to be married to the man Neill. The first I heard about Neill was from my daughter Laura who told me she had been introduced to him in London. This was about the end of November or early in December 1891. Shortly afterwards I received a letter from Neill asking my permission to pay his addresses to my daughter who was then staying in London. I wrote back to him asking particulars as to his age, prospects, antecedents, &c, and received a second letter in which he gave his age and went on to say that he was a surgeon and physician, but owing to ill-health had given up practice. He said his father and mother were both dead and he had no one to consult on his own side. He also said he was free from all vicious habits and that he was confident of his ability to make my daughter happy...*

*103, Lambeth Palace Road, London D.1.
December 22nd, 1891.*

*Christmas is coming, the goose is getting fat -- or shall be as soon as we are married, since, now that I have selected a wife, it is my ambition* *to bequeath to the world many sons who, from their earliest years shall be guided in their father's foot-steps. **And yet he is but one man: if he command to kill, they kill; if he command to spare, they spare; if he command to smite, they smite; if he command to make desolate, they make desolate.***

*Although it is December there is for me a heady touch of spring in the air; and, apart from the material advantages of a marriage with Laura, not least of which is the opportunity to set up a reputable weekday practice in the matriminonial home at Berkhamstead, I wonder if I am not for the first time since boyhood, a little in love. Quite refreshing in her naivete and high spirits, the girl has enabled me to recapture an element of joie de vivre. Happily, any affection I may feel for her is more than reciprocated, even though I have had occasion sharply to rebuke the dear love-Zorn creature for behaviour unbecoming to the future wife of Doctor Thomas N. Cream. Far from lessening Laura's attachment, however, the firm expression of my principles has, so it seems, served only to increase her respect.*

*Now that she has returned to her mother at Berkhamstead, Laura and I meet, perforce surreptitiously, over tea at the King's Arms Hotel. It seems mother is quite a dragon. Despite the old serpent already having consented to our engagement by mail, before agreeing to a marriage she stands on receiving evidence that I am in a position to support her daughter, declining until then to meet with me in person -- this despite making out a Will in Laura's favour which I have maintained cannot be revoked.*

*Impatient as I am to precipitate matters here and now, there seems nothing for it but to travel to Quebec, obtain proofs of my financial stability and return to beard the monster. But for her damned obduracy Laura and I might soon look forward to enjoying a state of connubial bliss, under the proper circumstances, instead of a chaste fare well kiss at the "Arms"-- enough to drive a hard-shell Baptist to dispsomania! Maybe, though, once we are wed my future mother-in-law shall be brought to the understanding that, far from losing a daughter she has gained a most estimable son-- one who can be counted upon to show her filial affection just so long as she shall live.*

The beginning of 1892 saw Cream boarding the S.S. "Sarnia" en route to the United States, with a rolling gait, though the ship had not set sail. William Fisher, a bed-room steward, assisted him to a cabin, where he became garrulous, confiding that his condition was the result of having fallen into the habit of taking morphia for medical reasons and had transferred to whisky instead. The physician continued to heal himself from a large brown bottle during the course of the conversation, regaling the steward with smutty jokes.

A day out at sea Cream emerged looking pale but passably sober and hailed a passenger on the opposite gangway with an invitation to join him.William Sellar allowed himself to be propelled upwards into the saloon, regaled by Cream's confidences, mainly on the subject of women.

"Allow me to introduce myself, Sir -- Doctor Thomas N. Cream is the name." Not pausing for Sellar's response, he rattled away: "I am a medical man, you know -- McGill University -- practiced in both Chicago and London -- travelling to Quebec to take care of some property -- to be married on my return to England. Here is a photograph of the young lady in question -- quite a pretty little piece, eh? First decent woman who ever took my fancy, as a matter of fact."

Sellar glanced politely at the picture, and made to take his leave, but Cream extended a restraining arm. "Now do be sociable, there's a good chap and join me in a few drams. Precious else to do for the next few days but drown our sorrows." He signalled the bar steward and Sellars, not wishing to appear churlish resumed his seat. The talk turned to the subject of London, and Cream's intimate acquaintance with its low life. Sellars, timid by nature and a model of Victorian propriety, was profoundly shocked by the crudeness of Cream's speech, making it quite clear that when in the capital he had certainly not, like Cream, availed himself of two or three women a night. "Don't know what you've missed, old boy, Cream commiserated. "Few limitations, I can vouch for that, and cheap at the price of a shilling or two. Try the Aquarium next time you're in town -- classy joint, best tail in town, don't you know, though you're expected to wine and dine that sort before getting down to serious business."

"I am afraid I am feeling rather unwell. Shaky stomach, you know". Sellar had risen again to his feet. "Do please excuse me, Doctor Cream. I must return at once to my cabin."

"Why, my dear fellow, it must be the movement of the ship. Allow me to provide a remedy." Cream withdrew the brown medicine bottle from his pocket and offered it across the table. "A little morphia -- will put you right in an instant."

Sellar, however, declined and hastened away, hoping fervently not to run into the unpleasant Doctor Cream for the remainder of the voyage. His hopes were to be dashed for later on in the evening Cream knocked on his cabin door, inquiring solicitiously after the sufferer's condition. Reluctant to appear downright uncivil, Sellar admitted him, noting with some apprehension that Cream was armed this time with quantities of whisky and gin; and had obviously already sampled some of their contents, Cream's proposal to "have ourselves a little fun and games" -- was received without enthusiasm by Sellar, who began to stammer his excuses. Cream would have none of them then, nor, what was even worse for Sellar, at unearthly hours on several consecutive nights when Cream rudely interrupted his slumbers, claiming he was suffering from nightmares and needed company. Only once did Sellar dare to protest, when Cream, as Sellar afterwards stated, "appeared much annoyed and looked very vicious." No hero, Sellar found it expedient to humour the restless and exciteable man; for way before the coast of Halifax hove in sight, he had begun increasingly to fear the consequences of doing otherwise.

PART OF A REPORT TO THE METROPOLITAN POLICE
BY
INSPECTOR FREDERICK JARVIS

*Montreal, Canada*
*19th July 1892.*

*... a letter from a Mr. McCulloch, stating he would like to see me as he had some important information to give me concerning Dr. Cream... His statement is as follows:*

I am a Traveller for an extensive grocery wholesale house...At the end of last Feb. and the first week in March I was in pursuance of my business in Quebec City and stayed at Blanchard's Hotel. I became acquainted with Dr. Cream there he occupied a room on the same floor as myself. About the second day I was there I complained to Cream of feeling unwell, he looked at me and said I was bi - ious. Come upstairs and I will give you something that will make you all right. I accompanied him to his room when he went to a drawer in the bureau and took out some bottles of pills he gave me from a bottle labelled "Blue Mass" and another from a bottle labelled anti-bilious. There were about 18 to 20 other bottles of pills in the drawer, he said he got them from an American firm as samples to sell in England, he intended selling them to Hospitals, Charitable Institutions and Medical men and that he expected to make a fortune out of it. He further said he could sell a bottle containing 500 pills at 40 cents and make money but that he should ask double that price for them. He further said he intended Navin, a little case made to carry the bottles in, about 4 tn. wide 8 deep and 12 long. While in his room he showed me the photograph of a lady whose name he said was Laura Sabatini, that he was engaged to her and expected to marry her on his return to England after getting his money from his father's estate. I went out in Town with him that evening to buy a musical instrument called an autoharp, he bought two which were to be sent from Toronto to him ... he deposited one dollar as part payment for the instruments, ten dollars to be paid when he received them ... not having the kind he wanted in stock. Next day Sunday about 10 a.m. as I came down to break-fast, Cream came in the office, he asked me how I felt and if the medicine he had given me had done me any good. I replied that it has operated very purpose-fully. After dinner on the same day I was in conversation with him when he asked me to show him my samples saying he would like to have an Agency for these in London. I went upstairs with him to his room to see some jewellery he said he had got back from a girl to whom he was engaged but who had married someone else. He then unlocked a yellow japanned tea trunk and took therefrom a dark japanned cash-box and from this he took the jewellery in question, two brooches, a set of earrings and necklace. it was old fashioned gold set with garnets and rubies. He next took a bottle out of the cash-box and said "Do you *know what this is." I replied No. He then said "It is poison". I said For God's sake what do you do with that? He replied, I give it to women to get them out of the family way. He then walked to the bureau (chest of drawers) from which he had taken the bottles of medicine...and took out a cardboard box about two and a half inches square by an inch deep and removing the lid showed me about 20 Capsules (empty) they were almost five eights of an inch long. He said when showing them "I give it to them in these." The bottle which he had said contained poison was about a third full of a whitish crystal, the particles being very uneven in size but averaging about the size of pinsheads, the bottle had a long mouth. was about two and a half inches long and about one and a half inches in diameter, it had no label on it. From the same Trunk in which he kept the cash box he produced a set of false whiskers; hair all round without mustache but divided and parted on chin. whiskers about 4 in. long of dark brown colour. I said what do you use these for? He replied "To disguise my identity so that they would not recognise me again, when operating on the women. He added that he had lots of fun in London in the Waterloo and London Roads, that he met many girls on these roads and that he never gave them more than a shilling, sometimes as many as three in a night. He never mentioned the names of any girls. He then came into my room and I showed him my samples consisting of spices, extracts, coffee. &c. He said on looking at them "I don't think I can handle these the freight duty and price being against them, and the commission not large enough." I afterwards went for a drive with him in a sleigh he had borrowed. when he showed me certain houses where he said his relatives lived, but that he was not on good terms with most of them, he also showed me the Yard his father formerly owned and where he Cream worked and lived as a boy. I was at the Hotel about 8 days and saw Cream every day, at meals; he spent money very freely and drank a good deal. He told me he took morphia pills and I advised him not to take so much. He said he took it on account of his eyes and head troubling him. Saw him on one occasion in a perfect stupor from the effects of the morphine...*

On March 19th, 1892 Mr. Douglas Battersby, shipping agent of St. James's Street, Montreal was expecting a client at three o'clock, one, Doctor Thomas Neill Cream, who had booked a saloon berth for his return to England. Punctual to the second, Cream strode into the office and proceeded to ensure that he would receive his money's worth while on board, fussing over every last detail concerning his creature comforts on the voyage. Having assured Cream that all would be attended to, Mr. Battersby breathed a sigh of relief at his departure. If he had hoped to hear the last of Cream and his numerous requirements, Battersby was due for a disappointment; for three days later he was contacted again.

> *"Montreal, 22nd March, 1892.*
>
> *D. Battersby, Esq., Montreal.*
>
> *Dear Sir,*
>
> *I am expecting a parcel and some letters and papers at the Albion Hotel some time to-day. Will you kindly get them for me and give them to the purser of the S.S. 'Labrador', and ask him to take charge of them for me, till I call on him in Liverpool for them? The parcel is a small one, and you can either give or send it to the purser of the 'Labrador' and much oblige.*
>
> *Yours truly,*
> *THOS. N. CREAM.*
>
> *P.S.,-I bought a ticket from you yesterday per S.S. 'Brittanic'."*

Mr. Battersby, on obtaining the parcel found himself wondering whether he should inspect the contents before passing them on. "Might be dynamite for all I know, what with all this talk of anarchy about these days." Mr. Battersby's fertile imagination had not led him entirely astray as it happened, since the parcel was certainly intended by Cream, in his habitual state of drunken maleficence, for a veritable load of dynamite. On cautiously opening it Mr. Battersby was mystified to find a stack of printed posters, topped by a first draft in Cream's handwriting, all bearing the same extraordinary message.

ELLEN DONWORTH'S DEATH

```
To the Guests of the Metropole Hotel
```

```
Ladies and Gentlemen,
```

```
I hereby notify you that the person who
poisoned Ellen Donworth on the 13th last
October is today in the employ of the
Metropole Hotel and that your lives are
in danger as long as you remain in this
Hotel.
```

```
Yours respectfully W. H. MURRAY
```

```
London April 1892.
```

Mr. Battersby, after some thought, decided he had better forward the parcel after all -- who knew but the man was actually a Government agent anxious to foil a plot! A further letter soon arrived from Cream to compensate him munificently for his trouble.

*"R.M.S. Britannic Apr. 7th, 1892.*

*D. Battersby, Esq.,*
*Montreal, Canada.*

*Dear Sir,*

> *Received goods per 'Labrador', all safe and your letter. Many thanks. The 'B' beat all previous records this time. We had a fine run, and was two days in ahead of the 'Labrador'. I enclose 15 pence in English postage to reimburse you for the 25 cents spent. Thanking you again for your kindness, I remain.*

> *THOS. N. CREAM.*

# PART 5

*Euston Hotel, London.*
*April 2nd, 1892.*

*Am putting up here at the Euston until my old room at the Sleapers becomes available on the 9th. The voyage was uneventful, since I spent most of it in my cabin, tight as a nun's cunt. In the same deplorable condition back in Montreal, just before sailing, I had five hundred bills printed up and sent on ahead, intending on my arrival here to have them distributed about the Metropole Hotel. I aimed, by announcing that there was a murderer loose in the hotel, to spread a fair amount of consternation among some of the residents -- several of whom last year complained of my intemperate behaviour and summoned the manager. A belligerent little bantam cock, I swiped him right off his perch, was set upon in cowardly fashion by several minions and forcibly ejected. The Circular stunt might have leveled me with the lot of them, and I should have gone ahead determinedly but for checking the bills this morning, only to find that when composing the draft I had again repeated an error, one to which my addictions for some reason render me prone -- that of referring to the use of poison in connection with those I had put to death, when only the executioner could have been privy to such a method. This in itself prompted me to pause and question the wisdom of proceeding further, but on reflection not to abandon the scheme there and then; for past experience has rendered my mind, if occasionally confused by intoxicants, ever alert on one point -- the absolute necessity of appending to certain communications any other signature than that of Thomas N. Cream. In the Metropole Circular, for instance, I generously credited the authorship to my old pal Murray from Pinkertons -- ergo there is little possibility it would be traced to me. Nevertheless, as the day draws to a close being still uncommonly sober and therefore particularly wary, I realize that the Metropole lark could run me into trouble after all, if not on account of the aforementioned slip, then because of potential complications concerning distribution of the material. With God's work yet incomplete, I cannot afford to take a chance, particularly for the sake of what is, after all, little more than* a practical joke. Mindful of my weighty responsibilities, I guess there is nothing for it but reluctantly to abandon the whole shenanigans.

Continuing on a note of caution it strikes me that, rather than pen anything else of that nature in my own hand, it might as be as well to persuade dear Laura to do so for me. Before calling upon her and the dragon I am off to the Prince of Wales Hotel at Chatham, said to be quite a lively town, accompanied by a spreeish old fellow I ran into at Gatti's, a retired physician by name of George Clifton, who, despite being sixty or more years of age, has asked me to show him a good time. I jovially suggested that he might, in pursuance of what I myself consider a good time, find himself needful of prompt medical attention, and that I was therefore an ideal companion for the trip! After this, if for no better reason than to attempt favourably impressing Laura's frightful mother, I must endeavor to be upon my best behaviour before showing up again at Berkhamstead.

To resume in a serious vein, now that my Sabbatical is at an end, it is time once more to take up the shield of faith --- **where with ye shall be able to quench all the fiery darts of the wicked. And take the helmet of salvation and the sword of the Spirit, which is the word of God.** (Reminding me to ensure that my room at Berkhamstead is equipped with a copy of the Holy Book.) Regarding Clover, I am aware I have sinned grievously in the eyes of the Lord, by placing temptations of the flesh before spiritual values, thus sparing the worthless lives of those sluts Masters and May. Impossible now to remedy the situation -- are not two women scorned doubly dangerous to a man? After much soul-searching I have reached the conclusion that there is but one way to obtain divine forgiveness; and that is to sacrifice unto the Lord, in their place, yet another pair of Jezebels.

EXCERPT FROM A SPECIAL REPORT.
METROPOLITAN POLICE
L. DIVISION.

13 April 1892.

P1294 William Eversfield reports:

*While at the hospital Emma Shrivell said they had made the acquaintance of a man named Fred -- height about 5 feet 8 or 9 inches, dark, stout build, bald on top of head, wears spectacles, dress black overcoat and high silk hat: whom they met on 11th Inst. and had tea with him. After which he gave each 3 long thin pills and after left them...*

LETTER FROM METROPOLITAN POLICE FILES WRITTEN ON NOTE-HEADING OF PRINCE OF WALES HOTEL, CHATHAM (this address crossed out)

*April 10th 1892. My Dear Alice*

*Just a few lines to say that all being well shall be in London tomorrow Monday and shall hope to have the pleasure of seeing you at 118 between six and seven in the evening pleased to accept your kind invitation to take tea with you we can then go to some place of entertainment for the rest of the evening.*

*Kind regards to your friend please remember me to her with best wishes to yourself believe me to remain*

*Yours faithfully*

*George Clifton.*

*A partly burned postcard found in the grate posted in London cancelling an appointment f or that date... sender is missing but there is a little similarity in the writing and that of the letter signed George Clifton.*

Cream had arrived back in England on All Fool's Day, April 1st, 1892, and shortly afterwards reassumed various pseudonyms -- excepting that of Jack the Ripper. He was particularly fond of presenting himself to the ladies as Colonel Frederick Hamilton, wealthy plantation owner of South Virginia or, in less illustrious circles, simply as Fred, a name put about originally by way of diverting suspicion for the murder of Ellen Donworth towards one, Frederick W. Smith, Member of Parliament. Alice Marsh and Emma Shriven were among those who knew him by the diminutive, as well as his new friend, George Clifton, to whom he had introduced himself as Doctor Frederick Neill. Marsh and Shrived, dismissed for immorality from their post as waitresses at Muttons Hotel in Brighton, had made for the bright lights of London, been invited by Cream to accompany him, together with an older acquaintance, on a trip to Chatham and, paid well for services rendered looked forward to a reunion once they had returned to the city. Not long after this a letter arrived for Alice at 118 Stamford Street, South East London, written by Cream, (signed "George Clifton"), dated April 10th 1892, and making an assignment for the following evening. Since George Clifton was unaware of having made the appointment he neglected to keep it; but his associate, convivial Doctor "Fred", bearing several bottles of stout, did not, though it was well after midnight when he arrived.

Fred having proved at Chatham far the more capable of the two men when it came to indulging in Emma's favourite pursuit, she in particular was pleasantly surprised; though Alice had from the first, despite Cream's geniality, found him rather intimidating. These were hard times though, and without a patron it was difficult to compete as well as they had hoped with the professionals of Stamford Street. Their savings were fast diminishing, so that neither girl could afford to turn away a potential customer. Alice thus had no option but to politely endorse Emma's prompt invitation to step inside and share a late supper of tinned salmon and a few crusts of bread.

"Why, this is mighty friendly of you, ladies. I shall be more than delighted to accept", said Fred amiably, removing his silk hat with a courtly flourish to reveal a bald dome gleaming with perspiration. Alice formed no higher opinion of Emma's admirer this time than she had before, particularly at close quarters, when the eyes magnified by gold rimmed lenses struck her as having a peculiar -- if not positively disturbing -- cast. To Emma, however, here was the perfect gentleman, if a trifle on the rough side in his habits; a flash dresser, spats and all, with an agreeable line in compliments and wearing expensive accoutrements. His soft persuasive accent enchanted her, as did his broad shoulders and winning smile. Instead of continuing to chance her luck on the streets, here was the perfect "protector", a doctor no less, so he claimed, who, with an option on both their services, would afford them a certain amount of prestige. This was a society where dual moral standards prevailed. For women without work or means there was rarely a choice other than promiscuity or starvation. Both Emma and Alice were aware that their only assets were youth, reasonably good looks and, in Emma's case, an outstandingly voluptuous shape. These she fully intended to market for the best possible price -- but, in common with others of her persuasion, would not have been loath to attain a modicum of respectablity into the bargain.

"Now just you settle down nice and cozy to your tea, Doctor Fred, dear," she said. "And then we'll treat ourselves to a bit of entertainment, like Mr. Clifton said in his letter, though he ain't here to enjoy it too, more's the shame."

"A proper shame," agreed Alice, who had seen *her* salvation in being an old man's darling.

"If Clifton has not the good form to show up nor send his apologies, I daresay we shall all manage well enough without him," observed Cream, and proceeded to show Emma how this might best be accomplished. A while later, downing the refreshments with gusto, he observed that Alice, after a few glasses of stout, was looking rather flushed and Emma more than a little peaked. "The onset of a fever, no doubt, Alice, my dear -- a good deal of influenza about at present."

Alice shivered slightly as if to confirm his diagnosis and averted her glance. "You do look a bit out of sorts, Alice," remarked Emma, "now that the doctor mentions it. Must be the fish, I fancy. A bit on the turn I shouldn't be surprised, it being opened yesterday lunch time and the weather so close for time of year."

Cream may suddenly have lost his appetite but not his party manners. "Nothing wrong with the meal -- excellent, quite excellent in fact, ladies, and I thank you for it. Why, had the fish been in the least unwholesome we should already be suffering the effects of severe poisoning. Even so, since Alice is off colour right now, and Emma the opposite, I suggest as a precaution that you both take three of these capsules before bedtime. Ideal cure for all ills, I assure you." He had removed from his waistcoat pocket the recommended medicine and also an impressive watch on a gold chain hung with a red seal, from which in turn was suspended, to Emma's admiration, a diamond horseshoe pin.

The watch indicating it to be nearly half past one in the morning he announced his imminent departure, in order to attend a pre-arranged night call. "Must be off at once, my dears, matter of life and death most likely!" He laughed mirthlessly, clapped his hat on, tipped it rakishly forward with his cane, and bade them farewell. Alice obeyed doctor's orders right away, almost as if in gratitude for his departure; as for Emma, who had always deep rooted dread of poisoning and still regarding the salmon with some suspicion, she too obediently downed her medicine.

In the early hours of April 12th, what with the dreadful commotion that ensued at 118 Stamford Street, a policeman was sent for, who heard the girls' piercing shrieks before he had entered the building and could never afterwards eradicate them from his memory. Inured as he was to human suffering, the appalling plight of these two benighted girls affected Police Constable Eversfield deeply. The spectacle of their agonizing ordeal, convulsions, arched backs, violent vomiting, with periods of spasm, muscular rigidity and all other symptoms of strychnine poisoning resulted in screams and groans pitons enough to soften the hardest heart. The constable finding them to be way beyond his own rudimentary knowledge of first aid at once summoned a cab, conveying the hysterical girls inside with the assistance of the entire household; and together with P.C. Cumley who had been on duty in the area, accompanied them to the hospital. Alice Marsh, the more fortunate of the two, never survived the journey; but Emma Shrivell, bellowing until she was blue in the face, was denied that merciful end for several anguished hours. "It was

Fred who poisoned us, Fred, Fred, FRED!" the girls had screamed, and the name continued to ring in the ears of P.C. Eversfield and his colleague P.C. Cumley long after those frantic cries were silenced. The ci-devant Jack the Ripper had achieved a second double event which equalled if not excelled the savage ferocity of the first; in that his last pair of victims had been exposed to the excruciating suffering of prolonged torture rather than being accorded the privilege of an abrupt end. The inflicting of such refined cruelty was now a hallmark of Cream's trade, and he would have plied it with ever increasing enthusiasm, had not his pernicious habits driven him inexorably towards his own destruction.

EXCERPT FROM A POLICE REPORT DATED MAY 16TH, 1892.

*Every effort has been made to find the man "Fred" and Sergt. Ward, while patrolling Westminster Bridge Road at 11 p.m. 13th inst. saw a man answering the description given of Fred, and kept him under observation, with the result that he picked up with a prostitute and accompanied her to 24 Elliotts Row, St. Georges Rd., where she resides; after leaving her proceeded to 103 Lambeth Palace Rd. where he let himself in with a key.*

*P. C. Ward has since seen the girl and ascertained that the man has made an an appointment with her at her residence on Thursday next, he also told her that he had recently returned from America and intended to return shortly, and that he lived solely to indulge in women.*

*This man is being kept under continuous observation by Sgt. Gray and P. C. Smale and Burgess C.E. Dept. His movements will be carefully watched,while inquiries respecting him are being made. P. C. Comley has also seen the man referred to ... believes him to be identical with the person he saw leave 118 Stamford St. at 1.45, 12th.*

### REPORTS FROM
### GEORGE HARVEY. LOCAL INSPECTOR.
### 19TH DAY OF MAY 1892.

*With ref. to attached reports; we beg to state that the man residing at No. 103 Lambeth Palace Road has been kept under observation. On 17th inst. he visited Violet Beverley, a prostitute at No. 3 North St. Kennington Rd. and remained nearly 3 hours, during that time he prepared what he called an American drink, which she declined to take and it was afterwards thrown away; he also showed her a leather case containing a quantity of pills and told her he was a Traveller for a Firm of Pill Manufacturers in New York and was in London for 4 or 5 weeks.*

*He also visited the girl 28th inst. staying some time and having connection twice with her, she has an appointment to meet him on Sat. which she will keep... this goes to prove that he is an extremely sensual individual...*

*It has been ascertained that the man referred to calls himself Dr. Neal and it is evident that he is connected with the Medical profession, he was seen 28th by Mr. Burdett, who is of the opinion that is the individual mentioned by him in his Statement.,.*

*At 9.15 p.m, 18th Dr. Neal with two other persons were being followed in Westminster Bridge Road by P.S. Brogan and P. C. Comley when one of the men with him evidently observed the officers and went to Kennington Rd. Station and complained of same. He gave his name as John P. Hayes ... thought he was being followed by some enemies to the Government ... could assist us in the enquiry relative to Dr. Neal.*

### 20TH MAY, 1892.

*With ref. to the appointment made by Dr. Neal, 103, Lambeth Palace Road with a prostitute at 24ElliottsRow on 19th inst. We beg to report that it was not kept, and we are acquainted with the reason, which is as follows.*

*When returning from Commsrs. Office yesterday afternoon with P. S. McIntyre we again met Dr. Neal to whom McIntyre spoke, and he told him that he had an appointment with a prostitute that evening; but he was not going to keep it, as the girl had told him she was put onto him by a detective, who told her to learn all she could about him. I heard this statement which shows how utterly unreliable these women are.*

GEORGE HARVEY, INSPECTOR.

Mrs. Sleaper heaved her cumbersome form from the fireside chair. Grossly overweight and almost totally inactive, rising to her feet was a major exercise and one which she performed as infrequently as possible.

"Em!" she called through the doorway, "What ever are you about with the vittals? Long past the dinner hour it is, and not a bite to eat. A fine figure of a woman like myself, so your poor dear father used to say, needs proper sustenance if she is not to fade away."

"Oh, ma, be patient do," called her daughter from the stairhead. "I've only one pair of hands and they've been occupied all day spring-cleaning."

"And not before time, it being Easter Monday already," bawled back Mrs. Sleaper ungraciously. "I wonder the lodgers put up with your slovenly habits. You don't know the meaning of a hard day's work, my girl!" Emily, lean as her mother was fat, and of necessity twice as spry, appeared presently, covered in dust, hair straggling untidily from beneath a mop cap, carrying a tray of bread, tea and the remains of yesterday's boiled hen.

"You might have troubled to run round the bakers for a hot meat pie or two, Em," complained Mrs. Sleaper. "In my state of health I could do with something more substantial than a bit of cold fowl." Mrs. Sleaper suffered from an as yet imaginary heart condition which conveniently precluded her from all physical effort.

Emily, long resigned to being put upon, passed her mother a cup of tea, poured one for herself, and sat down opposite. "Never mind, ma.

I'll light the coals before dark, and boil up that left-over beefsteak pudding and carrots I ordered in special last Sunday for Doctor Neill in the upstairs back, only he never ate it until Monday, the 11th that was, and then but half. Said he had an important appointment later and could not risk a bad stomach. The rest, with a few mashed spuds and a bit of jam tart for afters should set you up a treat, Ma!" Consoled by this prospect, Mrs. Sleaper relented sufficiently to indulge Emily in a few moments chat on the subject of certain strange "goings-on" in the household.

"You know, ma, I do believe there is something rum about Doctor Neill. Remember last year he asked me to pop down Lambeth Road, to find out if a young lady of his acquaintance had been poisoned to death, and you told me I had best keep my nose out of other people's business?"

"I remember it well enough, for he said Lord Russell, of all folk, had done her in. A proper card 'aint he, your Doctor Neill"

"I'll say, Ma, and that card being a right joker! Yesterday, Easter Sunday as ever was, he starts up again along the same lines, this time about those two Stamford Street girls, Alice Marsh and Emma Shriven who got done in a week or so ago. There was a report on the inquest in Lloyds this morning -- strychnine poisoning they say. While reading it I looks up for a moment to see Doctor Neill with his bald head around the kitchen door, watching me with that queer stare of his. He smiles and says, quite smarmy: "Good morning, Miss Sleaper. Would it be possible to take a glance at your newspaper, when convenient? I should like to check whether it contains an account of the inquest into the deaths of those two wretches poisoned by strychnine in Stamford Street. Such an unpleasant way to die -- must have endured the suffering of the damned, what? A cold-blooded crime, if ever there was one, Miss Sleaper. I am sure you would agree that the man who did it ought to be brought to justice!"

"Well, now, Em, even if Neill is an odd sort, it ain't so strange, him being a medical man, taking an interest in inquests, and suchlike."

"Yes, but Ma. Later, while I was doing out Mr. Walter Harper's room Neill comes in, taps my shoulder, giving me quite a turn, and asks a lot of questions about him; then goes and thumbs through his books and letters, if you please, asking what sort of chap he is, the kind of family he comes from and where they live. I told him Mr. Harper is soon to be a doctor, like his father before him, Doctor Joseph Harper of Barnstaple, who is ever so respectable and had put his son to board with us three years ago when Mr. Walter started studying at St. Thomas's.

`St. Thomas's, I was there myself for a while, quite a coincidence?' says Neill. `It would appear then that your Mister Harper and I have at least something in common, though he is, I must warn you Miss Sleaper, a man of extremely depraved tendencies -- a thoroughly bad egg.'

`Why, Doctor Neill,' says I. `Mr. Harper is as fine and decent a man as yourself, I am sure.'

`Oh no, Miss Sleaper, you are mistaken there, I fear,' says Neill, slick as a ha'porth of treacle. `Without wishing to disturb you unduly, I believe it is my duty to pass on, in the strictest confidence of course, certain facts that have recently been made known to me, which establish beyond a doubt that Harper was the fellow who poisoned those Stamford Street girls. I am in two minds as to whether to inform the police, not wishing to have a man's life on my conscience, though of course the scoundrel should undoubtedly be hanged.'

Well, Ma, I was so outraged on behalf of poor Mr. Harper that I hardly knew what I was saying, and told Neill straight he must be mad.

`It is not I who am the madman, I assure you, my dear lady,' he answered, cool as a cucumber. `The police have the proofs, you see. This I know from word received through a detective friend of mine from America. He told me that, to his certain knowledge, letters now in the hands of the police had been forwarded to the Stamford Street women warning that Harper was out to kill them, and that they would be ill-advised to accept any medicine from him.'"

Emily had taken this at the time to be yet another example of the man's tweaked humour, but it struck her now with delayed shock that if Neill had chanced to be telling the truth it would seem Harper, whom they had considered for three years to be a pleasant and entirely innoffensive young man was in fact a monster who went about distributing strychnine at random, deriving intense pleasure in the certain knowledge (no doubt acquired in the course of his studies as a medical student) that his victims would die in unspeakable agony. There was no guarantee, if this were so, that he might not one day take it into his head to select the Sleapers as his next victims. Mrs. Sleaper, however, dismissed the suggestion as ludicrous.

"Don't be so daft, girl; Walter Harper is no murderer but a gentleman born and bred. Comes from a decent family, he does, pays his way regular; and that's a good enough character reference for the likes of me. I declare, Em, my heart is in quite a flutter with all this nonsense. Why, the way you do go on, Jack the Ripper himself might be back -- and residing at 103!

The following day, inoffensive young Walter Harper endeavoured to pass by Cream on the landing without exchanging a word. Harper had prudently decided to avoid a confrontation with the sinister Doctor Neill, despite having heard from Miss Sleaper that not only had the man had been snooping about his rooms but implied that he, Harper, had been involved in some disgraceful incident concerning the murder of two prostitutes. Assuming the fellow to be out of his mind, he had managed to avoid Neill until now.

"Good morning, Harper. And how are you today?" inquired Cream, solicitously.
"Morning, Neill," Harper replied shortly, but was prevented from moving on by Cream's burly form barring his way at the stairhead. "Would you not care to take breakfast with me today, Harper? I understand we have a good deal in common, since I too was at St. Thomas's for a while. Mostly Obstetrical and Mortuary. As a matter of fact, some of my patients were quite cut up about it, ha-ha!"

Harper winced. "Thank you, but I seldom take breakfast." The curt dismissal of his overtures inflamed Cream's anger to such an extent that he would have attempted to throw Harper back down the stairs had Harper not anticipated the move and managed to ease by. Miss Sleaper appeared en route to Cream's room, with a tray of toast and milk. Cream shouted after Harper: "Think your shit smells of roses, you snooty little sod!"

"I never heard such language, nor don't wish to again, if you please!" exclaimed Miss Sleaper, turning pink and losing her grip of the tray. "Now look what a bother you've caused with your dirty talk. Ought to be ashamed, Doctor Neill, really you ought. If I tell my Ma she'll send you packing, and so you deserve!"

"My dear Miss Sleaper, pray forgive me. We men are accustomed when alone to express ourselves in rather, shall we say, indelicate terms, at times. I should not of course have spoken so bluntly had I realized there was a lady present." Slightly mollified at the term -- Cream was a master of flattery, by which means he had already exerted his influence on Miss Sleaper to a considerable extent -- she retreated to fetch some cleaning materials and a new dish of toast and milk for that wicked Doctor Neill.

*London, 25th April, 1892.*

*Dr. Harper, Barnstaple.*

*Dear Sir,*

> *I am writing to inform you that one of my operators has indisputable evidence that your son, J. Harper, a medical student at St. Thomas's Hospital, poisoned two girls named Alice Marsh and Emma Shrivell on the 12th inst., and that I am willing to give you the said evidence (so that you can suppress it) for the sum of £1500 sterling. The evidence in my hands is strong enough to convict and hang your son, but I shall give it you for £1500 sterling, or sell it to the police for the same amount. The publication of the evidence will ruin you and your family for ever, and you know that as well as I do, To show*

*you that what I am writing is true, I am willing to send you a copy of the evidence against your son, so that when you read it you will need no one to tell you that it will convict your son. Answer my letter at once through the columns of the London Daily Chronicle as follows: "W.H.M. -- Will pay you for your services. -- Dr. H." After I see this in paper I will communicate with you again. As I said before, I am perfectly willing to satisfy you that I have strong evidence against your son by giving you a copy of it before you pay me a penny. If you do not answer it at once I am going to give evidence to the Coroner at once.*

*Yours respectfully*

*W. H.MURRAY.*

# PART 6

103, Lambeth Palace Road, London S.E.I.

May 16th, 1892.

*April was, all in all, quite an eventful, if not to say doubly eventful month, in the case of those two degenerates, Alice Marsh and Emma Shrivell. By all reports their torments were, as the sluts so richly deserved, trenchantly prolonged -- affording me extreme satisfaction not only on that score but also on brilliantly having achieved the second twin coup of my career.*

*The contempt, not to say downright anger, so easily aroused in me by most women, was reinforced last month by the disagree-able attitude of Laura's mother, to whom I was finally presented. The deaf shrew was demonstrably unimpressed with my qualities; treating me with positive disdain. Suppressing my rage only with the utmost difficulty I feigned tender concern for her health. Being however unaccustomed as Laura to communicating through an ear trumpet I found the effort of yelling down the tube an altogether too taxing exercise, and promised, more from irritation than sympathy, that I should make it my business to obtain suitable medical help. For all this, the harridan for some reason refused to consent there and then to my marrying her daughter; she may have been a model of virtue but I could cheerfully have throttled her. Afterwards escorting them both to a festival of song at the church, I almost drowned out the choir in loud voiced resentment -- though apparently less to the annoyance of mother than of Laura, who declared later, with rather more spirit than I had expected of her, that she had been quite put out by my calling so much attention to myself, particularly in the presence of the vicar's wife, and that I was kindly never to do so again. I should at once have struck another woman for such boldness, but there is about Laura, even when cross, an air of fragile vulnerability which rouses a man's protective instinct. A stranger to sentimentality as a rule, damned if I am not for once in danger of growing soft on a girl; and had better retain a firm grip on myself, if I am not to succumb to the sweet Delilah's charms.*

*Towards April's end I heard, disconcertingly, of some servant who was putting about a rumour that Matilda Clover had died last year in suspicious circumstances, which, reaching the attention of Inspector Harvey of the Yard resulted in his obtaining permission on the 30th to exhume the body. Whether or not it is my uneasy imagination playing me tricks, I have since begun to suspect 103 to be under surveillance, and said as much to Sleaper, suggesting that it might be that snooty sod Harper who was the subject of a police investigation. The impudent chit replied: "If they are watching anyone It is you, Doctor Neill. "To which I responded that if so, it could only be because I am an American. Anticipating that the woman would at this point recollect my having not only displayed uncommon curiosity (and perhaps a certain degree of specialized knowledge) in the way Marsh and Shrivell had met their end, but also an untoward interest in Clover's death, I took the opportunity of mentioning that since there was now to be an inquest, Sleaper had done well to have avoided calling by Clover's house to pry -- thus panicking the impressionable idiot into assuming that had been her own idea, and f or all we knew it was actually she the police were following. If they are in fact on to me, Inspector Harvey and the others will find that two can play at the game of cat and mouse, and that the best man will win.*

MRS. MARGARET ARMSTEAD
examined by
THE ATTORNEY-GENERAL AT
CREAM'S TRIAL FOR MURDER IN JULY 1892

-- I am the wife of William Armstead, a photographer, of 129 Westminster Bridge Road. A person named Haynes came to lodge at our house in March last, about Easter. I think I made the prisoner's acquaintance through his coming to be photographed in my husband's studio. There he made the acquaintance of Haynes, and they became intimate. In May, when the prisoner was at our house, I became aware that some observation was being kept on our place, and I called the attention of my husband and the prisoner to the fact. The prisoner said nothing then. I went to have some refreshment with him, and at the place we went to he pointed to a person and asked me if he was one of the men who was watching the house. I said that I could not see from the distance at which we were sitting.

--Did he say anything about the Stamford Street case?

--He said what a dreadful murder it was, and that whoever did it ought to be hanged.

--Did you say anything further?

--I asked him if he knew the girls Marsh and Shrivell. He said he knew them well, that they used to solicit up at the Bridge of an evening.

--Did you ever see the prisoner in a square-topped hat?

--I cannot remember.

--The cases of Marsh and Shrivell were being talked about at that time?

-- Yes.

Cross-examined

-- Was it the common talk of the neighbourhood? -- Yes.

-- Was it through you that the prisoner first became acquainted with Haynes?

-- Yes.

-- Did you tell the prisoner that Haynes had been a detective?

-- I may have done so, or else my husband may have done so; I do not know.

-- Did Haynes say anything about having been a detective?

-- I believe he did. I believe my husband told the prisoner that Haynes had been a detective or engaged in detective work. I do not know whether the bridge he mentioned would be Westminster or Waterloo.

*103 Lambeth Palace Road, London S.E.I.*

*May 18th, 1892.*

*Last night I dreamed again of Anderesmann. Though my anger at his abandonment has never been properly assuaged -- I scorned even to look the fellow up when last in Chicago -- he still on occasions visits me in the night, mouthing as always his righteous platitudes -- a nightmare if ever there was one! Rousing this morning, in a lather of fury, not unmixed with a thoroughly unreasoned sense of remorse it took me a while to get a hold on myself -- Anderesmann, in dreams or otherwise, having an uncanny knack of putting the other fellow in the wrong, and vice versa.*

*This dream was one that has become unpleasantly repetitive, featuring Anderesmann, dressed in the regalia of a High Court Judge, addressing in mournful tones a jury composed, but for one faceless male, entirely of wanton women -- those upon whom I had been appointed by a Higher Court than this to impose a stern sentence of my own. Marsh, Shrivell, Clover, Eddowes, Stride and all the other morally myopic trash, each and every one thoroughly deserving to be wiped systematically off the face of the earth, these I realized with horror, had been called to sit in judgment upon me. It was I, the man commanded by God to despatch these abandoned sluts to hell, I, Doctor Thomas Neill Cream, saviour of mankind who stood, a prisoner in the dock, entirely at their mercy.*

*"Ladies and gentleman of the jury," intoned Anderesmann in a voice of doom, "I direct you to find the accused guilty as charged of murders so foul as never before equalled in the annals of crime. A wise man is cautious and turns away from evil, but a fool throws off restraint and is careless. Rise, lost souls, and declare your verdict." Whereupon, the bloodless shades, Eddowes, Stride, Marsh, Shrivell, Clover and the others rose in unison, pointing skeletal fingers in my direction.*

*"Guilty as charged! Sentenced to hang -- hang by the neck until he is dead!" screeched the harpies. Roused to wakefulness by a violent fit of choking, this unnerving dream, as always, played upon my mind to such an extent that I had, and continue to have at this moment, the greatest difficulty in shaking off it's disagreeable effects. My resentment of Anderesmann is at these times indescribable, since even in my dreams he has set himself up to judge of my behaviour without the least consideration of his own dereliction; and by remaining absent from my life when most needed during the past few years, can blame only himself for any misfortunes which may transpire as a result of any jam I may be unfortunate enough to get myself into. Chilled to the soul by even the faintest prospect of this dream, due to some unwitting slip on my part, ever becoming a reality, I shall resume my practice over the past several months of retiring with a nightlight. How childlike and unreasoned are our fears, how oft do we poor vulnerable beings allow ourselves to become the victims of our own fevered fantasies?*

*With each dawn there is for me, thank heaven, a return to rationality, and a resurgence of courage -- a quality, though I say it myself, lacking only in my dreams. After a liquid breakfast and a spot of medication I have entirely regained my normal sublime assurance in being able to beat the bastards at their own sport; the confident expectation based upon startling success of recent manoeuvres, which have actually enabled me to tap in on the intelligence of Scotland Yard itself. This I managed to contrive by promoting a relationship, via Armstead the photographer and his wife Maggie, with their lodger, John Haynes, a former government agent, who in turn happens conveniently to be acquainted with Police Sergeant McIntyre of the Yard. Haynes claims to have conducted some secret investigations in the United States for the Treasury; hinting though not confirming outright, that these were in connection with with the Whitechapel Murders of '88. Convinced, from various details he let fall of the matter, that this is so, my cultivating of Haynes, and through him McIntyre, has to be the masterstroke of all time; an addled agent and a plodding policeman being now regular drinking partners of agreeable Doctor Neill's alter egos -- namely Jack the Ripper and the Lambeth Poisoner -- a double event for the law, if ever there was one, had they only the wit to know it! Dropped it to Haynes that Walter Harper murdered Marsh & Shrivell, Donworth,*

*Clover and Lou Harvey, even pointing out where Lou had lived -- knowing full well he would pass it all on to McIntyre, whom, if and when he questions me about this, I intend to prime with the idea that my ubiquitous friend detective Murray was my secret informant. Downing on invitation a few John Collins, the fools invariably become quite free in their confidences, particular in the case of McIntyre, who can then be relied upon to keep me well abreast of developments concerning the Yard's latest abortive efforts to get their man -- little suspecting that man to be considerably closer than they think!*

Inside the Crown and Cushion Public House, Lambeth, during the latter week of May 1892 two men were engaged in subdued conversation. Police Sergeant McIntyre of the Criminal Investigation Department, Scotland Yard was a shrewd little Irishman with a bristling moustache, waxed to spiky points and an equally prickly personality. He was fortunate in possessing a strong stomach for drink and when off duty was never loathe to sample a few pints in the company of friends and colleagues, with no adverse effect. Professionally he had been known to put this facility to advantage, conveying a quite erroneous impression of drunken stupidity that had snared many a none too wary crook. His companion, John Haynes, whom he had met in April at the Armsteads and knew to work undercover for the Treasury, had a less hardy stomach; and having formed a drinking relationship of several weeks standing with the convivial Cream, was on one occasion thrown sufficiently off his guard to reveal rather more of his background than was prudent. When conducting a criminal investigation however, the contents of Haynes's glass was commonly assigned to the nearest aspidistra. Plants were to flourish in pubs the length and breadth of Lambeth when Haynes had introduced McIntyre to Cream and started after a while to compare notes. Unknown then to McIntyre, the Yard, at a higher level, were proposing to step up their investigation into the poisoning of Marsh and Shrivell, and indeed had already begun to take an interest in the activities of the so-called Doctor Neill, whose appearance fitted admirably with the description of a police witness on the scene at Stamford Street. As a result, Cream gradually became aware that he was being followed and complained to both Haynes and McIntyre, requesting them to make inquiries as to the reason for such a disgraceful invasion of privacy. The display of injured innocence was, however, to McIntyre's mind, hardly in keeping with Cream's brag of having slickly foiled a police conspiracy to entrap him with a prostitute -- or, as he put it, "rip". The detective, who had until then no reason to regard Cream as anyone other than a law-abiding businessman -- obliged with an inquiry post haste. The result of this was to enlighten him to the fact that his superiors regarded the apparently respectable Doctor Neill as their prime suspect in the Lambeth Poisoning cases.

As it emerged from their discussion across the bar-room table, Cream, when overly intoxicated, had boasted to Haynes of having known the late Marsh and Shrivell intimately, and had warned him and McIntyre against one Walter J. Harper -- who, in his opinion was undoubtedly the murderer, having, so Cream claimed, asked him to obtain strychnine. Furthermore, the unaccountably well-informed "Neill" went on to assert that a women called Clover had, like the girls from Stamford Street, died of strychnine poisoning -- not to speak of an Emma Donworth and a Lou Harvey who had also shared that fate. How had he come by this intelligence? Why, through his close friend, a private detective called Murray. McIntyre, now hot on the case, was aware that Clover's body, as a result of information received, had recently been disinterred and, though the inquest was not to take place until June 22nd, had been confidentially advised that it was indeed as full of strychnine as those of the late lamented Marsh and Shrivell. In that there had not yet been any public announcement of this, Cream's detailed knowledge of the matter was, to say the least, surprising. That McIntyre was subsequently unable to trace the passing of a Lou Harvey came as an even greater a surprise, since she happened still to be enjoying excellent health and recall: eventually furnishing a detailed description of the man known as Neill, who had, she was convinced, the previous year attempted to poison her. The conversation continued *sotto voce*, since Cream was due to join them shortly.

"Tell me, Pat, do you know anything of this man Murray?" asked Haynes.

"Only what we have heard from our friend the Doctor", said McIntyre drily. "I made an appointment with Neill on the 24th which he cancelled on a pretext of ill health. Just the same I called upon him later that evening at his lodgings -- not ostensibly on official business, of course, but to commiserate. I explained any inquiries I might make were intended only to protect him from a possible misunderstanding between himself and Scotland Yard -- which, conscious he was being followed, seemed to put him at his ease. "I have some indecent portraits about me, and I've been knocking about with women a good deal. The authorities may have got to hear of it, I daresay." He treated me to one of his meaning smirks. "I hardly suppose a worldly chap like you would consider *that* a crime." Continuing gregariously despite his indisposition, he volunteered that this Murray, a detective, had approached him in Lambeth Palace Road a week or so before the inquest on Marsh and Shrivell. Neill maintained the man had asked him some intimate questions about his fellow lodger, Walter Harper, Neill declining to answer on grounds of discretion. Murray then, according to Neill, handed him a post-marked letter apparently written by himself to the Stamford Street girls, warning them to beware of Harper, since he would serve them as he had done Matilda Clover and Lou Harvey. Again according to Neill the man in question was about 40, around 5 feet 8 or 9 in height, wearing a dark cut-away coat, light trousers and a hard felt hat."

"A heavy moustache and straggling grey hair," Haynes added, the description being identical to that which Cream had also offered him of one, Murray, though without his notes to hand he could not quite place the occasion, nor the context of the conversation.

"Right." McIntyre pulled at his own moustache thoughtfully. "Does it not all strike you, John, as a remarkably accurate description, in all but the straggling hair, of Neill himself?"

"Dashed if it does not!" said Haynes. "Did you manage to get a specimen of his handwriting?"

"Oh yes, he was as usual quite forthcoming. Scrawled a few words on a fine sheet of stationary with a watermark, `Fairfield, Superfine Quality'. Same brand of American paper, as a matter of fact, that was used on a blackmailing letter in our possession, also accusing Walter Harper of murder by strychnine and sent to his father at Barnstable."

"What was his explanation of that?"

"None, for I did not request one at this stage -- like yourself I want him to continue regarding me as a trusted pal -- encourage a few more confidences in a friendly sort of way, you see. I merely observed that he seemed very well posted with regard to the Lambeth Poisonings. 'Yes,' said Neill, quick as a flash, 'I have followed the matter closely in the *British Medical Journal*. Being a medical man, I take an interest in matters of this kind.'"

"Lambeth Poisoner or not, he certainly is an odd enough customer," said Haynes. "I was on an omnibus with him not long after the Marsh and Shrivell murders, when a newsboy cried out that a suspect had been arrested in the Stamford Street case. Neill turned positively green, and would have dashed down then and there amid the traffic but for my persuading him to remain on board until we had reached Charing Cross. This he did, though obviously in a state of great trepidation; and at the station descended the steps three at a time. He then bought four copies of the evening papers and scanned the contents like a man possessed; though quite unable to focuss on the print what with his faulty eyesight and the news-sheets quivering in his hands like Autumn leaves. Finally he exclaimed: "For mercy's sake, John, read this out to me." I duly obliged and when he heard the account had no connection with the poisoning of Marsh and Shrivell, appeared much relieved; but noting my own dubious expression passed the whole incident off as a mark of his great anxiety to ensure that the murderer had been brought to justice."

"I trust we shall be able to put his mind at rest on that score," commented McIntyre, directing a stream of saliva accurately into a nearby spittoon. "Thinks he's too clever by half for the likes of us, our Doctor Neill. Not enough evidence to act on yet...but we shall have him in the end, John; for I have not the slightest doubt that he's our man."

"Perhaps in more senses than one, Pat" mused Haynes, who had been struck by an astounding theory -- one which might never be proved, but which nevertheless, effectively linked the sadistic Lambeth Poisoner with an equally vicious prostitute killer -- one who had apparently disappeared off the face of the earth four years ago, and yet whose psychological makeup certainly bore the same stamp as that of the Lambeth Poisoner. He drew a cigar from. his waistcoat pocket and fumbling at the tip with his thumb nail found that Cream had come up behind him. "Pray allow me," he said silkily, preferring Haynes his own platinum cigar cutter. "Just in the nick of time -- am I not a pretty sharp fellow, my friend, ha-ha?" The humour, if it could be construed as such, was lost on Haynes and McIntyre, though not the note of triumph in Cream's peculiar laugh.

*103, Lambeth Palace Road, London S.E.1.*

*June 1st, 1892.*

*The Bosses are now undoubtedly closing in, I have it both from McIntyre and Haynes; but am however supremely confident from what McIntyre has let out that the Yard have not a jot of concrete evidence against me, and what is more must fail to obtain any, even though the inquest on Clover starts this month. I am of course always one step ahead of the bastards, owing to information readily obtainable from the peeler, who when he has had a few too many can be counted upon to keep me abreast of the Yard's movements. As for Haynes priding himself on being a secret agent -- what a laugh -- after a drink or two he continues equally loose tongued as McIntyre, childishly easily to control and with a commendable eagerness to tell all he knows. Between both, they could not bag a blind beggar!*

*Only as a precaution, since the Yard have been watching me since April, I had already passed on most of my writings to Laura, who has sworn on the Bible never to betray me. She can be relied upon absolutely to obey my instructions, hiding everything in the Japanned box buried beneath a rose-bed in her garden. The soul of honour, I am certain the dear girl will respect my wishes to abstain from reading the material, which I have anyway placed in sealed envelopes and wrapped in oilcloth. For obvious reasons, from now until the whole affair blows over I shall discontinue writing my journal, mailing this last sealed episode to Berkampstead for safekeeping. Sleaper, like Laura, is also governed in most respects by my wishes and can be relied upon to prevent other of my possessions falling into the hands of the police. Returning from a long weekend and duly noting, with some amusement, a fellow posted across the street holding an inverted copy of* **The Police Gazette,** *I took the precaution of destroying an old note-book containing a few Ripper references, and had Sleaper burn them. Also placed in her safekeeping was my cash box, wrapped in newspaper and securely tied with string, containing one or two trinkets and other personal items, thus covering myself should they manage to obtain a warrant to search my premises.*

*Thanks to my skillful manipulation of Haynes and MacIntyre I am sitting pretty. That the Yard cannot support a single charge against me I am one hundred per cent sure. The fact remains there never has been and never will be a man among them smart enough to outclass Thomas N. Cream.* **The Lord is on my side, He is my helper, and I shall gloat over my enemies.**

On the 25th of May Patrick McIntyre had called again on "Doctor Neill", for the purpose of receiving a general record of his activities while in England. Cream had pronounced himself quite agreeable to supplying such details as he could recollect, though, in bed pleading debility, had appointed the ever obliging Miss Sleaper as his scribe.

McIntyre read:

`I arrived in Liverpool on the 1st October, 1891; came ashore on the 2nd October; spent three days in Liverpool; arrived in London on the 5th October; put up at Anderton's Hotel; spent two or three days there; then removed to 103 Lambeth Palace Road, where I remained till the 6th of January, 1892, on which night I returned to Liverpool, on my way to America. There I remained until the 23rd of March, on which day I sailed from New York for Liverpool. I arrived in Liverpool on the 1st April;*

> *in London on the 2nd of April; returned to Liverpool on the 4th or 5th of April; spent two or three days in Liverpool, after which I returned to London; put up at Edward's Hotel; spent two or three days there; then went down into the country, where I spent several days, after which I came to live at 103 Lambeth Palace Road, where I still reside.*

> *THOMAS NEILL.*

There were two omissions from this statement, one which McIntyre spotted instantly, the other relating to a fact he was not as yet acquainted with -- to wit that "Neill" had actually visited London way before October 1981 and studied at St. Thomas's Hospital under his real name. Had Cream revealed this, there was always the slight risk that on further inquiry his questionable relationship with the late Fordyce might at last come to light, maybe through criminal associates who had been privy to their dodge. In which case, thought Cream, it was always possible that some bright spark like his former attorney Marshall Hall, now a prominent criminal lawyer, would hear of it and make a connection with Cream and that mysterious 'Fordyce' he had defended on a bigamy charge in 1888, the year of the Ripper -- when Cream was supposed to be still inside. Why, they might even now nail him for the Whitechapel jobs, should Hall identify Cream as his former client; thus establishing that he had actually been in England during the Ripper crimes. Cream had trouble enough, heaven knew, without chancing that eventuality.

McIntyre folded the statement and snapped it safely inside his bag. "'Phis should keep everyone satisfied down at the Yard, Neill, except on one minor point..1 believe Miss Sleaper we may dispense with your company for the present."

"That point being?" McIntyre remained silent until Miss Sleaper, her ears practically flapping, had reluctantly left the room. "Come man, speak up. what is your problem?" Cream sounded jittery.

"Not mine but yours, Neill," corrected McIntyre, noting the drops of sweat which had which appeared on his adversary's brow and which were not, he suspected wholly accountable to his poor state of health. "There is here some slight discrepancy which can, I am sure, be easily cleared up."

McIntyre fully enjoyed dangling his adversary on a string, if not yet a rope, pausing deliberately for several moments before adding: "Would you be so good, just for the record, to tell me what you were doing on the night of the Stamford Street poisonings, so that I may set you straight with my colleagues; for I see no reference at all to April 11th last in your statement."

"By all means, old chap." Cream unwound, confident that he could through Laura easily arrange an alibi. "So soon as I get out of bed, and I am able to look up some dates, I will be able to fix my whereabouts at that particular time, but," -- beaming -- "I believe I was down at Berkhamstead on the 11th, come to think of it."

Next day McIntyre ran into him in Lambeth Palace Road -- not wholly by accident, as Cream at once realized. It was an unpleasant surprise, since he had thought now to have put the Yard entirely off the scent. Managing, however, to maintain an icy calm Cream announced: "I am going away today at three o'clock" -- asking, just a shade too casually:" Will I be arrested if I do so, do you suppose, old man?"

McIntyre's response set Cream even more on his guard. "I cannot tell you; if you walk across with me to Scotland Yard I will make inquiries." Cream made as if to go along with him until they were halfway across Westminster Bridge, when, unable to conceal his increased misgivings he turned on the detective.

"I will not go any further with you," he rapped. "I am suspicious of you, and I believe you are playing me double. You sent a 'rip' after me to meet me outside the *British Medical Journal* office."

"Are you out of your mind, Neill? How could I do so when I was unaware you were going there?" Cream, with some effort, affected to accept this reasoning. He had to his peril revealed himself to be rattled, and sought hastily to excuse the outburst.

"Forgive me, Pat, I am not yet quite recovered from my sickness --still feel a trifle on edge; and convalescence is hardly aided by having been, for reasons even you and Haynes cannot comprehend, selected by the Yard as scapegoat in the Lambeth Poisonings. It occurs to me, and may indeed not be far from the truth, that I am in fact being persecuted by your colleagues only because of my American accent. Quite disgraceful that a man's speech can be held against him by those in authority, if such is the case." Cream, true to form, had talked himself into a mood of angry recrimination. Tension escalating, his voice rose above the clatter of passing traffic on the bridge to a choleric roar. "These investigations are a slur upon my reputation and I intend to protest to your Bosses at the highest level.

"And so you should, so you should." McIntyre had never had any valid reason to question Cream's sanity; but the absurdity of these assertions and the manner in which they were delivered struck him as falling not far short of a madman's ravings. He elected to humour them on the same paranoid theme. "Between ourselves, old chap, the Yard has been riddled with prejudice against you Yankees since '88, when it was generally thought that Jack the Ripper was an American. We at the Department came under a great deal of criticism, I can tell you, for letting that devil slip through our fingers; and as a result, to this day the Force have quite a down on anyone with the even slightest drawl."

"I shall instruct Waters without further delay to forward a strong letter of complaint to whoever is responsible. Or maybe on second thoughts I should consider hiring myself a better Solicitor." He lowered his voice conspiratorially. "Say, Pat, can you suggest someone who can get me out of this fix?"

"Indeed I cannot Neill. It would not be consistent with my position to do so." With a tremendous effort of will Cream forced himself to appear calm. He could not afford to lose McIntyre's good offices at this stage. "Come, let us say no more about it. How about a drink?" McIntyre hesitated and, to avoid the very real possibility of Cream absconding before the Public Prosecutor had been applied to for a warrant, decided for the last time to play along.

Next day "Doctor Neill" was paid another visit at his lodgings in Lambeth Palace Road, this time by Inspector John Bennett Tunbridge, ostensibly responding to Cream's complaint of being watched. His fiancee, Laura Sabbatini, dressed becomingly in a bonnet and gown of lavender silk, had been sent for and sat primly holding a paper parcel; supplying that very air of polite respectability that had somehow eluded Cream.

Tunbridge was a heavy built, florid faced, bluff character looking thoroughly ill at ease in a plain-clothes outfit of black bowler hat, dark suit and starched shirt, all of which seemed at least a size too small. Cream in contrast was dressed in the latest cutaway jacket, silk shirt and tie secured with a diamond pin, and an impeccably creased pair of pants. A stiff dose of cocaine had set him way above the experiences of yesterday, the Inspector receiving the impression of a man admirably in control of the situation.

"Good afternoon, Inspector. What may I do for you?"

"Afternoon, Doctor Neill. Afternoon Ma'am. Good of you to see me at such short notice, I'm sure, Sir." Tunbridge fiddled uncomfortably with his collar, embarrassed at being obliged to conduct his investigation in the presence of a lady.

"It is perfectly in order to speak before my fiancee, Inspector." Cream gave Laura an affectionate peck on the cheek. "You and I have nothing to hide from one another, do we, my dear?"

"Thank you, Doctor Neill. I shall try to be brief. I have called on behalf of Scotland Yard, concerning a letter that arrived by hand this morning from your Solicitors, Messrs. Waters and Bryan, registering a complaint, Sir, that you are being watched by the police."

"I am under that distinct impression, Inspector, and have no intention of allowing myself to be stalked like a common criminal. This unwarranted outrage is interfering with my business, and I do not intend to tolerate it. Unless the Yard call off their hounds immediately I shall sue for damages."

"You must pardon the Doctor for speaking so plainly, Inspector. He has, I am sure, done nothing to be ashamed of, and has every right to protest," said Laura.

"Indeed he has, ma'am, and may protest as much as he sees fit. Now, Sir, speaking of business -- what, if I may make so bold, is the nature of yours in this country?"

"I have already made an account of that to Sergeant McIntyre," snapped Cream impatiently; "but if you insist on wasting my time further, I will state again that I came to England for the first time in October last, 1891, to consult an occulist; that I am as you know a doctor of medicine, practised in America, underwent a serious illness some time ago, as a result of which night calls no longer agreed with me. In consequence I gave up my practice and since February have acted as an agent for the Harvey Drug Company of Saratoga Springs, New York. I had been travelling as their representative throughout Canada until arriving here."

"Quite so, Sir." Tunbridge had been taking laborious notes, and now paused to shoot a question at Cream: "In connection with your new occupation would you not be obliged to carry about a supply of drugs, including certain poisons such as, perhaps, strychnine?"

"Of course, Inspector. Let me show you my medicine case. Here for instance is a bottle labelled one sixteenth of a grain of strychnine."

"What are these pills composed of, Sir?"

"I have just detailed that, Inspector. One sixteenth grain of strychnine and a little sugar coating,"

"At that rate this bottle contains quite a large quantity of strychnine, and would be highly dangerous if it fell into the hands of the public, would you not say, Sir?"

"It is not intended to sell them to the public direct, but only to chemists and surgeons, who will dispense them in their proper quantities.

"On the 26th May last year had you, by chance, any knowledge that a woman called Matilda Clover died from strychnine, Sir?"

"I have no such knowledge, and no suggestions had been made to me that the woman had died of strychnine. I had heard her body had been exhumed." Under such pressure Cream's nerves were tending once more to fray. "Now see here, Inspector, I do not know what you are getting at, but in view of the seriousness of your implications, I refuse to answer any further questions without my Solicitor. Now kindly show at least some consideration for a man's privacy and get the hell out of here!"

"Language, Thomas, dear! Laura was highly startled, "What ever will the Inspector think?"

"Don't upset yourself, Miss. The doctor is bound to be just a bit put out by my questioning, him being a respectable medical man and all. But I'm only doing my duty -- no offence meant, Sir, and none taken."

Tunbridge's next interview was with Doctor Harper of Barnstable and his son Walter. Comparing the threatening letter they had received with the example of Cream's handwriting obtained from McIntyre and from a chemist who had supplied him with strychnine, the Inspector returned at once to London. On the 3rd of June 1892 Tunbridge applied for a warrant to arrest Doctor Thomas Neill for extortion. The warrant was duly executed as dusk began to fall in the Lambeth Palace Road. Cream had exited his lodgings top hat and tailed for a pleasant night's entertainment, which as it turned out was to be spent in an unsalubrious cell at Bow Street police station. When Tunbridge, accompanied by McIntyre, had made his arrest, Cream, full of cocaine and certain they could not make the charges stick, cockily announced:

"You have got the wrong man. Fire away!" Tunbridge showed him the envelope in which the letter had been posted to Doctor Harper:

"This is what you are accused of sending." Cream glanced at the writing on the envelope. "That is not my writing."

Tunbridge withdrew the letter. Cream made no comment. At Bow Street he was equally non-commitaL Demanding to communicate with his Solicitor he was supplied with a telegram form, but snapped:

"I write nothing. You can send it for me."

Now that their suspect was in custody, the police lost no time searching his premises and came up with one or two items which Cream, in his cleaning up exercise, had overlooked, including:

> a medicine case containing assorted drugs and poisons
> a morphia injector
> a sheet of waterproof
> a Gladstone bag
> 6 copies of "The Medical Journal"
> 4 obscene photographs
> 2 memorial cards
> a soft felt hat
> a note of Alice Marsh's address, in her own handwriting; and
> a scrap of paper on which was scrawled:

> "Oct. 19, M.C. Oct.19; Oct.13; Ap. 11, E.S., Apr.11; Oct.23, .L,. H. Oct.23.

It recorded the premeditated murder of Matilda Clover, October 19, 1891 (and duly accomplished on that date), that of Ellen Donworth, Oct. 13, (1891); Emma Shrivell, April 11, (1892) -- and Louisa (Lou) Harvey, a.k.a Harris, whose death Cream had recorded as October 23rd, (1891). However the following letter was received by the Bow Street magistrate during the June 1892 hearing of Cream's case, proving that lady to be very much alive.

## PROOFS OF IDENTITY OF NIELL.

*Sir,*

*Met a man outside of St. James Hall regent St. 12.30 one night in October, about the 20th. Had been to the Alhambra and seen him there, earlier the same night. Went with him from St. James to an hotel in Berwick St. Oxford St. Stayed there with him all night left about 8 oc. in the morning. Made an appointment with him to meet the same night at 7.30 on the Embankment. Met him same night opposite Charing X. Underground R. Station. Walked with him to the Northumberland Public-house, had glass of wine, and then walked back to the Embankment. Were he gave me two capsules. But not liking the look of the thing, I pretended to put them in my mouth. But kept them in my hand. And when he happened to look away, I threw them over the Embankment. He then said that he had to be at St. Thomas's Hospital, left me, and gave me 5s. to go to the Oxford Music Hall. Promising to meet me outside at 11 oc. But he never came. I had told him that I was living at Townshend Rd. St. Johns Wood but I gave him the wrong number. I never saw him again till about 3 weeks after. When I had moved from St Johns Wood to Stamford St. When I happened to be at Piccadilly Circus and I saw him, I spoke to him. he asked me to have a drink, I had a drink, in the Regent, Air St. He promised to meet me at 11 oc. on the same night. He had not seemed as if he knew me while we were drinking. So I said to him don't you remember me. he said no. I said not that night when you promised to meet me outside the Oxford. He then said whats your name. I said Louisa Harvey. He seemed surprised, said no more, and walked quickly away. And never turned up that night. I saw him once again, about a month afterward with a young lady down the Strand, and I never saw him again. I have a witness who saw him give me capsules on the Embankment who could identify him. I had not troubled to read the case particular till Friday night, when I happened to read it in the star. I was struck with the resemblance. So I got the Telegraph next morning, saw my name mentioned. so I was almost sure. He being under the impression that I took the capsules, and either dropped dead in the street, or music hall.*

*I had told him that I was a servant. He wore Gold rimmed Glasses and had very Peculiar eyes. As far as I can remember he had dress suit on, and long mackintosh on his arm. He spoke with a foreign Twang. He asked me if I had ever been in America. I said no. He had an Old fashioned Gold Watch, with an Hair or silk fob Chain and a seal. Said he had been in the Army. I noticed he was a very hairy man, he said he had never been married.*

*I enclose paragraph cut from Daily Telegraph of Saturday.*

*Address*
    *Mrs Harris*
        *87 Upper North Street Brighton*

When the case closed on June 28th 1892, Cream remained in custody.

# PART 7

On Wednesday, 22nd June, 1892, Mr. A. Braxton Hicks, the Mid-Surrey Coroner, opened an inquest at the Tooting Vestry Hall, in connection with the death of Matilda Clover, aged twenty-seven, a single woman, which occurred at 27, Lambeth Road, on 21st October, 1891, from the effects of strychnine poisoning. The exhumation of the body took place on 5th May, in consequence of certain facts which came to the knowledge of the police during their investigation of the charges against Thomas Neill, who was under remand at the Bow Street Police Court, accused of sending letters attempting to blackmail Dr. Harper of Barnstaple, and others. One letter, which mentioned that Matilda Clover died through being poisoned by strychnine, was dated 28th November, 1891, five weeks after the death of the deceased, and was addressed to Dr. W. H. Broadbent.

## DEPOSITION OF WITNESSES.

DR. WILLIAM HENRY BROADBENT, M.D., of 34, Seymour Street, Portman Square, W., stated that he was physician to St. Mary's Hospital. On 30th November, 1891, he received by post a letter (produced). He had never heard of the Miss Clover mentioned in the letter, and he had never been at 27, Lambeth Road. He knew nothing whatever of the writer of the letter. Having read it, he immediately handed it to the police authorities. The handwriting was not that of any person he was acquainted with.

The Coroner read the letter, which was signed "M. Malone," and demanded 2,500 pounds for information relating to Dr. Broadbent's connection with the death of Clover.

ANNIE CLEMENTS, a charwoman, of 18 Joiners Street, Westminster Bridge Road, said that she knew a young woman named Ellen Donworth, who died on 13th October. She lived at 8, Duke Street, Westminster Bridge Road. Witness used frequently to see her, living in the same house. She also knew a young man named Ernest Linnell. On the Saturday before her death Donworth received a letter by the first post, which she said was from a gentleman. She also received a letter on the Tuesday morning by the same post, which, she said, was from the same gentleman, whom she was to see outside the York Hotel, Waterloo Road. She was to take back the letter to the gentleman to prove that she had received it. She said she expected to hear from him every other day. The gentleman she told witness, was bald-headed and cross-eyed. When Donworth went out she was quite well, but an hour and a half afterwards she was brought back, very ill, by a gentleman. Dr. Lowe's assistant saw her. She said the tall man had given her something to drink out of a bottle -- some white stuff. She did not say where the stuff was given her, but said it was the same man who had written the letter.

ELIZABETH MASTERS:

On the 17th inst. she was shown some men at Bow Street police station. She did not recognise Neill at first but she did when she saw him with his hat off. She had no doubt he was the man who went with her and afterwards to the music hall. When he was at the music hall he was wearing a hard bowler hat with a flat top and a black, dull waterproof coat. She noticed he had a heavy gold chain and a watch. On Friday he wore a silk hat. She remarked how different he looked in it.

ELIZABETH MAY:

At the music hall she noticed that Neill's eyes looked very strange. The witness identified a photograph of Clover. When Neill passed the house Masters remarked how different he looked without a hat.

EMILY SLEAPER, landlady at 103 Lambeth Palace Road...Dr. Neill came to reside there on 7th October, having taken the second floor front room on the previous day...He stayed there until 6th January...A week after he came there he began to wear spectacles, and he bought a new silk hat...She understood that he came to England for the benefit of his health. In October she remembered his asking her to take a letter round to Lambeth Road. She asked him what it was for, and he replied, "I know a girl there, and think she has been poisoned. I want to find out if she is dead or not."...Witness said, "No, you had better go yourself, as I do not like to go under the circumstances." After she had declined to go he said he would inquire himself, adding "I think I know who poisoned her." Witness asked him who he thought it was, and he replied, "Lord Russell." That was about the time the Russell matrimonial suit was on...In January he went to America, returning to England on 7th April, when he engaged the second floor back room. When he came back he told her he was agent for the Harvey Drug Company, and showed her the case of pills ppr~oduced. He remained in her house until he was arrested. He always seemed to have money, but never saw any one on business... She had another gentleman stopping as a lodger in her house, named Harper. One day when Mr. Harper was away Neill came into his room, where witness was, and spoke about him. He asked what kind of gentleman he was and where he lived...She remembered hearing about two girls, named Marsh and Shrivell, being murdered by strychnine poisoning and Neill told her he wanted to see the inquest in a Sunday paper, remarking that it was a cold-blooded murder. About three weeks after the newspaper incident Neill came in in a very excited state and spoke about the deaths of Marsh and Shrivell. He said, "Do you know who poisoned these two girls in Stamford Street?" Witness said, "No", and he said, If I tell you, you are not to tell any one; it was Mr. Harper...After that he said the girls had received a letter warning them that Mr. Harper was poisoning them, and not to take the stuff he would give them...When the detectives were watching Neill the latter remarked to witness that it was a very good thing she did not go to the house in Lambeth Road, as they were going to exhume the body. He came in one morning, and said the house was being watched. He did not say why, but witness said, "They are watching you." He replied, "They have made a mistake, but as I am an American they are suspicious of me." He afterwards said they were watching the house for Mr. Harper. When she asked him why he took such a interest in the inquest of Marsh and Shrivell, he said he thought the scoundrel ought to be brought to justice.

THE COUNTESS RUSSELL stated that in December last she was staying at the Savoy Hotel. While there she received a letter addressed to herself, which she showed to several persons, including Mr. George Lewis. In that letter her husband was accused of the murder of a woman named Clover. It was addressed from the Lambeth Road. She could not remember whether strychine was mentioned, but it certainly said "by poison". Witness was positive, the name mentioned was Clover, and fancied the Christian name was Matilda, but could not swear as to that.

CHARLOTTE VOGT, the landlady of 118 Stamford Street, stated that Alice Marsh and Emma Shrivell lodged at her house, ocupying the front and back room on the second floor. On 11th April witness saw them both during the day. She retired to rest between eleven and twelve, and was wakened about half-past two by her husband. In consequence of what he said, she went downstairs, and found Marsh lying on her face in the passage. As she seemed vey ill, witness sent for the police and a cab. She afterwards heard Shrivell screaming, and upong going upstairs to her room she found her on the bed calling for "Alice." Marsh was only partially dressed.

Police-Constable GEORGE CUMLEY, 211L, said that on the night in question he was about ten yards from 118 Stamford Street when he saw a gentleman leave the house and walk away. There was a lamp opposite the door, and witness saw his profile. He was wearing gold-rimmed s ectacles, and was between forty-five and fifty years of age. He was about 5 feet 10 inches in height, and was wearing a dark overcoat and a silk hat. Shortly afterwards witness was called into the house and saw Marsh in the passage in great agony. Having administered emetics to the two girls, he placed Marsh in a cab and conveyed her to the hospital, but she was dead when she arrived there. He had asked her what she had eaten, and she replied, "I have had some supper, and a gentleman gave us three pills each." Witness said, "Was it the gentleman you let out at a quarter to two with glasses on," and she replied, "Yes,: adding that they called him "Fred". She described the pills as being long, thin ones. On the night of 12th May witness again saw the gentleman in Westminster Bridge Road, but he was then wearing a short coat. He believed Neill was the man2 as he had seen him several times. The man went in the direction of York Road.

Police-Constable EVERSIELD, 194L, stated that he found Shrivell in the second floor room also in great agony, He questioned her, and she said that she had been three weeks in London from Brighton. She explained that she and Marsh made the acquaintance of a man named Fred, who was very bald on the top of his head, and wore spectacles and a silk hat. He said he gave her three long pills. Witness made a note of the description she gave to him.

MR. WALTER JOSEPH HARPER, M.R.C.S., L.R.C.P., of the Terrace, Braunton, North Devon, said that until April last he was a student at St. Thomas's Hospital. For two and a half years he had lodged at 103 Lambeth Palace Road...He never knew or heard of Alice Marsh, Emma Shrivell, Ellen Donworth, or Matilda Clover. The first he heard of the names was when they came out at the inquiry. He had never heard of the name of Lou Harvey. He had never spoken to any one about the poisoning of these girls. He never had anything to do with a Mr. W. H. Murray.

MISS LAURA SABBATINI stated that she resided at Chapel Street, Berkhamstead, Herts. She made the acquaintance of Dr. Neill in November last, when she was in London. He was introduced to her as Dr. Thomas Neill Cream, and he told her he was a doctor in America...Shortly after she became known to him he proposed marriage to her, and she accepted him... The letter produced contained the proposal of marriage. On 6th January Neill went to America for the purpose, as he said, of seeing about his father's estate. Previous to this, on 23rd December, he made a Will in her favour, in which he described himself as "Thomas Neill Cream, physician, late of the city of Quebec," and left her the whole of his property. (Will produced)...The letter proposing marriage and the will were both in his own handwriting.

THE *CORONER* proceeded to sum up, remarking that the object of the inquiry was *prima facie* to ascertain the cause of the death of Matilda Clover. He would ask the jury if they had any reasonable doubt that the letter written to Dr. Broadbent was penned by Neill. He could not guide their opinions, but he had no doubt in his mind that the handwriting was the same as that contained in the will and other documents. If that person were Neill, he was the man who knew that the deceased died from strychnine poisoning, that her name was Matilda Clover, and she lived at 27, Lambeth Road, and that she died in October. It was impossible to deal with the case of Clover without bringing in the others, but it must be borne in mind that Neill was the only person that assumed to have a knowledge of the death of Clover from strychnine poisoning, for he mentioned it, not only in his letter to Dr. Broadbent, but also to the witnesses M'Intyre, Haynes and Sleaper. Could they, then, have any doubt, on the face of it, that Clover died from the effects of strychnine administered to her by Neill, who in that event ought to be charged with her murder?

Neill was sworn:

CORONER: -- What is your name?

NEILL -- I decline to answer any question in regard to that.

CORONER -- But you must tell me that.

NEILL -- No, sir; I have got my instructions what to do, and I shall abide by them whatever the consequences are.

CORONER: -- Is your name Thomas Neill Cream?

NEILL -- I decline to answer that question.

CORONER -- Are you a qualified medical man? --(No answer).

The jury retired, and, after twenty minutes' deliberation, returned into Court with a verdict, "That Matilda Clover died from the effects of strychnine poisoning, and that the poison was administered by Thomas Neill with intent to destroy life."

THE CORONER said that was a verdict of "Wilful murder" against Neill.

**BEFORE THE VERDICT WAS ANNOUNCED, THE CORONER STATED THAT HE HAD RECEIVED THE FOLLOWING LETTER, ADDRESSED TO MR. HICKS, VESTRY HALL, TOOTING:-**

*"Dear Sir, -- The man that you have in your power, Dr. Neill, is as innocent as you are. Knowing him by sight, I disguised myself like him, and made the acquaintance of the girls that have been poisoned. I gave them the pills to cure them of all their earthly miseries, and they died. Miss L. Harris has got more sense than I thought she had, but I shall have her yet. Mr. P. Harvey might also follow Lou Harvey out of this world of care and woe. Lady Russell is quite right about the letter, and so am I. Lord Russell had a hand in the poisoning of Clover. Nellie Donworth must have stayed out all night, or else she would not have been complaining of pains and cold when Annie Clements saw her. If I were you: I would release Dr. T. Neill, or you might*

*get into trouble. His innocence will be declared sooner or later, and when he is free he might sue you for damages.*

*Yours respectfully, JUAN POLLEN, alias JACK THE RIPPER.*

*Beware all. I warn but once."*

Dr. T. Neill was not, however, freed on the strength of this, and on the 18th July was formally re-charged by Inspector John Bennett Tunbridge with the wilful murder of Matilda Clover. Cream was relatively unconcerned, since in his view they had not sufficient evidence to convict him of any of the Lambeth Poisonings. Later however he demanded of Tunbridge with greater anxiety as to whether "anything is going to be done in the *other* cases?," adding "You will be sure to let me know."

Tunbridge assumed him to be referring only to the murders of Donworth, Marsh and Shrivell. In that he may not have been entirely correct.

The venue of this bizarre melodrama now transferred to the Old Bailey, featuring much the same cast, including, large as life, the miraculously resurrected Miss Louisa Harris.

-- "Thomas Neill, you are indicted for the wilful murder of Alice Marsh, Ellen Donworth, Emma Shrivell, and Matilda Clover; also for sending to Joseph Harper a letter demanding money with menaces, without any reasonable or probable cause; for sending a similar letter to William Henry Broadbent; and for attempting to administer to Louisa Harris a large quantity of strychnine with intent to murder her. Do you plead `Guilty' or `Not Guilty'.

--"Not Guilty."

THE ATTORNEY-GENERAL: "The prisoner, whose name is Thomas Neill Cream, stands indicted under the name by which he was better known in this country, namely of Thomas Neill, with the murder of a young woman named Matilda Clover on 20th October, 1891, the means employed being the administration of strychnine."

EXCERPTS FROM LETTERS TO MISS LAURA
SABBATINI FROM THOMAS NEILL CREAM, WHICH
HE WROTE WHILE IN CUSTODY DURING 1892

### June 28th, 1892.

*I was perfectly safe till you swore a ainst me, but how it will end now I do not know. You know, dear, you never saw me write a letter in your life, and yet you went on the stand and swore that my will and my letter which you gave to the authorities were in my writing. Now, my dear Laura, you must correct this. The next time you are on the stand you must swear positively that you never saw me write and that you cannot identify any of my writings. If you do this you will help to save me. Mr. Waters win tell you how to do it and correct this terrible injury you have done me. When the officers ask any questions about me, tell them you don't know, as you don't remember. When they submit my writing to you and ask you if it is mine, tell them "you do not know". For God's sake burn anything you have with my writin, on. If you annoy me in any way or do me any injury in my time of trouble, you are going to get into terrible trouble, and I cannot save you from it; but my solicitor and I will protect you as long as you are true to me and do me no harm. I may want the loan of some money from you until I get some from America. If you should run short, dear, borrow some from Winnie, and I will make it all right with her by and by; you know I paid her what you owed her before. Let me know, dear, the least money you can live comfortably on till I can get out of my troubles, as I want to make some arrangement for you.*

### July 4th, 1892.

*I shall never threaten you, my darling. All I ask of you, dear, is to say and do nothing that will hurt me, or annoy my counsel. I would not have written as I did, but I was afraid you would bring terrible trouble on your own head by your conduct. I shall say no more, now, darling. In future say you don't remember, or you don't know, to every question you are asked about me. I do not blame you now, for I have found out it was mother made you tell about the letters. This is mother's gratitude for what I did for her. I cannot tell how long this will last. They are putting it off from week to week, trying to get evidence against me, but they cannot get any evidence that I committed murder or sent blackmailing letters to any one. They are getting desperate, and have sent more detectives to America to try and get evidence there. They have put more detectives on the case to try and get more evidence, and I am sure they are watching you, and they will watch you till this is all over. They think you know a great deal more than you have told. They will be after you again, you may depend on that. I wish we could manage it so that we could get married, then you could not testify against me; for a man's wife is never allowed to testify against him. Many thanks, darling, for your great kindness in lending me the ten pounds. I wanted it badly till I get more from America. They searched all my trunks and clothing at 103 Lambeth Palace Road, but they got nothing for their pains; I was ready for them. If the authorities had a strong case or a big pile of evidence against me, they would not have put my case off till next Thursday, but they cannot prove that I committed any; now, like Micawber, they are playing a waiting game -- waiting to see if something will turn up; but it won't, my darling. You need not be afraid of that. Now, my dear Laura, you must cheer up; be brave, my darling. I would be glad to have you come to Holloway and see me, but I cannot hear you, my darling, and it is not safe for you to come, because you are being to closely watched; they are trying hard to get more evidence against me. It makes me feel terribly bad, too, after you go away. I am so lonely without you. Why did you not let me know you were so fond of me when I was with you? Your letters are a revelation to me. I know now that you love me, but I never felt sure of it before. I was always fond of you. I could not help it. I became infatuated with you, and the longer I knew you the fonder I became. If I had known then, as I know now, that you are so fond of me, how much happier I should have been. It is that knowledge that is worrying me so much now that I am away from you. I am glad that you are sticking to me, for if you ever left me I would Madly lose my life. I care nothing at all for life without you.*

*July 14th, 1892.*

*Do not believe Sergeant M'Intyre's evidence that he swore to yesterday when he says I spoke ill of you to him. So help my God, it is a lie. They are doing this to make you angry and get you to swear against me.*

*26th July, 1892.*

*My dear Laura.*

*Was at Bow Street yesterday, and heard such **good** news that I have not been able to sleep since. A member of Parliament sent me word that he had over two hundred witnesses to clear me if I wanted them. I am going to use some of them, as their evidence **will clear me.** Mr. Waters will have some news for you on Saturday orMonday next. Be sure and look your best in Court next week, as my friends are always in Court now.*

*Yours for ever*

*NEILL.*

*August 5th, 1892.*

*My darling Laura,*

*I really do not understand you. Last week you found fault with me because I did not recognise you in Court, and on Tuesday I could not get you to look when I turned round. What do you mean by it? I cannot write from Holloway unless you acknowledge receipt of every letter I send you. How am I to know the police are not getting hold of my letters if you do not let me know you are receiving them? I am very ill with bowel complaint, and when I think of the harm you have done me in giving up my will and letter to the police, it makes me wild. I hope to God I will never meet your mother again.*

*London, 16th August, 1892.*

*My dear Laura,*

*The fact that I have never been seen with Donworth, Clover, Marsh, or Shrivel/ ought to satisfy you that the authorities cannot **prove** I **murdered** them. **Constance Lingfield swore I was not the man she saw with Donworth. Lucy Rose** refused to identify me as the man **she saw with Clover** on the night of her death.*

***Policeman Comely** refused to swear I was the man **he saw coming out of Marsh and Shrivell's house on the morning of their death.** Now, how are they going to prove I murdered them. Dr. Stevenson's evidence is very favourable to me, and it alone would clear in the Clover and Marsh and Shrivell case. The strychnine pills I bought from the Harvey Drub Company were sold to a passenger on the ".Britannic and we have sent for him to prove it. So, you see, I have a complete answer to that. Three witnesses at the Coroner's inquest swore falsely, and the authorities knew it, and did not call them at the Police Court. Robert Taylor, Clover's uncle, was one of them. If the authorities could prove I murdered these girls, do you think my case would have dragged as it has done since last June. The blackmailing case has become very weak through your evidence that you could not swear to my writing.*

***The longer the authorities drag the matter shows they cannot get the evidence they want and require to convict.** Be sure and send every pill-box and every bottle you have with the labels of Priests or the Harvey Drug Company to Mr. Waters at once. Do not degrade yourself by conversing with Ward or Tonbridge. **We caught Haynes and Tonbridge***

**swearing falsely last week.** *Love to you now, my dear little girl, from*

*Yours affectely,*

*NEILL.*

Despite Cream's assidious manipulation of Laura, it had, infuriatingly, been her evidence which turned out to be among the most damaging.

"The third time he came", she had testified, "he asked me to write some letters for him. I asked him why he wanted me to write them. He refused to give me any reason; I do not recollect exactly what he said. I don't think I asked him more than once. He dictated some letters to me. Yes, this is one of the letters --

*London, 2nd May, 1892.*

*To Coroner Wyatt,*
*St. Thomas's Hospital,*
*London.*

*Dear Sir,*
*Will you please give the enclosed letter to the Foreman of the Coroner's jury, at the inquest on Alice Marsh and Emma Shrivell, and oblige,*

*Yours respectfully*
*Wm. H. Murray.*

I wrote the address on the envelope -- I wrote this letter to the Foreman of the Coroner's jury:-

*London, 2nd May, 1892*

*To the Foreman of the Coroner's Jury in the cases of Alice Marsh and Emma Shrivell.*

Dear Sir,

*I beg to inform you that one of my operators has positiveproof that Walter J. Harper, a medical student of St. Thomas's Hospital, and anon of Dr. Harper, of Bear Street, Barnstaple, is responsible for the deaths of Alice Marsh and Emma Shrivell, he having poisoned those girls with strychnine. That proof you can have on paying my bill for services to George Clarke, detective, 20 Cockspur Street, Charing Cross, to whom I will give the proof on his paying my bill.*

Yours respectfully,

WM. H. MURRAY.

I also wrote this other letter at the prisoner's dictation, and the envelope also –

*To George Clarke, Esq., Detective,*
*20, Cockspur Street, Charing Cross.*

*London, 4th May 1892.*

*Dear Sir,*

*If Mr. Wyatt, Coroner, calls on you in regard to the murders of Alice Marsh and Emma Shrivell, you can tell him that you will give proof positive to him that W. H. Harper, student, of St. Thomas's Hospital, and son of Dr. Harper, Bear Street, Barnstaple, poisoned those girls with strychnine, provided the Coroner will pay you well for your services. Proof of this will be forthcoming. I will write you again in a few days.*

Yours respectfully,

Wm. H. MURRAY.

"The prisoner took these letters and envelopes away with him, returning to town that night. When I wrote the letters I asked him if he had that evidence, he said that a friend of his, a detective, had it; he did not mention his name. I asked him why I should sign the name of "Murray", he said that that was the name of his friend. When I asked him what he knew of this, or of Murray, he said he would tell me all about it someday."

"Thomas Neill," intoned Mr. Justice Hawkins, "The jury, after having listened with the most patient attention to the evidence which has been offered against you in respect of this most terrible crime, and having paid all attention to the most able arguments and the very eloquent speech which your learned counsel addressed to them on your behalf, have felt it their bounden duty to find you guilty of the crime of wilful murder, of a murder so diabolical in its character, fraught with so much cold-blooded cruelty, that one dare hardly trust oneself to speak of the details of your wickedness. What motive could have actuated you to take the life of that girl away, and with so much torture to that poor creature, who could not have offended you, I know not. But I do know that your cruelty towards her, and the crime that you have committed, are to my mind of unparalleled atrocity. For the crime of which you have been convicted our law knows but one penalty -- the penalty of death. That sentence I must pronounce upon you, in accordance with my duty. I would add one word: to beseech you, during the short time that life remains to you -- to remember that when you descend the steps from the spot where you now stand this world will be no more to you --- to endeavour to seek your peace with Almighty God. Pray Him to pardon you for your great sin; He alone can grant you pardon. The crime which you have committed, I have already said, can be expiated only by your death. I proceed, therefore, to pass upon you the dread sentence of the law, which is, that you be taken from hence to the place whence you came, and thence to a lawful place of execution, and that there you be hanged by your neck until you be dead, and that when you are dead your body be buried within the precincts of that prison within the walls of which you shall have been confined last before the execution of the judgment upon you. And may the Lord have mercy upon your soul."

Since only one charge was proceeded with at the trial, that of the wilful murder of Matilda Clover, the Judge's subsequent decision to admit evidence in the other indictments had weighed heavily against Cream. Indeed, he had up until the last counted on there being insufficient evidence to convict him; remaining at most times confident that he would be freed to go about his business just as the Good Lord intended. He had, however, reckoned without Mr. Justice Hawkins. Cream stood in shocked silence during the sentencing, but afterwards vowed darkly to "give it to Hawkins" -- though quite how he proposed to do so from the strict confines of Newgate jail remains a matter for conjecture.

# PART 8

On the Monday before Cream was due to die Kennedy Jones, with much trepidation, stepped across the threshold of Newgate's condemned cell. Though the bearer of unwelcome tidings, he was sanguine enough to believe that Cream might still be willing to honour their bargain, if only for the opportunity of being seen, at least by posterity, as he apparently saw himself -- a dedicated physician who had forfeited his life in the battle against corruption.

Cream was seated hollow-eyed at his table, on which was a neat brown paper parcel tied together with string and sealed with crimson blobs of wax. Saint or sinner, he had now no option but to accept the ugly truth -- that his life was shortly to be choked out of him by a biting band of hemp. A stench of fear pervaded the atmosphere, the pungent reek of an animal at bay. Jones endeavoured not to retch.

"At your request, Doctor," he faltered, "f have called upon Miss Laura Sabbatini at Berkhamstead; but regret to inform you, that on the earnest advice of her mother, the young lady has declined to visit you before your --ahem -- impending departure." It struck even Jones that his choice of words might in the circumstances have been improved upon; and yet he was wholly unprepared for Cream's hysterical tirade.

"What perfidy! May she and that malevolent old mother of hers burn in hell! *All wickedness is but little to the wickedness of a woman.* Bunch of whores, the fucking lot of them!"

It required the combined strength of four burly guards to prevent Cream from flinging himself on the petrified journalist with the avowed intention, in the regrettable absence of the beloved, of ripping out Jones's guts instead. He stood his ground only in consequence of being rooted to it with fright; and remained paralysed until Cream had been forcibly re-seated in his chair, confined by a straight-waistcoat. Only then did Jones summon enough nerve to reach for Cream's manuscript. There was widespread interest in the Lambeth Poisoner, particularly now that his execution was imminent; and Jones, who had guaranteed his editor the greatest scoop of the century, might well be out of a job should he fail to deliver. Extracting from his wallet an order for five hundred pounds he placed it gingerly on the table before Cream. He then drew towards him the manuscript which, hopefully, included sensational revelations as to the identity of Jack the Ripper.

"Well, now, Doctor Cream, this will serve to complete our little transaction to the advantage of us both, I trust." Cream's face was blotched and livid, as much from fury as the herculean effort he had made to hold his own. However, if his captors considered him helpless as a trussed turkey, they were wrong. Before Jones had managed to lay hands on the manscript Cream sprang to his feet, launched a hefty kick at the table, and succeeding in knocking the journalist and his silly bowler flying.

"The Jezabel, the dirty traitorous Jezabel", Cream raved. "An insignificant dressmaker whom I, a doctor of medicine, have raised way beyond her station -- the two-timing bitch is now ungrateful enough to turn down a dying man's request. Oh no sir, let not Miss Laura Sabbatini nor yet her cursed mother expect to receive a penny now from me! Take your money, you obsequious little worm, and get out of my sight! As for Andersmann, he can shove his goddamned ethics up his rear!"

Cream's legs were knocked from under him with a sharp blow of a warder's cane, as Jones, minus the precious manuscript but with the greater good fortune still to be in possession of his life, was escorted, bruised and shaken, through the studded iron gate. Cream meanwhile had been spreadeagled on the floor, still ranting crazily, the heavy oak table reversed across his knees and weighted effectively by the posterior of an eighteen stone guard.

When the prisoner had regained some semblance of self control he was released from restraint and, as of right, his Solicitor sent for. Waters arrived to find six guards instead of four stationed inside the condemned cell and another posted strategically outside, ready to raise an alarm. Cream now spoke dispassionately.

"Both you and I am aware, Waters, that there was a want of proof as to my identity touching the murder of Matilda Clover, yet I am to swing for it in the morning. So much for justice and fair play! However, it may ease your mind to know that I am now resigned to my unlucky fate." His insatiable craving for publicity prompted him to add: "Say, what is the feeling about me outside?"

The Solicitor commented only that opinion against him was rather strong; a monumental understatement in that he had been obliged to fight his way into Newgate through an enormous throng of cheering, jeering ghouls. Cream shrugged. In any case, he cared for nothing now, except vengeance. That the financial deal with Kennedy had been revoked was sufficient punishment for the Sabbatinis; but there was still a score to settle with the authorities.

They may have been spared the ridicule his published confessions would have heaped on them, but the damned Bosses should not, if he could help it, evade some sort of poetic justice. Let them be denied what above anything, would have afforded them their greatest triumph --the discovery, should his confessions fall into their hands, that they had done for Jack the Ripper.

"My last wish, John, is that you take these papers away and burn them," The game may have been up for Cream, but he had made his winning move. "Catch me when you can," the Ripper had taunted them. The day would never dawn, so far as the police were concerned, in the absence of a solemn confession from Thomas N. Cream. That he had finally "set the sons-of-bitches up as an all time bunch of losers" provided what little worldly pleasure remained to him, and lessened any regret he might otherwise have felt in sacrificing the task on which, to complete by deadline, he had expended all his energies.

Waters, ever obedient to his duty, went home and immediately carried out his instructions; consigning the brown paper package unopened, to the blazing hearth. Watching wax dripping in blood-red streaks over Cream's labours lost, Waters found himself, despite the fire's heat, shivering slightly. Inquisitive though he may have been as to its contents, the Solicitor made no move to rescue the singeing bundle before incineration was complete. As one of a team who had come close to achieving an acquittal for Cream, in John Water's philosophy some things were better left unread.

Cream spent most of his last night on earth engaged in agonizing self analysis. Where in heaven's name he had gone wrong? How had he, a physician, a man of moral and religious principles, come to such a pass? Not for the first time, though seldom for long, he began seriously to question his motivations. Could it be a sickness of the mind he had once feared instead of a devout desire to serve trod that had driven him to the deeds for which he was now to pay the price? There certainly had been times when his confounded headaches had threatened to drive him mad. He sure had better avoid that line of thought, though -- the mere prospect of insanity always scared him shitless -- and he had no intention of dying badly before those smug sods. If only he could spend a while with Anderesmann, that would straighten him out. "Easy, now, Tom, you're as sane as the next man; who knows that better than I?" Anderesmann would reassure him, just like old times.

Stark images of childhood began to flood his memory; the relentless beatings he had endured in infancy, imposed less often by his weak father than a fanatically religious mother who, seeing her woefully cross-eyed son spit at his younger sister, feared him demonically possessed. Was the skipping-rope burn which later appeared on her screaming daughter's neck indeed the mark of Satan, or Mary Elder's self-fulfilling prophecy?

Ruminations such as these preoccupied Cream's mind until, on the morning of Tuesday, November 15th, 1892, his final hour struck; starting at eight o'clock with breakfast and the equally unappetising arrival of the prison chaplain, the Reverend Mr. Merrick. He, as was his wont on such occasions, appeared to be in a worse state of composure than the prisoner -- clothes in disarray and with what few hairs he possessed straggling in ungovernable wisps from an otherwise shiny pate. Cream, without spectacles and squinting at the chaplain myopically in the cell's dim light, thought with perverse amusement how like the fellow was to his inventive description of Murray, to whom he had ironically ascribed the initials W.H. in revered memory of his late and loaded parent, William Henry Cream. The fabrication, even if they did consider themselves pretty damn smart nowadays, had in the event served well enough to dupe McIntyre and Haynes, since neither one, nor any of their colleagues, had ever caught on to his small slip in telling McIntyre that Murray had sent that warning note to Stamford Street, and Haynes that he had done so himself. Someone someday would latch on to that fact, though, and show them all up for the fools they were -- though he unfortunately would not be around to enjoy their discomfort. Neither should they enjoy his, for the matter of that. None should see him cringe, oh no Sir, he should never afford the bastards that satisfaction -- the chaplain failing dismally to elicit the least expression of remorse, nor yet admission of guilt on any count whatsoever. Cream, indeed, toying with his food, remained unrewardingly silent during the entire interview.

The great bell of the Church of St. Sepulchre, which had always signalled a hanging, began tolling ominiously at quarter to nine. Cream clutched at his Bible, praying silently that he might continue to face his ordeal like a man. The others joined Merrick, a mournful retinue consisting of the Governor, Colonel Milman, bearing a warrant for the execution, who, with no fondness for Cream, nevertheless obviously disliked his task, accompanied by Under-Sheriff Metcalfe, Dr. Gilbert and Scott, the chief warder. Last but not least, Billington entered the cell carrying a set of straps. Cream rose and with a look of the coolest contempt, turned his back on the hangman, allowing his arms to be pinioned without the least resistance. Flanked by his guard of dishonour, the prisoner was marched for what seemed to him like an eternity, but was in reality only a short spell, down the dank prison corridor and into the hanging shed. He made out with difficulty the one inch width of hemp suspended from a beam, and even in that awful moment mustered enough courage to step firmly, almost jauntily on the trap. Just prior to Billington drawing the white cap over his eyes, Cream saw Merrick's blurred face:

"Thomas Neill Cream, you are about to enter the Kingdom of Almighty God, there to be judged for your sins. Before your life upon this earth is ended, I solemnly commend you to unburden yourself of all wrongdoing. Repent before it is too late, so that by His divine mercy you may yet be granted heavenly grace. Our Father ...”

Yet in Cream’s last moments of awareness he perceived not the chaplain but, incredibly, Anderesmann. “For my sake, Tom, confess truly now and save your immortal soul.” This was beyond belief! How had he taken Merrick’s place -- and as to confessing for his benefit, who in tarnation did Anderesmann think he was, anyway?” As if Anderesmann had read Cream’s thoughts, he cried out loud and clear:

“I am your conscience and your light.” But there was no light, only suffocating darkness, as Billington lowered the hood. The hangman had heard nothing of Anderesmann, but he would be willing to swear to Cream’s last words:

**“I am Jack ---”.**

Simultaneous with Cream’s five foot descent the customary black flag was hoisted outside the prison over debtors’ gate, to be received with enthusiastic applause from a dense audience. Among them were Haynes and McIntyre.

The pair of sleuths repaired to Cream’s old haunt in Lambeth, “The Crown and Cushion”. McIntyre raised his glass: “A toast to the Lambeth Poisoner, God damn his black soul! Pity that for all our efforts we could not send Jack the Ripper” -- his forefinger stabbed towards the floorboards --”in a like direction. Same sort of cunning sadistic bastard as Cream, don’t you know, Haynes.”

Haynes did know, and rejoiced.

R. B. Graham, K.C., prosecutor at the murder trial of Earle Nelson in Canada, November 1927:

“My learned friend Mr. Stitt used the words “the chain of circumstantial evidence’. Circumstantial evidence, members of the jury, is not a chain -- it is a rope, which is not as strong as its weakest strand only, but has the strength of all its strands combined. In the story of this crime how thoroughly the evidence is borne out and amplified by the details, weaving all together in such a way that every strand has been spun out and bound and twisted with its fellow strands, into a cord that is almost perfect!"